"The sex scenes were some of the sexiest, most intimate and quite frankly, sensual I have read in a while. Jenny Frame had me hooked and I reread a few scenes because I felt like I needed to experience the intense intimacy between Finn and Bridget again. The devotion they showed to one another during these sex scenes but also in the intimate moments was gripping and for lack of a better word, carnal."—*Les Rêveur*

"The sexual chemistry between [Finn and Bridge] is unbelievably hot. It is sexy, lustful and with more than a hint of kink. The scenes between them are highly erotic—and not just the sex scenes. The tension is ramped up so well that I felt the characters would explode if they did not get relief!…An excellent book set in the most wonderful village—a place I hope to return to very soon!"—*Kitty Kat's Book Reviews*

"This is Frame's best character work to date. They are layered and flawed and yet relatable…Frame really pushed herself with *Charming the Vicar* and it totally paid off…I also appreciate that even though she regularly writes butch/femme characters, no two pairings are the same."—*The Lesbian Review*

Unexpected

Jenny Frame "has this beautiful way of writing a phenomenally hot scene while incorporating the love and tenderness between the couple."—*Les Rêveur*

"If you enjoy contemporary romances, *Unexpected* is a great choice. The character work is excellent, the plotting and pacing are well done, and it's just a sweet, warm read…Definitely pick this book up when you're looking for your next comfort read, because it's sure to put a smile on your face by the time you get to that happy ending."—*Curve*

"*Unexpected* by Jenny Frame is a charming butch/femme romance that is perfect for anyone who wants to feel the magic of overcoming adversity and finding true love. I love the way Jenny Frame writes. I have yet to discover an author who writes like her. Her voice is strong and unique and gives a freshness to the lesbian fiction sector."
—*The Lesbian Review*

Royal Rebel

"Frame's stories are easy to follow and really engaging. She stands head and shoulders above a number of the romance authors and it's easy to see why she is quickly making a name for herself in lesfic romance."—*The Lesbian Review*

Courting the Countess

"I love Frame's romances. They are well paced, filled with beautiful character moments and a wonderful set of side characters who ultimately end up winning your heart...I love Jenny Frame's butch/femme dynamic; she gets it so right for a romance."—*The Lesbian Review*

"I loved, loved, loved this book. I didn't expect to get so involved in the story but I couldn't help but fall in love with Annie and Harry...The love scenes were beautifully written and very sexy. I found the whole book romantic and ultimately joyful and I had a lump in my throat on more than one occasion. A wonderful book that certainly stirred my emotions."—*Kitty Kat's Book Reviews*

"*Courting The Countess* has an historical feel in a present day world, a thought provoking tale filled with raw emotions throughout. [Frame] has a magical way of pulling you in, making you feel every emotion her characters experience."—*Lunar Rainbow Reviewz*

"I didn't want to put the book down and I didn't. Harry and Annie are two amazingly written characters that bring life to the pages as they find love and adventures in Harry's home. This is a great read, and you will enjoy it immensely if you give it a try!"—*Fantastic Book Reviews*

A Royal Romance

"*A Royal Romance* was a guilty pleasure read for me. It was just fun to see the relationship develop between George and Bea, to see George's life as queen and Bea's as a commoner. It was also refreshing to see that both of their families were encouraging, even when Bea doubted that things could work between them because of their class differences...*A Royal Romance* left me wanting a sequel, and romances don't usually do that to me."—*Leeanna.ME Mostly a Book Blog*

Praise for Jenny Frame

The Duchess and the Dreamer

"We thoroughly enjoyed the whole romance-the-disbelieving-duchess with gallantry, unwavering care, and grand gestures. Since this is very firmly in the butch-femme zone, it appealed to that part of our traditionally-conditioned-typecasting mindset that all the wooing and work is done by Evan without throwing even a small fit at any point. We liked the fact that Clementine has layers and depth. She has her own personal and personality hurdles that make her behaviour understandable and create the right opportunities for Evan to play the romantic knight convincingly…We definitely recommend this one to anyone looking for a feel-good mushy romance."—*Best Lesfic Reviews*

"There are a whole range of things I like about Jenny Frame's aristocratic heroines: they have plausible histories to account for them holding titles in their own right; they're in touch with reality and not necessarily super-rich, certainly not through inheritance; and they find themselves paired with perfectly contrasting co-heroines…Clementine and Evan are excellently depicted, and I love the butch:femme dynamic they have going on, as well as their individual abilities to stick to their principles but also to compromise with each other when necessary."
—*The Good, The Bad and The Unread*

Still Not Over You

"*Still Not Over You* is a wonderful second-chance romance anthology that makes you believe in love again. And you would certainly be missing out if you have not read *My Forever Girl*, because it truly is everything."—*SymRoute*

Someone to Love

"One of the author's best works to date—both Trent and Wendy were so well developed they came alive. I could really picture them and they jumped off   nd their sexual
dynamic wa   characters and
the storyline   vritten and well
handled."—   *ry (UK)*

Wooing the Farmer

"This book, like all of Jenny Frame's, is just one major swoon."—*Les Rêveur*

"The chemistry between the two MCs had us hooked right away. We also absolutely loved the seemingly ditzy femme with an ambition of steel but really a vulnerable girl. The sex scenes are great. Definitely recommended."—*Reviewer@large*

"This is the book we Axedale fanatics have been waiting for…Jenny Frame writes the most amazing characters and this whole series is a masterpiece. But where she excels is in writing butch lesbians. Every time I read a Jenny Frame book I think it's the best ever, but time and again she surprises me. She has surpassed herself with *Wooing the Farmer*."—*Kitty Kat's Book Review Blog*

Royal Court

"The author creates two very relatable characters…Quincy's quietude and mental torture are offset by Holly's openness and lust for life. Holly's determination and tenacity in trying to reach Quincy are total wish-fulfilment of a person like that. The chemistry and attraction is excellently built."—*Best Lesbian Erotica*

"[A] butch/femme romance that packs a punch."—*Les Rêveur*

Royal Court "was a fun, light-hearted book with a very endearing romance."—*Leanne Chew, Librarian, Parnell Library (Auckland, NZ)*

"There were unbelievably hot sex scenes as I have come to expect and look forward to in Jenny Frame's books. Passions slowly rise until you feel the characters may burst!…Royal Court is wonderful and I highly recommend it."—*Kitty Kat's Book Review Blog*

Charming the Vicar

"Chances are, you've never read or become captivated by a romance like *Charming the Vicar*. While books featuring people of the cloth aren't unusual, Bridget is no ordinary vicar—a lesbian with a history of kink…Surrounded by mostly supportive villagers, Bridget and Finn balance love and faith in a story that affirms both can exist for anyone, regardless of sexual identity."—*RT Book Reviews*

By the Author

A Royal Romance

Courting the Countess

Dapper

Royal Rebel

Unexpected

Charming the Vicar

Royal Court

Wooing the Farmer

Someone to Love

The Duchess and the Dreamer

Royal Family

Home Is Where the Heart Is

Wild for You

Hunger for You

Longing for You

Wolfgang County Series

Heart of the Pack

Soul of the Pack

Blood of the Pack

Visit us at www.boldstrokesbooks.com

HOME IS WHERE THE HEART IS

by
Jenny Frame

2021

HOME IS WHERE THE HEART IS

© 2021 By Jenny Frame. All Rights Reserved.

ISBN 13: 978-1-63555-922-4

This Trade Paperback Original Is Published By
Bold Strokes Books, Inc.
P.O. Box 249
Valley Falls, NY 12185

First Edition: July 2021

CREDITS

EDITOR: RUTH STERNGLANTS
PRODUCTION DESIGN: STACIA SEAMAN
COVER DESIGN BY TAMMY SEIDICK

Acknowledgments

Thank you to all the BSB staff for their tireless hard work. Thank you to Ruth for always helping my books be the best they can be, and thanks to my family for their support and encouragement.

Lou and Barney, you give me the life and love I never dreamed I could have. I'm grateful beyond words for every day I spend with you, and I can't wait for the adventures we still have to experience together.

We three are family.

To Lou and Barney,
My home and my heart are always with you

CHAPTER ONE

Y̶ou pig!"
         Steff Archer felt the shock of cold liquid and ice hitting her face and heard the gasps of those around her in the packed wine bar.

"Jesus Christ, Naomi." The alcohol from the drink nipped her eyes. She grasped the napkin in front of her and brought it to her face.

"You brought me out tonight to dump me? Couldn't you have saved all this time and just phoned me?"

Archie opened her eyes and looked at the irate woman standing across from her. "I didn't deceive you. I never said this was serious, but—"

Naomi cut her off. "Two months we were together, Archie. Forgive me for thinking that meant we were in a relationship. I'm thirty-seven. I haven't got time to waste on casual dating."

Archie dabbed at her soaking wet shirt and became acutely aware of the people at the tables around them staring at them. She had brought Naomi out tonight to hopefully end their dating in an amicable way. They had been dating for two months, but Archie never had long-term relationships, and she'd felt Naomi was getting a little serious. But it was going all wrong.

"Naomi, please—"

Her now former date wouldn't sit down. She was a ball of fury. "I know about your glitzy party in Rosebrook."

"Glitzy party?" Archie said in confusion.

Naomi pulled out a popular gay magazine and showed her a double-page spread on Rosebrook. It was a story about Evan Fox and the Duchess of Rosebrook, Clementine. Evan had bought Clementine's ancestral home and village, with plans to make an ecological community, to set an example of how the future could be greener and safe for all to live in.

Clementine had fallen in love with Evan, and together they were striving to make a green, diverse environment for all those who needed it, especially those in the LGBTQ+ community.

Although they'd had the ribbon-cutting ceremony earlier, this party had been the press launch. All the media had been invited, including many gay magazines and social media outlets, to publicize their new eco community.

"You never invited me as your date, and I know why. It's because of *her*, isn't it?"

Naomi threw the magazine at her. Archie looked down and saw a picture of her and Ashling O'Rourke dancing together at the party. Naomi had gotten entirely the wrong end of the stick. She and Ash didn't even have the closest working relationship, not since Archie had asked her to make the tea like a good little secretary, not the PA to the duchess that she was.

Archie had been paying for that ever since.

"Don't be ridiculous. Ash is thirteen years younger than me. My friend Evan simply asked me to—"

Naomi didn't let her finish. "You've already dumped me, so why continue to lie? Look at the way you're looking at her." Naomi slipped on her coat and picked up her bag. "Well, she'll find out what a heartless prick you are, soon enough. Goodbye."

Archie looked down at her red wine-soaked shirt and sighed. "That went well."

A waiter approached carefully and said, "Could I get you something to mop that up?"

"That's okay. Just the bill, please. I'm sorry about the mess."

Bill paid, Archie made her way out to the London street. Her shirt was soaking wet and uncomfortable. She looked at her watch, which also had been splashed and was now all sticky, and saw it still wasn't even eight o'clock yet.

She was actually a lot closer to her dad's house than her flat. Maybe he could give her a change of shirt? Archie took out her phone and dialled her dad's number.

"Hello? Adam Archer speaking."

"Hi, Dad. It's me. Are you in tonight?"

"For the next hour and a half, Archie. Then I've got a dinner date. Are you nearby?" Adam said.

"Yes, just five minutes away. I wondered if I could drop in. I need a change of shirt. I'll explain when I get there."

"Of course. Come over. We can have a chat while I get ready."

Archie hung up and flagged down a taxi. When she sat in the back seat, she realized she'd stuffed the magazine that Naomi had thrown at her in her pocket. She pulled it out and looked at the picture of her and Ashling dancing.

She couldn't see what Naomi saw in that picture that made her think she and Ash had something between them. All Archie could remember was bickering all through that dance. The photographer must have caught them between bouts of sniping at each other.

She'd only asked Ash to dance after prompting from Evan, who had noticed Ash's continued discomfort from the close attentions of another partygoer. Ash had grown up in a very sheltered existence in Rosebrook and hadn't developed the tools to tell someone to back off, so over went Archie to mark her imaginary territory and rescue her damsel in distress.

The taxi stopped at her destination. Archie paid the driver and walked up the steps of a mid-terrace Victorian house. She was just about to knock when her dad opened the door.

"Archie—oh." Her dad looked her up and down. "Who did you piss off?"

"I made a woman angry, and apparently I'm a pig."

He smiled. "Well, you better come in. You look like you could do with a drink."

❖

The cool early evening breeze blew across Rosebrook beach. It was a welcome change for Ashling O'Rourke after enduring an exceptionally hot June day. After a hot, busy day in the Rosebrook Trust office, Ash routinely came down to read a book on the beach. She always brought her deckchair up to the water's edge so the water would lap at her feet while she read. Ash was a few pages from the end of her favourite romance novel, *The Dastardly Duke*. Despite having read the book countless times, Ash's breathing grew short, her heart pounded, and she dug her toes into the cold wet sand beneath her feet in anticipation of the final declaration of love.

Ash was never bored of her favourite books—in fact, rereading them over and over gave her a safe, relaxed feeling. Even though there might be angst throughout the story, she knew for certain it would all be all right in the end.

She loved fairy tale and Regency romance novels, and any downtime Ash had in the day was spent reading her beloved books. Her love of romance fiction, and her large collection of books, had been passed down to her from her mother, Kate.

When Ash reached the marriage proposal on the last page, she was reminded of how she and her mum talked about that scene, every time one of them read it. She looked up from the paperback and watched the gentle waves roll into shore. She could hear her mum's voice as they talked giddily over their favourite book.

She was sure that was why these books were so important to her. They and her memories were all she had of her mum now. But they also allowed her to escape. The small village of Rosebrook was dying by the time she was born, and so books, and especially romance novels, became her escape from the dull world she was living in.

Ash's books gave her the only chance to experience the excitement of love in all its forms, because here in Rosebrook, still living with her dad, books were the only excitement she got.

She gazed back to the page and smiled. This was her favourite part, and she knew it by heart. Ash brought the book to her chest, closed her eyes, and recited those final words of the love story.

"*The dastardly duke thought his heart was impenetrable, but that was until the obstinate Diana Carlton came along, and his heart had been pierced by Cupid's arrow. All that had seemed important, like the glamourous London parties, the many women he pursued and seduced, gambling at the cards table, and travelling all over the world, were now so unimportant. All that mattered was making a home for Diana at Glassford Castle and spending forever loving her. The dastardly duke was now the deeply loving duke and all because of the power of love."*

Ash let out a sigh of happiness and opened her eyes. If you couldn't experience real love, then living vicariously through your favourite fictional characters was the next best thing, and where better to read about them than on the beach, in the cove below the village.

She didn't think there was any beach in the world that came close to Rosebrook's unspoiled beach, as long as the weather was fine, which it had been this summer. Rosebrook beach hadn't been a tourist trap for a long, long time. Her grandma used to tell her about the flock of visitors they got every spring and summer, who brought much needed revenue to the village.

Ash looked to her left and saw her father's small fishing boat sailing towards the wooden pier at the end of the beach. She got up and folded up her deckchair. The breeze gusted and blew her straw sun hat off her head. Ash picked it up, then brushed her hair behind her ears.

She'd said she would meet her dad after he came in from his afternoon booking, so she lifted her deckchair and carried it up to the beach huts that ran along the sheer cliff face at the back of the beach. The huts were among the many improvements since Evan Fox had come to their village.

The CEO of Fox Toys and an avid environmentalist, Evan Fox had come to Rosebrook determined to revitalize the village she and her parents had visited as a child. Evan bounced in full of energy and sold the villagers on her vision to build a new kind of village— an ecological village where they made the environment, and saving it, their top priority. Bringing back the Victorian style beach huts was one of the things that Ash loved. She opened the door and placed her deckchair in, then locked the hut up and began walking along the beach towards the boat shop, holding her shoes in her hand. Walking on the cool sand was a heavenly way to end the day. Evan's vision hadn't exactly been an easy sell to her father and the traditional country farmers, but after the village was almost destroyed by flooding last year, they finally came around to a decision that if they didn't do their part to save the environment, then they would eventually lose everything, not to mention the money Evan was pouring into their village to revitalize it.

Meanwhile, her dad's fishing party bookings had more than tripled since this time last year, so that income, along with her job working as the duchess's PA, meant life was now a bit more comfortable for the O'Rourkes.

Up ahead she could see the fishermen her dad James had taken out were now gathering their gear and making their way up the beach walkway to the car parking area above. She made her way onto the wooden jetty and waited for her dad to tie up and secure the boat.

Her dad's business might be doing a bit better, but he still cut a lonely figure. Of course he had a few people he counted as friends, who he had a drink with at the pub, but nobody could ever relieve his pain and loneliness at losing Kate, her mother, the love of James's life.

That was why she could never leave him. She gave up her chance to go to university to look after her dad when her mum died, and that had been very isolating for her, but now she had a career in the village, and new friends that had enriched her life.

When Evan Fox married their very own Duchess of Rosebrook, she brought more than hope for the future. The new Rosebrook village was planned to be a safe place for LGBTQ+ people. A haven where all those people often marginalized by society could come and sign on to the village charter of safety, tolerance, and inclusion.

For a gay woman like herself, it was wonderful to be surrounded by like-minded people.

"Ashling," James said in his lilting Irish brogue.

Ash gave him a kiss on the cheek. "Hi, Daddy, did you have a good fishing trip?"

"We did. They were businessmen from London—they booked for next month too, and they're going to recommend me to their friends," James said.

"That's great, Daddy."

"Let's get the shop all closed up, and you can tell me about your day."

They walked into the fishing shop, and James went over to the till to book in the fishermen's next date. The small shop sold bait and fishing equipment, but the majority of his income came from his fishing and boating trips.

"They gave me a fifty pound tip too."

Ash was delighted. At least one part of his life was getting better. "Well done, you deserve it."

"So, tell me about your day, my girl."

"It was busy. The duchess and I were going through some more applications to join the community," Ash said. Now that the first block of refurbished cottages were filling up, the next phase would be starting soon.

"Are the duchess and Fox ready to leave?" James asked.

"Just about, I think. They're leaving after lunch tomorrow."

Having gotten married a few months ago, Clementine and Evan waited till the summer months to go on their honeymoon. They hadn't wanted to leave Rosebrook when there was so much still to do. Plus they hoped the weather would be better in the summer for their honeymoon destination in Scotland.

"Clementine says it's a working honeymoon," Ash said.

James looked up from the till as he counted money. "Is there such a thing?"

Ash smiled. "I think where Fox is concerned, there is. She never shuts down from working, but in a good way. She just wants to make the world a better place."

"Where is it they are going?"

"Thistleburn in Scotland. You know how Clementine's full

title is Duchess of Rosebrook, Countess of Thistleburn, Baroness Portford?"

James nodded.

"Well, Clementine's grandmother sold the lands in Thistleburn when she was short of money. Evan bought them back for Clementine as a wedding present. So they're going to visit, see what needs to be done there. I think Fox thinks it might be a second eco village, once Rosebrook is working well," Ash explained.

James finished counting the cash, put it in a locked box, and tucked it under his arm. "That Fox is driven. Oh well, as long as she keeps her focus on Rosebrook just now, and my girl has a good job with the duchess, that's all I care about."

"I've to meet with Clementine in the morning to go over some of the things she wants done while she is away."

James walked over to the door and held it open for Ash. "So, is Archie in charge while they are away?"

Ash frowned. "No, she's not. We each have our own responsibilities from the duchess and Fox."

She hadn't hit it off with Steff Archer from the start of working together, when Archie mistook her for the office tea girl.

James locked the door to the boat shop, and they walked up the steps from the beach to the village.

"It's not like you, that frown. You're like your mum—you always seem to get on with people."

Ash frowned again and deep down had a visceral reaction when thinking about how much Archie annoyed her. "I do like everyone, Dad, but Archie is pompous, patronizing, and…" Ash hesitated. "Something else beginning with *P*."

A prick.

❖

Archie was much more comfortable now. She was sitting at the kitchen island, wearing one of her dad's T-shirts, while her shirt soaked in the sink. Her dad was ironing his own shirt for his dinner date.

She took a sip of wine. "This is really nice."

Adam looked up from his ironing. "It is, isn't it? It's a new line I've added. Selling really well."

Her father was a wine merchant and supplied many of the country's top restaurants, as well as the public via his online store. No one knew more about wine than Adam Archer.

Adam was a great dad. He'd been the first one to call her Archie, after her teenage self told him that she didn't feel comfortable with her given name, Stephanie. He didn't hesitate to support her and her natural affinity towards her more masculine side, in appearance and energy.

Now only her mum called her Stephanie, and there would be no budging her, not that Archie ever saw her these days.

"So what did you do to deserve wine in the face?"

"I took my date out to, as kindly as possible, tell her I didn't want us to see each other any more," Archie said.

"Naomi? I thought you liked her."

"I did—I mean, I do. But she was getting a bit too serious."

"My daughter, the perennial bachelor," he said.

"You can talk, Dad. You've never had a long-term relationship since you left Mum."

He lifted the shirt and inspected it for creases. "That's because I had a lot to work through after splitting from your mum. A lifetime of being in the closet is stifling, and I needed time to work out who I was. I don't want that for you."

Her dad hung the shirt on its hanger and started to put the iron and ironing board away. "I want you to find happiness."

"I am happy, in small chunks. I feel trapped if I'm in a relationship too long," Archie said.

He walked over to sit at the island with her and poured himself a drink. "That's your mother's and my fault."

"Don't say that, Dad," Archie said. "I make my own choices." The truth was, living in the midst of her parents' toxic marriage had put her off commitment for life.

"So that's why you got the wine in the face?"

"Yes, I am a pig, and apparently she was too old to waste time with someone who wasn't interested in a long-term future," Archie said.

He took a drink of wine and said, "She has a point. Most people are settled down at your age. Marriage, kids."

Archie shivered. "Not me, and neither did you."

"That's different. I bowed to family pressure and married a woman when I was gay. I was trapped in a loveless marriage. But if I had been brought up in your generation, I would have liked to have gotten married to a man and had a family. A kid, just like you. You were worth going through all the pain and the arguments." He smiled.

Archie squeezed her dad's hand. "Thanks." She pulled the magazine from her pocket and handed it to him. "This didn't help. Naomi was angry that I didn't take her to this party at Rosebrook."

Adam looked over the page. "Why didn't you?"

"I just like to keep my life in Rosebrook separate."

Her dad stabbed a finger at the page. "Who's this pretty woman that you're smiling at adoringly?"

"What? I am not," Archie said defensively. "The photographer just caught us in between bouts of arguments."

"That not the famous Ashling, is it? The one who annoys the life out of you at the Rosebrook office?"

"Have I mentioned her before?"

Her dad nodded.

"Well, yes. That's the one. We got off on the wrong foot, and it's been acrimonious ever since."

"Lovely looking girl."

Archie didn't want to talk any more about her and said, "Shouldn't you be getting ready for dinner?"

He looked at his watch and jumped up. "You're right." He took his shirt off the hanger and put it and his tie on quickly. "How do I look?"

"Handsome as always, Dad."

Her father kept very fit and took care of himself. The grey streaks in his hair only made him look more distinguished.

"How is Stuart?"

Stuart had been going out with her dad longer than anyone had in the past. She'd met him and liked him, but like her own, her dad's relationships never seemed to last.

"He's well. I—I was thinking of asking him to move in with me."

"What? Really?" Archie said with surprise.

"Yes, I love him, and I'd like to share my life with someone. You've got to grab happiness where you can. Life is short, Archie."

Archie was taken aback. No one had gotten that close to her father or made him want to share his life. She got up and said, "If he makes you happy, Dad, then I'm all for it." She gave her dad a hug.

He said, "Thanks. I hope you will find love someday, Archie. Don't judge relationships by me and your mum."

That was easier said than done. Being brought up in that horrible toxic marriage had left some deep scars on her psyche, and she didn't have the courage to face healing them.

"I love you, Dad."

CHAPTER TWO

Clementine undulated her hips as she straddled Fox's waist. Fox held Clementine's buttocks in her hands and helped her grind down deeply on her strap-on.

"Oh God, it's too much."

Clementine's arms started to shake, as they always did when her orgasm was close, especially when Fox was so deep inside of her. Fox said, "You always say it's too much, and it never is. I'm always here."

Clementine hastened her thrust, then went completely still and let out a low primal groan. Fox loved to make her wife feel like this.

Clementine fell forward onto Fox and kissed her. "That was so good," she breathed.

Fox held Clementine's hips tightly, and within a few thrusts a wave of orgasm swept from her groin to the tips of her fingers and toes. "Jesus Christ."

While Fox got her breath back, Clementine kissed Evan on the nose. "We were supposed to be finalizing our packing, Foxy."

"Everyone needs a break. I say our honeymoon has officially started."

Clementine lifted herself off carefully and rolled to the side. "Not till tomorrow it doesn't. Besides, it's been one long honeymoon since we got married," Clementine said.

Fox gave her a big grin. "It has, hasn't it? It must be fun being married to me."

Clementine playfully pushed her, and then sat up against the headboard. "You really are full of yourself, Foxy."

Fox sat up beside her. "No, really, it takes a special woman to be able to put up with my manic craziness."

Clementine lifted Fox's hand and kissed it. "There's no one better for the job than me."

She looked around the Duke's bedroom and sighed with contentment. The months she had spent living back in her family home, along with Evan, had been the happiest that she could remember. Clementine had longed to be here her whole life, and now through her love for Evan, she got to be duchess in her family seat again.

When Fox bought her run-down home, she resented her and everything Evan Fox did to the house, but she'd slowly realized Evan was here for the long haul, and she began to fall in love.

Fox had a vision, a dream for Rosebrook, and Clementine bought into that after a lifetime of resenting her grandmother Isadora, who had similar dreams and lost the family fortune. Now she and Fox both fulfilled so many dreams for the community and had many more to bring to fruition.

"What are you thinking?" Fox asked.

"Thinking how happy I am and how happy the village is that you came bouncing in like Tigger, with all your wonderful ideas."

"We're making good progress, aren't we? The original tenants' houses refurbished, the empty cottages done and new tenants given their keys, the beach improved, and walkways made safe—it's all coming together, but still so much to do."

"That's the thing, Foxy. Work is never finished."

Fox furrowed her eyebrows. "You think I can't finish what I started?"

"No, it's not like that. I mean an estate, a village and all the land surrounding attached to a title, is never finished. Since these lands and title were created, it's been an ongoing job, passed down from generation to generation. As duchess I'm only a caretaker, making all the improvements I can, until my heir, Lucy, inherits my title."

"And lands, remember," Fox said.

The title and the estate had been split apart when Clementine's father had to sell up due to mounting debts. Hundreds of years of unbroken history came to an end. By Clementine's marriage to Fox, the estate and title had been reunited—but temporarily.

Even if they had children together, Clementine couldn't pass on her title to them as only children conceived by both parties in the marriage could inherit a title, something that made Clementine angry but hopefully would change in coming years.

Luckily, unless Clementine died before her elderly cousin, his daughter Lucy would inherit, and a lovelier girl you could not meet. She had come to stay with them for a holiday, and both she and Fox fell in love with her.

Fox had insisted that the house go back with the title, both in Rosebrook and in Thistleburn. She wanted everything returned to the way it was before Isadora Fitzroy had to sell the land. It really touched Clementine that someone would love her so much and be willing to do that.

They had decided that if they had any children of their own, their children would share the responsibility of the family's lands and be equally provided for, even if they couldn't have titles.

"But I'll have lots of time to keep improving the estate when we come back," Clementine said.

"I'm not sure what we will be coming back to," Fox said. "Archie and Ash are brilliant individually, but together…not team players."

Clementine had an idea percolating in her mind and she smiled at her partner. "How about we throw them into the water, tied to each other, and see if they both come up for air?"

"I like the way your mind works, Your Duchess-ship."

❖

"You'll keep an eye on Agatha and Ada?" Clementine said.

It was Sunday afternoon, and Ash and Clementine were in the

Rosebrook Trust office. They were going over all the duties Ash would need to take responsibility for, while Clementine was away. The former medieval banqueting hall was the oldest part of the estate, and the only remaining building from the original Rosebrook Castle.

"Of course I will. They are the closest I have to a granny. Besides, I know Kay will be in to see them every day."

Kay was Clementine's best friend, and almost a big sister to Ash, and always helped take care of the old women, Agatha and Ada. Both Kay and her husband Casper gave up high-paying jobs in the city to move to Rosebrook and buy a small holding where they could be as self-sufficient as possible.

"Okay…" Ash watched Clementine look down the list she had on her iPad. "I'll send you a copy of this, don't worry. I just wanted to talk through them first."

"These are all my responsibilities? Just so I know, because Archie thinks she's the boss of everything, and with you and Fox not here, she'll be impossible, no doubt."

"Don't worry. Fox is giving Archie her instructions as we speak. So, next there's the mini parliament. Can you take the chair and go through the agenda with everyone?"

"Me? Take the chair? Wouldn't Archie expect to?" Ash said.

The village mini parliament was part of Fox's grand vision for this new kind of community. The idea came from Clementine's late grandmother, Isadora Fitzroy, who first had the noble thought of having a truly representative community.

"Archie won't be here in the evenings. She'll be going home to London after workt. Anyway, you'll be great. Now, first on the agenda should be getting a volunteer to take the beekeeping role in Bee World."

Ash took a note on her notepad. "I wish I had the time to take that job on. It would be fascinating to learn about beekeeping. It would be fun."

"I know, and so essential to our ecosystem. When Fox first came here and told me that she wanted to open Bee World, I had visions of some kind of weird theme park, not a large piece of land given over to a bee habitat."

Ash had taken a keen interest as the patch of land was dug up, the right flowers to attract the bees were planted, and then the first beehives arrived from the supplier. But her day job, which often spilled into the evening, didn't allow her enough time to dedicate to the little bees. "So Mr. Skinner the beekeeper will still be looking after them, meantime?"

Since the bees had arrived, Fox had arranged for a professional keeper to visit the village a few times a week to take care of the hives.

"Yes." Clementine's fingers whizzed across the iPad screen. "I've just emailed you the application pack for the short beekeeping course. Have anyone interested fill that out, and then email it back to the college," Clementine said.

"Got it. Anything else for the meeting?"

"Nothing other than any issues the community brings up. If there's anything you're not comfortable dealing with, just wait for us to come home. Next, the new doctor's surgery is nearly ready. Blake tells me the equipment is arriving tomorrow, so if you can check if she needs any help with anything, and keep an eye on Eliska."

Ash knew how hard Clementine and Kay had worked to make Eliska Novak feel welcomed into the community, as had Ash, but she was still so quiet, so shy. Dr. Blake Campbell had met Eliska and her daughter in a refugee camp, in the war-torn country of Ustana. She got her out and back to Britain, and after a lengthy immigration process, Eliska now had permission to stay in the UK.

"Okay," Clementine said, "there's still a few more things on the list."

Ash could have felt overwhelmed by all this new responsibility, but she loved it. After years of stagnating and simply looking after her dad, she now had time to see what she was capable of. Ash couldn't wait for what came next.

❖

Archie picked up the last few cases in the entrance hall of Rosebrook house and followed Fox out to the driveway. She had been helping Fox lift both her and Clementine's suitcases out into a waiting Volkswagen camper van.

Fox swung her bags into the open back door of the van and said, "That's the lot."

Archie put the bags in and sighed. "Are you quite sure you've got enough luggage?"

"Just about," Fox said.

Archie leaned her hand against the side of the van and said, "I bet most of it's yours too."

Fox grinned. "I've got to keep up the dapper Fox image."

"Are you sure Clementine is happy about going on her honeymoon to Scotland in a camper van? You didn't just bulldoze her into it?"

Fox raised an eyebrow. "No one can bulldoze Clem into anything. She's excited by the adventure and to go back to her land in Scotland. Besides, I've done enough travel by air for business this year. I just can't justify it, ecologically." Fox shut the back doors and patted the van. "She's a beautiful beast, isn't she?"

Archie followed Fox as she walked up to the front of the van. "Beautiful isn't the first word that springs to mind," she said.

"Oh, come on. You have no soul, Archie. Bertha is beautiful."

"Bertha?"

Fox gave her a cheesy grin. "Bertha. Not only is she beautiful, but she's electric, so the duchess and myself can have a more ecological honeymoon. But down to business." Fox clapped and rubbed her hands together. "I've emailed you a list of responsibilities I want you to concentrate on while I'm away."

Archie took out her phone and opened up her email. "Okay, got it. Open up in the morning, chair the mini parliament, give help to Blake at the surgery…"

Fox was way ahead of her. "Griffin will be arriving sometime this week, so make sure she's all set up in her cottage. The old beer factory has to be fitted exactly as per her instructions. Whatever she needs is okay."

In Clementine's grandmother's day, the beer factory had been the source of employment for the village, along with the now long abandoned machinery factory.

"Didn't she say what day?" Archie asked.

"You know Griff. It could be tomorrow, it could be a week. She's a free spirit."

"That she is."

Archie had shared a good few beers and lagers with Griffin and Fox, when Griffin was in town. Fox and Griffin were different. Where Fox was the perfect dapper gent, Griffin looked as though she had just returned from a gap year, wandering the globe, with nothing but the possessions that would fit in a rucksack, which had some truth to it.

Griff was a traveller and had a large social media presence after she'd travelled the world to find the perfect beers and learn how to make them. Fox first met her back in her student days and had always kept up their friendship. When Fox introduced Griffin to Archie, Archie wasn't sure what to make of her but soon was charmed. Griff was that special kind of character you'd always want to have a beer with.

"How long will she stay?" Archie asked.

"She's promised to stay at least until the factory is up and running. Maybe we can persuade her to stay longer," Fox said.

"I doubt it. She'll get itchy feet and want to get back out on the road."

Fox slapped her on the shoulder. "But she hasn't been to Rosebrook before. Magical things can happen in Rosebrook, like love."

Archie rolled her eyes. Magic and love were not the feelings she had when she thought of insular, small villages. She felt suffocated at the very thought.

She gazed down at the list of items in the email and spotted one called The Big Idea. "What's this Big Idea all about?" Archie asked.

"Oh yes." Fox held her hands up and gave the impression the phrase was up in lights. "The Big Idea. Clem and I want you and

Ash to come up with ideas to help publicize the village. We had the press night but need some sort of splash to reach people in all four corners of the kingdom. We need a diverse group—individuals and families—to join us in this new community."

Archie sighed internally at the thought of working with Ash. "Maybe we should wait till after you come back from your honeymoon."

"Why?"

"Ash clashes with me whenever we have to work on anything. We couldn't even dance at your wedding without Ash sniping and complaining. I'm used to leading teams of mature businesspeople, not placating a young woman with a chip on her shoulder."

"Ash is an intelligent, bright woman with lots of ideas. Be open to them, and be positive, Archie. No bickering."

Archie was insulted. "I don't bicker. I'm thirty-six years old. I'm a professional."

Fox folded her arms and gave her a questioning look. "Well I think she must bring out your inner child because it sounds like the playground sometimes."

"So says the CEO who has dance breaks in the office?"

Fox just laughed, and said, "Oh, and as well as Griffin, remember—Patrick Doyle is arriving in a few weeks. Make sure he has everything he needs, and show him around the place. I'd like him to work with Griffin at the beer factory. I think Griff's influence would be good for him."

Patrick Doyle was the latest new member of the Rosebrook community, having applied for a place with them. Rosebrook wasn't like other villages. Whereas a lot of villages up and down the country suffered when wealthy city people bought up the houses and priced out the locals and their next generation, Rosebrook was a closed community.

Fox and Clementine owned the land and almost all the houses. This gave them the power to make Fox's dream of a village community with low-cost housing a reality.

The cottages were nowhere near even half full yet, and more

were still to become available, but they weren't in a rush. Fox and Clementine wanted to slowly build up their community, piece by piece.

Rosebrook's mission was to be a place open to all, a safe place for the LGBTQ+ community to live and work, and for everyone to share the common goal of ecology and protecting the environment. Patrick Doyle, like all comers to Rosebrook, was granted a new home, a safe place to live, and a new job on arrival.

Archie looked forward to meeting their new resident. Even though she had long been Fox's environmental consultant, her job had changed and broadened to helping make this community a success. Welcoming new residents and giving them a start at a new life was a great part of this job.

"I'll make sure Patrick feels at home," Archie said.

"Fantastic." Fox fished a bunch of keys out of her pocket and handed them to Archie. "These are the keys to the house. I know you said you won't stay at the house, but just in case you change your mind. The maid and housekeeping service won't be there, but I'm sure you could fend for yourself."

Archie took the keys and said, "Thanks. I'll stick to going home every night, but I'll keep an eye on the place."

As inconvenient as the commute from London was, there was no way she wanted to spend her evenings as well as her working days in the village. Village life brought back too many unhappy memories.

"So, you think you'll be away for a month?"

"Something like that, depends on how things go in Thistleburn. Clem has a couple of ceremonial duties, and then we'll see how the land lies. I'm excited to see what Thistleburn is like. Maybe it can be our second Rosebrook." Fox grinned.

Archie laughed. "You're going to come back with more dreams, aren't you?"

"Hopefully, but don't worry—Clem is good at keeping my feet on the ground. After Thistleburn we'll go further up north."

They started to walk back to the house.

"I hope you've got some nice hotels booked for her ladyship," Archie said.

Fox stopped and said with mock shock, "Do I look like I would have a duchess sleep in a camper van every night? No, the camper is just for comfort. I've got some nice five star hotels booked, as we slowly make our way to Scotland, and then I have a surprise for Clem for the last part of our honeymoon."

"What can you tell me?"

"A private yacht to sail around the Scottish islands. It will be beautiful."

"Gossiping again, you two?"

Neither of them had noticed Clementine walking up from the office. Luckily she didn't seem to have heard anything.

"We love a good gossip," Fox said.

"Well, from tomorrow, no more." Clementine looked at Archie and said, "Unless the village is on fire, I don't want any work emails or phone calls while we're on our honeymoon. You and Ash can sort out anything that comes up."

"Of course, don't worry, Your Ladyship."

CHAPTER THREE

On Monday morning Archie arrived at work for eight o'clock after a long commute. She wasn't a morning person, and it made having to leave so early so hard. But apart from the early hour, she was quite looking forward to being in charge and doing things her way for a change. No music breaks or trampolining sessions while Fox was away.

She loved Fox and knew she got the best out of the staff, but Archie was more traditional and didn't want to take part in dance breaks every couple of hours. A day of quiet office work would be just be what the doctor ordered.

Archie grabbed her case and got out of the car. She set it on the ground while she plugged in her car at one of the charging points outside the office. Electric cars were important to Fox. She made sure there were plenty of charging points installed throughout the village, and everyone that worked for Fox Toys or the Rosebrook Trust was given a car as part of their pay package.

Once the car was charging, Archie grabbed her case and walked to the office door, taking out her keys as she went. She was just about to put her key in the lock when she spotted a light on and heard music being played.

She tried the handle and the door opened. Immediately on alert, she went inside as quietly as possible. Who would break in here, an office in the middle of nowhere?

Mind you, there was a lot of expensive equipment in here to steal. After a few steps her worry about a break-in changed to feelings of annoyance. Ash was sitting at her desk, reading a book and twirling her brown hair through her fingers.

Ash jumped when Archie marched into the open office. "Oh my God. You nearly gave me a heart attack."

Archie slammed her case down onto her desk. "What are you doing here? I thought we were being burgled."

Ash placed her bookmark in carefully and set down her book. "I work here. I mean, I know you think I'm the tea girl, but I do work here."

Archie got even more annoyed. Ash would never let that first interaction between them go. "You're getting boring now," Archie said with a sigh.

The song that was playing through the speakers changed to the love song that had been at number one for what seemed like a year to Archie. Every time she turned on the radio, her ears were assaulted by that sentimental nonsense.

"Please, not that bloody song."

Ash shot her a dirty look. "You are grouchy in the morning. It's part of my romance reading playlist, but I'll put it off if it offends you so much."

She pressed pause on her phone, and the music stopped abruptly.

"I'm not grouchy. I'm here early to open up"—Archie shook the keys—"and find you already here and playing awful music."

"It's not awful. You just need to lighten up, Archie. Besides, I have the keys just like you." Ash shook them the same as Archie had done. "Clementine gave them to me to open up."

Archie opened her case and took her iPad out. "I can see that it makes sense for you to have them in case of emergency, but it's really the office manager's responsibility to open up in the morning."

The bloody cheek, Ash thought. Archie was trying to act like the big boss and assert her dominance, like a wolf or something. Ash wasn't going to let that happen. She was the duchess's personal assistant, not just some secretary.

"The last time I looked, you were an environmental consultant, not office manager."

Archie sat down and turned on her computer. "Well obviously when Fox isn't here, I'm her deputy."

Archie was obstinate and dismissive, and it was really starting to annoy Ash now. "Look, I'm the duchess's PA, and she's given me the keys and specific tasks to take care of. There's no boss—we're a collective."

Archie looked over from her computer and gave Ash a serious look. "There's always a hierarchy in a team, always a leader. I'm the oldest and most senior, so the task naturally falls to me. Besides, Fox gave me a list of tasks to be responsible for. So you do yours, and I'll do mine."

Ash didn't want to argue any more, or she might say something she'd regret. As Archie said, she'd stick to her own tasks and hopefully they wouldn't cross paths too much.

Ash loved the early summer. The birds were singing, and you could smell the sea air in the soft breeze. Beautiful. Although she had a dream of seeing the world outside Rosebrook one day, nowhere could ever substitute for her home. Rosebrook was in her heart, and now that it was slowly getting back on its feet, Ash was feeling so optimistic about the future.

As she turned the corner into Rosebrook estate, she was surprised and irritated to find that Archie's car was parked outside the office.

"Bloody Archie," Ash said under her breath.

God knew what time she would have had to leave her London home this morning, just to beat Ash to the office. Was she so insecure that beating Ash to open up the office was important to her?

Ash marched up to the office and through the door, ready to have words with Archie, but she caught her breath just as she was about to say something snarky. Archie sat with her head resting on the desk, fast asleep.

Ash chuckled to herself and then put her bag on her desk. "I think Sleeping Beauty needs some coffee."

She walked up to the back of the room where the coffee machine was and made coffee for them both, then grabbed a bottle of water from the fridge for Archie.

Archie was still sleeping when she placed the cup of coffee on her desk. Ash didn't disturb her yet, but instead got her book out and started playing her romance playlist. She thought the music would wake Archie quite quickly, but she continued snoozing.

Ash found herself smiling as she watched Archie's sleeping form. Archie was different from the gorgeous Fox but still as good-looking. She had her own special kind of dapper. Instead of a full three-piece suit, Archie wore the best designer jeans, a dress shirt, and a waistcoat, with a gold pocket watch chain. Brown distressed boots and an undercut hairstyle with a topknot finished off her hipster style.

All that and her tall, strong physique meant Ash couldn't deny that Archie was good-looking. If only she wasn't so disagreeable. She picked up her book and took a sip of her coffee.

She'd started a new book last night, and it was just heating up. The story was about an older earl who fell in love with his younger secretary. One of Ash's favourite tropes in romance fiction was age gap. There was something so sexy to Ash about an older, more worldly person. Maybe it was because she was the complete opposite to worldly.

The only time she'd been out of Rosebrook was to go to school, and although she'd met a girlfriend at school, and they'd tentatively explored their new-found sexuality, that was nothing to what someone had usually experienced at her age.

She gazed at Archie. *You're thirty-six. I bet you've seen a lot of the world.*

Ash shook herself from her thoughts. Rupert, Fox's PA, would be here soon, along with the other staff, and as annoying as Archie was, she didn't want the staff to see her at a disadvantage. Plus, her coffee would be getting cold.

Ash got up just as the song that annoyed Archie so much

yesterday started playing. That was the perfect wake-up song for her. She shook Archie gently on the shoulder.

Archie gasped and sat up, not appearing to know where she was.

"Nice sleep?" Ash said.

Archie scrubbed her face. "I wasn't sleeping. I was resting my eyes."

"Of course you were. Here, I made you coffee."

Archie looked down at it. "It's black. You remembered."

Ash sat on the edge of the desk. "Of course I did. I'm the tea girl, remember?"

Archie took a sip and hummed. "Thanks. I didn't get a chance to pick up breakfast."

"Breakfast? This is elevenses time for country folk. You must have left incredibly early, just to beat me in here."

Archie gave her a look of disdain. "I wasn't trying to beat you. I'm not a child, and please put that stomach-churning song off."

"Tired and grumpy?" Ash stood up and leaned over the desk. "Well, think about this. I only have to roll out of bed, and I'm here. So unless you want to continue this game of trying to be the alpha wolf of this pack and leave your home in London at midnight, you'll see it only makes sense for me to open up."

Archie was going a little red in the face, with anger, Ash guessed, so she turned and walked back to her desk. She was walking on air. She was normally quite a quiet, easy-going woman, but Archie always brought out the stubborn in her.

Ash enjoyed their sparring. It was exciting in a way and made her more confident in herself than she ever had been before. Ash was so grateful to Clementine for giving her this job. It was opening up her world and helping her find her strengths. Before she started working here, she would have shied away from a confident, older person like Archie, but now she was proving to herself that she could be so much more, that she was worth so much more.

Just as she sat down at her desk, Archie slammed down her coffee mug and said, "Fine. I'll allow you to open up. Just make sure the office is always open on time." Archie got up and stomped off to the office bathroom.

Ash rubbed her hands together with glee. "I won. Ash fifteen, old grumpy-drawers, love. This working together is going to be fun."

CHAPTER FOUR

The next week was anything but fun for Archie. She and Ash continued pushing each other's buttons and competing for the rest of the staff's time to work on their own list of duties.

This morning Archie was supposed to be working on one of her research projects, but instead of looking at her computer screen, she was staring over at Ash with simmering anger. She never usually had a problem at work with office politics. She was a mature team player—well, normally she was leading the team, but still a team player.

But there was something about Ash that brought out a different side to her. The other morning when she fell asleep at her desk had been embarrassing. Nothing like that had ever happened to her before, but she'd had to leave home at four in the morning, and she hadn't gotten to sleep till half-past one.

If Rupert and the other staff had seen her asleep at her desk, it would have destroyed her authority and the standards she set for the team. At least Ash had woken her before that happened. But she did realize opening up the office was a battle she couldn't win. Ash lived here, and it made sense for her to take care of that duty.

What did it even matter anyway? She had thought about delegating that responsibility, but because Ash had assumed it was her job, it brought out Archie's stubbornness.

"Archie?"

Archie was so engrossed in her thoughts and looking over at Ash that she jumped. "Yes? What?"

It was Rupert, Fox's PA. Archie knew him well from the time they'd worked with Fox at Fox Toys. He was really good at his job, and a hard worker. When Fox asked him to come to Rosebrook with her, he jumped at the chance for a new life with his partner Jonah. They lived in one of the Seascape cottages. Jonah was a big bear of a man who had been a bar manager in London. He was a perfect fit to run the refurbished village pub, The King's Arms.

"Sorry to interrupt, but I'm going for the sandwiches now." The pub made up platters of sandwiches, wraps, and pies for the office workers' lunch, which Fox paid for. "What would you like from the shop while I'm out?"

Archie stood and got some money from her wallet, then gave it to Rupert. "Yes, could you get me an energy drink? I need something to wake me up."

"Will do. I won't be long."

She sat back down and brought her attention back to her work, where it should have been all morning. She was researching electric farm vehicles for Fox. She wanted to encourage their resident old-school farmers, Mr. and Mrs. Murdoch, and Mr. Mason, to farm in more environmental and sustainable ways.

But so far today, she'd hardly made any progress. She smelt a beautiful aroma of perfume that set off tingles in her body. She looked up, expecting to find one of the other members of staff, and instead found Ash standing there.

To her surprise the tingles didn't dissipate—they only increased, strangely.

"Can I help you?" Archie asked.

"No, I just wanted to let you know I'm going to eat my lunch and read my book at the beach lookout," Ash said.

Archie looked at the book tucked under Ash's hand. Its nauseating title was *The Earl's Price of Love*. She pointed at the book and said, "You know that sentimental claptrap will rot your brain."

Ash looked furious. "Only someone with an emotional bypass could think that, but I'll leave you to your own personality flaws. I won't be back after lunch for a while—I'm going to do the duchess's walkabout."

Every few days or so, Lady Clementine took a walk through the village and spoke to the residents about any concerns or troubles they had. Archie would say this for the duchess—she did really care about people here and took her role as leader of the community very seriously.

"What about lunch? Rupert's just left to pick it up," Archie said.

"I brought my own. So I'll go and rot my brain, apparently, with this book and be back later."

Archie watched her walk out of the office and an idea popped into her head. Maybe there was a way to get her own back for that morning and show Ash and the staff who was boss.

She grinned and quickly typed out an email to all the staff. Fifteen–love Ash said it was this morning? She thought it would be fifteen all now.

❖

Ash finished her lunch at the point overlooking the beach. It was right next to her house, so it was a favourite place of hers. The sound of the waves and the sea air made it such a relaxing spot.

She put her book away and said, "That's enough brain rotting for now."

It really aggravated Ash that people had such a bad opinion of romance fiction. These books gave her joy and were as well-written as any other genre. Over the years she had added to her mother's collection with some lesbian romance of her own. The books fuelled her dreams, and she never gave up hope that she would find someone who would make her feel love and passion like the characters in her books.

After all, the same happened for her mum and dad. There were few young people in the village when her mum was young, but one day a young Irish wanderer arrived in the village, looking for a few weeks' work with her grandfather on the fishing boat, and never left. There must be someone out there for her surely.

"Back to work."

Ash usually accompanied the duchess on her walkabouts, with notepad in hand, to write down any issues. She enjoyed it a lot. It meant she got to know the newcomers to the village well, and she didn't think they'd mind seeing just her.

She walked down the road at the entrance of the village and headed towards the Seascape cottages. These were her favourites, but she was biased, given her love of the sea. Each cottage had seashells from Rosebrook beach embedded into the walls, one of Clementine's great ideas.

Ash walked by the first cottage, as she knew the residents were at work. Jay and Erica Strickland were a couple in their late fifties, brought into the village to run the shop. She would see them later.

Next up were Prisha and her toddler son, Rohan. She saw them in the cottage's front garden and waved. Prisha wore her long black hair held in a ponytail today and always managed to look beautiful, despite being the harassed mother of a lively toddler.

"Good morning, Pris."

Pris stood up from her weeding and smiled. "Hello. Look, Roh, it's Ashling."

The little boy toddled to the gate. Prisha joined him and lifted him up.

Ash took his hand and gave him a kiss. "Hi, Rohan. How are you today?"

"He's in quite a good mood today, so we thought we'd do a bit of gardening."

"And how are you, Pris?"

Prisha's smile faltered, and she went silent. Ash liked and admired Prisha so much. Life hadn't been kind to Prisha, recently widowed then made redundant, but she was a strong woman, and instead of giving up on life, she saw Fox's advert for people to join them here in Rosebrook and decided to hope for a new life for her and Rohan.

She'd enrolled for an online degree in English and Communication, and Clementine hoped to get her involved in the tourist programme they were working on.

After the short silence, Prisha said, "Okay. I'm just taking things day by day. It's all you can do, isn't it?"

Ash knew the pain of losing someone you loved, but to be left with a young child to bring up on your own must be unbearable.

"Yes, you just keep going because if you stop—"

"You think too much," Prisha finished for her.

Ash nodded.

"Listen to us getting morbid," Prisha said. "At least it's a beautiful day. Summer in Rosebrook was just what I needed."

"It doesn't seem that long since we had the Great Storm last year," Ash said.

"Oh yes, Lady Clementine told me about it. Sounds awful."

Ash smiled. "It was, but luckily we have the most enthusiastic of community leaders in Evan Fox. She didn't let us feel sorry for ourselves, and now the village is as good as new."

"You would never know the village had been through something so damaging. I hope the duchess and Fox are having a nice honeymoon, although I've heard the weather has been rainy this summer in Scotland."

Ash chuckled. "That won't deter Fox. She doesn't allow things like rain to ruin her fun. Anyway, I better get on. I'm doing the duchess's walkabout today."

"Thanks for dropping by."

Archie looked down at her iPad to check her notes. She had been leading the rest of the staff in a meeting for the past twenty minutes, and unlike the rest of the day, she didn't have the annoyance of Ash trying to involve herself in it.

"Okay, to recap, I want a report on the sourcing of equipment for the proposed toy and sensory equipment manufacturing scheme for the former machinery factory, and that's everything."

After everyone had filed out, Archie checked her emails and replied briefly to a couple. She stopped when she felt a presence behind her. Archie turned her head and saw Ash standing there. She stood up and turned to face her.

Ash looked at her with a mix of anger and hurt. "You had a meeting without me?"

Archie felt immediately guilty. "You were busy. I was just leading a quick team meeting."

"That is not why you did it," Ash said angrily.

Archie saw Rupert and some of the other staff in the main office watching. She shut the conference room door to give them privacy.

"Listen—"

Ash cut her off. "I mean, I could just about live with being the office tea girl, but to be deliberately left out of a meeting? That's something else. Are you so insecure that you would show me who's boss by having a meeting without me?"

"You were busy. I didn't…" Archie couldn't finish the sentence.

"I should have left you sleeping the other morning. Left you snoring your head off while everyone filed into the office. I suppose you think you've put points on the board now, that it's fifteen all. Fine. But just to let you know, I'm not going to back down. I will do what the duchess asked of me, and your fragile ego won't stop me."

Ash turned on her heel and marched out of the conference room. Archie's guilt had turned to anger, and she hurried after her.

"I do not have a fragile ego."

She then realized that every face in the office was looking at her. Archie could feel her face burn with embarrassment.

She quickly shut the door and gathered herself. Never in her professional career had someone gotten under her skin like Ashling O'Rourke. Occasionally she had butted heads with some men who didn't like to take advice from someone like her, but that was soon addressed by her depth of knowledge and natural leadership skills.

This was childish, and she vowed not to be caught up in Ash's silliness.

CHAPTER FIVE

By the time Friday came, Archie was finding her vow difficult. They had been stepping on each other's toes all week. This afternoon Archie thought she'd get out of the firing line and take care of one of Fox's instructions. She'd check on Blake Campbell and her wife, Eliska, at the doctor's surgery.

According to Clementine there hadn't been a doctor's practice in the village for thirty years. Getting Blake, with her background of working with the Red Cross, was quite a coup for Rosebrook. The community and especially their elder residents would greatly appreciate a local doctor.

It wasn't just important to build a community to work in harmony with the environment. It was also equally important to have a healthy population, in order to make it all happen.

Archie walked up to the door of the surgery, based in the old building that had originally housed the doctor's office.

She knocked and said, "It's Archie, anyone at home?"

"Come in."

Archie walked into a bright reception area, with the smell of fresh paint and the furniture wrapped in plastic. Blake was behind the reception desk.

"Good morn—"

Blake looked at her watch. "It's just turned twelve. Afternoon, Archie."

"Afternoon. How's things?" Archie asked.

Blake walked around the reception desk and shook Archie's hand. "Going well, I think. The furniture arrived yesterday, and the IT and phones came this morning."

"Excellent. I just thought I'd make sure you have everything you need."

"We're popular this morning. Ashling arrived ten minutes ago."

Archie's heart sank. *Can I do anything without that woman interfering?*

At that point Ash and Eliska walked out of one of the treatment rooms.

"Eli?" Blake said. "Archie's come to make sure that everything was going well, just like Ashling."

"Hi, Archie," Eliska said.

Eliska was still so quiet, but more talkative than when she first arrived. Archie turned her gaze to Ash.

"Ashling."

"Archie," Ash said tersely.

The tension and silence in the room was deafening. Blake must have felt it because she said, "Why don't we all have a nice cup of tea."

But Eliska chipped in, "Blake, Ash and I were going to have a coffee and a chat. Why don't you get something to eat at the pub with Archie. Ola is playing with Kay and her boys."

Blake turned to her and said, "Archie, would you like to join me?"

"Yes, I'd like that." Archie was more than happy to get out of this frosty atmosphere.

Blake kissed her wife on the cheek, and then she and Archie walked up to the pub. "It's a beautiful country pub, isn't it?" Blake said.

The pub had been carefully restored to its original design from six hundred years ago, with modern amenities of course.

"It is. Fox and Lady Clementine wanted to marry the old and the new, a bit like themselves," Archie joked.

"True." Blake laughed.

As the village wasn't even at half-capacity yet, the pub was never busy, but two of the old-timers were in for a lunchtime pint. The pub would be important in bringing a very diverse village population together. The first ingredient was Jonah, the bar manager. He looked like a big strong farmer, and so the older locals respected and liked him.

Apart from Mr. Fergus, Jonah and his partner Rupert were the only gay men the original villagers knew, and Jonah certainly broke stereotypes.

Another way the pub would help change attitudes was that Fox and Clementine had insisted on new unisex toilets, so no one was subjected to the awkwardness that some in the LGBTQ+ community experienced outside the bubble of Rosebrook.

It had taken some time for the older residents to accept this change, but now everyone was used to it.

"Afternoon, gentlemen," Archie said to the three men sitting at the bar, then turned to Mr. Murdoch and Mr. Mason. "How are your animals doing on the new feed?"

"They're enjoying it. Eating like never before," Mr. Murdoch said.

"Good, good." Archie then said to Blake, "Our resident farmers are trialling a new environmentally friendly animal feed."

They got two bottles of no-alcohol lager and took them to a table next to Fergus, who was enjoying lunch.

"How is the surgery looking, young Blake?" Fergus asked.

"Looking shipshape, Mr. Fergus. Not long now."

"I can't tell you how much better it will be having a doctor on our doorstep, especially for the old 'uns like me."

"We're nearly ready for you," Blake said.

Once Fergus turned his attention back to his food, Archie asked Blake, "So how are things, really?"

Blake took a sip from her bottle. "At the surgery, finding my way around the computer appointment system is my biggest challenge. It's been a long time since I worked as a GP, so I'm a bit rusty. I'm more used to bullets flying and bombs exploding."

"How long were you with the Red Cross?" Archie asked.

"Twelve years. It's a long time, but I enjoyed every minute of helping all the people I could. It was a vocation."

"It sounds like a quiet country practice isn't really your scene."

"Eli and Ola need a quiet country practice, so I'll learn to adapt," Blake said.

"It's an important career and way of life you've given up."

"You'd give up anything for the woman you love. I'll still be a doctor, just in a different way, and it'll be a welcome relief from the stressful asylum process."

Blake had given up everything, it seemed, for love. Archie wondered what it was like to love someone that much you'd give anything to make them happy.

Blake continued, "Eli and Ola have seen things and had to endure things no one should have to. When I met her, I vowed I'd get them both back here and give them a safe home. Rosebrook is perfect."

Archie didn't know the personal details, but you could read between the lines. "You're a good person, Doctor."

"I'm not, believe me. I still have my moments. It's hard trying to support someone who has PTSD and anxiety. Every day is a challenge for her, and for me to help her, but it is so easy to love Eli. She's a beautiful soul."

Archie was touched by those sentiments. She had never been around truly loving relationships before she met Fox's parents, and then Fox and the duchess. Could love be that pure?

Blake added, "Ola is recovering much faster, children do. She's made great friends with Kay and Casper's boys, which is letting her be a child again. I promised Eli a good and a safe life here, and I hope she can be happy with me."

"You can tell she loves you," Archie said.

Blake looked down at the table and played with the beer mat. "I hope so—she says she does, but—"

"But what?"

Blake cleared her throat. "I thought you all might realize. Technically, I married Eli to help her become a British citizen. Don't get me wrong, I fell in love with Eli from the first moment I saw her and would have wanted to marry her anyway, but I don't know if she would have. We don't have a full relationship."

Archie was so surprised. "I would never have guessed. I mean, I'm no expert in love and relationships, but you look at each other with such adoration, that I just assumed."

"You think so?" Blake asked. "She tells me she loves me, but I don't know if it's in the same way I love her."

"It looks like she does. I'm not one to give advice—the longest I've been out with someone is about three months, if that—but I'd say, give her time. You've given her safety and a new life, and love. I'm sure she just needs to settle in."

"Sometimes it feels like I'm getting closer to her, but then she has a bad day and pushes me away. I'm a doctor, and psychologically I understand it, but emotionally it's still hard."

"I can imagine," Archie said.

But could she imagine? It was hard to put herself in Blake's shoes. In some small, barely acknowledged part of her soul, she did wonder what it would feel like to love, to not be alone. Being alone never really worried her as a younger woman, but she started to think about it more and more recently. She supposed it was Fox getting married that shone a light on that part of her soul, forcing her to think about it.

"Love is a funny thing, Archie. It can make you the sappiest, most sentimental person alive, but it can also make you annoyed, angry, frustrated," Blake said.

Now that was something she could understand. There was one face that leapt to mind when Archie thought of anger, annoyance, and frustration—Ashling O'Rourke.

The evening came quickly for Ash. It was the village's weekly meeting at The Meeting Place, as Fox liked to call it. It served as the village's mini parliament where the community came together to take, hopefully, collective decisions.

Ash had dinner with her dad and left early to walk up to the deconsecrated church building that had been transformed into The Meeting Place. She always attended the meeting every week, but this one would be different. Ash would be chairing the meeting, and she was nervous.

She had gained so much confidence since starting work with the duchess and the trust, but chairing a meeting with all the residents, some of whom had strong opinions, was daunting.

Ash didn't know if she had it in her, but she was determined to try. At least one thing was true—if she did make a mess of it, she wouldn't fall flat on her face in front of Archie. Archie rarely came to these meetings, unless her expertise was needed, as she wasn't a resident. Plus Ash always had the impression that as soon as Archie's work was done, she liked to get back to London as quickly as possible.

Ash walked up the steps to the building and put her key in the lock, but it was already open. Her heart started to beat faster. Had someone broken in? She walked through the front door and saw the light on, in what was the main body of the former church.

She stood on tiptoe and peeked through the glass-panelled window on the doors and saw Archie sitting on the stage, next to the wooden lectern. "Blimey, her again."

Frustration was coursing through Ash's veins when she burst through the doors.

"What are you doing here?"

Archie looked up, then glanced at the clock on the wall. "You're early for the meeting."

"I'm here to set up."

"Set up what?"

Ash marched down the aisle, to the stage. "You're everywhere I go this week."

"Tell me about it," Archie said. "Set up what?"

Ash walked up the steps onto the stage and put her bag on the desk. "Set up for the meeting. I'm chairing while Fox and Lady Clem are away."

Archie laughed. "*You* are chairing?"

Archie's laughter hurt her. "Yes, why is that so funny?"

"You have no experience."

Ash stabbed a finger at her. "And you have no experience living in a village. You get out of here as quickly as you can every day." Archie's smile faltered, and she cleared her throat.

Ash continued, "Why do you keep popping up every time I go to do a task that the duchess has given me, like this lunchtime at the doctor's surgery?"

"The duchess may have suggested you check in with Eliska, but Fox gave me the responsibility of helping to get the surgery up and running, just like every other task you've turned up at."

Ash frantically looked in her bag for her work iPad. She opened the document Lady Clementine had given her and put it in front of Archie on the desk.

Archie read down the list and said, "Why have they done this?"

"What?" Ash asked.

Archie put her iPad next to Ash's. "Look at the list."

Was this some sort of joke? Because if it was, it was just making everything harder. "It's the same. Why?"

"Before she left, Fox told me to make sure I worked well with you. Possibly because we butt heads and don't work together well. Maybe they want to force us to find ways of getting along."

Ash sighed and plopped down on the seat. "We don't make a good team."

"That's one thing we agree on."

At that comment, Ash smiled at Archie. It was the first genuine smile she had gotten from Ash—and she liked the feeling.

"So what do we do?" Ash asked. "You're the one from the corporate world—you must have done millions of courses on team building."

"I have, but I usually lead the teams."

"I did get that impression. You're usually top dog, leader of the pack, and I'm—What am I?"

Archie could have made many barbed comments in response. "An independent mind."

"Is that the polite way of saying annoying and stubborn?"

Archie wanted to say yes. Ash was aggravating, but she made life interesting. This week had certainly not been boring.

"No, but I think we have to call a ceasefire and go through these responsibilities. Fox and Lady Clementine obviously think our working relationship is a problem for the trust, so we have to find a way to fix it."

"You're right, but what about tonight…"

"What?" Archie asked.

"I didn't want to let Clementine down, but I've been so nervous about tonight. I mean, I've grown up being the little girl of this village, and now I have to stand up in front of them and lead them. Imagine Mr. Murdoch and Mr. Mason listening to me."

Archie saw a vulnerability in Ash then, one that immediately tugged at her heart and made her feel protective.

"You should have confidence in yourself. You certainly do with me. I'm thirteen years older than you and have more experience, but you don't mind telling me what's what."

Ash sat back in her chair and sighed. "That's different. You're Archie."

Archie didn't quite know what that meant. "Okay, well how about we co-chair the meeting. I can lead initially, if you feel nervous, and then you can come in on any issues that come up?"

Ash smiled. Two genuine smiles she had gotten out of Ash now, more than the whole time since she'd arrived in Rosebrook.

"Yes, let's do that." Ash went rummaging in her bag again and brought out a pile of papers held together in an elastic band. "I made up little leaflets with our agenda on them."

"Perfect. Why don't you greet the people as they arrive and hand them out? You know them better than me," Archie said.

"Okay, I will."

"Wow, we agreed on something. That's new."

Ash looked at her and simply said, "Yes, it's new."

They held each other's gaze, and Archie felt her heart thud and her stomach tighten. There was a silence that neither seemed able to fill, so Archie cleared her throat and said, "How was Eliska after Blake and I left today?"

"She was okay. I think Eliska is happy here with us, certainly with Blake."

"I think Blake would like to know that," Archie said.

"What do you mean? Did she say something to you?"

Archie didn't want to give away any secrets, so she tried to skirt around the issue. "I know Eliska had a terrible time in her country, and Blake tried to save her, so they—"

"Oh, you mean the fact they got married so Eliska could become a British citizen? Yeah, I know that—didn't you?"

"No, my relationship intuition isn't very good. But Blake said she would have married her anyway. She's the love of her life."

Ash placed her hand on her heart and gave an exaggerated, whimsical sigh. "What an amazing experience it would be, to be the love of someone's life."

Archie looked away. She could only picture unhappiness at that thought. Instead of responding, she said, "Blake doesn't want to push her and doesn't know if she loves her or is *in* love with her."

Ash said, "Eliska wanted advice on how to let Blake know how she feels and how to move their relationship to the next level, but she didn't know how to."

Archie couldn't imagine Ash having much if any experience to impart. "What was your advice?"

Ash's face became animated and excited. "I lent her a book from my collection, where the couple are living in this exact same situation."

Archie couldn't believe it. "You gave her a romance novel? Seriously? Ash, this is not a school romance. This is real life, with real emotions and real people that can be hurt."

Ash lost her smiley animated look, and the face that Archie was more used to seeing returned. "You don't know anything about romance fiction, or romance probably, so you can keep your opinions to yourself."

"*Fiction* is the operative word. Fiction is exactly what those books peddle, and what your idea of love is."

"Oh, I see grumpy-drawers is back. You don't know what

you're talking about. These books let people experience all the different kinds of love there is. When you read them, they give you an ideal to strive for in your own life."

"What do you know about the pain and hurt of love? You're young, and you've lived your life sheltered in this village."

Ash had hurt strewn across her face. "I've been in love, and I've had my heart broken, so you don't know anything about me."

Archie immediately wanted to ask who, what, and why— because who would break Ash's heart?

"Ash—"

Before Archie could say sorry, the doors to the hall opened, and Mr. Fergus walked in.

"I'm not too early, am I?"

"Not at all, Fergus," Ash said.

Ash didn't look at Archie but picked up her leaflets and said, "I'll greet everyone at the door."

Yet again Archie had put her foot in it. She didn't mean to hurt Ash's feelings, but a romance novel was not going to fix a serious relationship like Eliska and Blake's.

Archie watched Ash open the doors and warmly greet those who had arrived. She tried to imagine sitting across from Ash and telling her it was over, like she did with Naomi, and breaking her heart. The thought made Archie profoundly sad.

Ash seemed to believe Archie thought she was lacking in some way, and didn't like her, but it wasn't true. Just because Archie didn't think she was ready for a leadership role, and they bickered a lot, didn't mean that she didn't think Ash was good at her job.

Archie admired the way Ash, without a formal university education, had listened and learned from others at the trust and become a valuable member of the team. Maybe she needed to show Ash that.

❖

Almost everyone was here, thought Ash as she waited at the open door of the former church. She saw Alanna Wilson coming down the road in her wheelchair with her next-door neighbours from the Countryside cottages, Whitney and Christian Kingston.

Alanna, a beautiful redhead with porcelain-white skin, was a few years older than her. After a car accident left her in a wheelchair, she came to Rosebrook for a new start in life.

Similar to Kay and Casper, Whitney and Christian left high-flying jobs in the city to make a fresh beginning. Christian had suffered a massive heart attack and so needed a slower pace in life. Fortunately, they were both able to work from home, so they could live in Rosebrook, still work freelance, and get heavily involved with the environmental projects in the village.

Ash smiled. She was so happy this evening—no one came alone. Neighbours walked to the meetings together, both old-timers and new arrivals. There weren't many in the village as yet, but the community spirit was strong with them all.

"Hi, Alanna, Whitney, Christian."

They all replied, and Christian said, "Are we late?"

"Not at all, but everyone's here. Come in."

Christian pushed Alanna's wheelchair up the ramp and in the building.

"It's my fault we're a bit late," Alanna said. "I was talking to Whitney about an idea I had for the community."

"Sounds interesting. Are you going to tell us at the meeting?" Ash asked.

"We sure are," Whitney said.

"Great, let's go before grumpy Archie gets any grumpier."

Alanna and Whitney laughed. "Archie's grumpy?"

"Well, she is with me, anyway."

Ash led them in to their seats, then took her place beside Archie. She saw Archie trying to smile at her, but she just ignored it.

Even though the pulpit was on a raised stage, when they held their mini parliament, whoever was leading the meeting stood at the front of the pews on the main floor. It was important to Fox that everyone in the community was on the same level, and no one less important than the other.

To emphasize that point, when The Meeting Place was

refurbished, she'd had the pews moved into a semicircle, so there wasn't a feeling of us and them, giving a more inclusive feel.

The sounds of chatter came to an end when Archie clapped her hands together. "Good evening, everyone. Thanks for coming. Since Evan and the duchess are on their honeymoon, you're stuck with me and my co-chair, Ashling."

Co-chair? Was that Archie's way of trying to make up with her?

"There's not too much on the agenda tonight, apart from anything you want to bring up." Archie looked down at her iPad and said, "First item Evan wanted me to bring up was Bee World. She's looking for a volunteer to learn to take care of the bees. We've found an online course for beekeeping, which the trust will fully pay for. Are there any volunteers?"

Ash looked out to the audience. Some looked horrified and shook their heads. Prisha shivered, and Ada said to her sister Agatha very loudly, "She wants us to keep fleas?"

The villagers around them chuckled.

"No, Ada, bees, Evan wants us to keep bees."

"I don't think we've enough room for bees, Aggie," Ada replied.

Ash chuckled to herself. The old ladies were adorable. One thing she did notice was an intense whispered conversation between Blake and Eliska.

Blake seemed to be encouraging her to speak, but Eliska sank lower in her seat and shook her head. Did she want to do it and was too shy to say so? Ash couldn't imagine Blake trying to push her into anything. She would need to check on that after the meeting.

"Anyone?" Archie repeated.

Casper said, "Christian and I are pretty busy with our own work and the community fields."

Casper was an expert on planting after running his own small holding since he and Kay arrived in the village. Fox had asked him to take a leadership role within the village and teach whoever was interested in vegetable growing.

Christian quickly volunteered when he and his wife Whitney arrived in Rosebrook. The land they were cultivating was small enough for them both to handle, but the plan was to turn more land over to cultivating food as the Rosebrook population grew.

Eventually Kay put her hand up. "If nobody else is willing, I could do it."

"Thank you, Kay. I know insects aren't everybody's favourite thing, but they are essential for the preservation of the food chain."

Archie looked back down at her iPad and continued, "On the subject of the vegetable fields, we'll soon be needing volunteers to pitch in with the harvest. How long will it be, Casper?"

"Maybe four or five weeks. I'll let you know and make up a work schedule."

"Thanks, Casper. Just like our friends the bees, the community fields are one of the cornerstones of what we're trying to do here in Rosebrook. One of our mission statements is to have food sovereignty. In other words, keep control over the way our food is produced, traded, and consumed here. The less reliant we are on the big supermarkets, the more money is kept in the community, with our resident farmers, Mr. Murdoch and Mr. Mason, our fisherman, Mr. O'Rourke, and now our own vegetable growers, Casper and Christian. Plus the less waste and deadly plastic packaging there will be, and the safer our plants and animals will be."

Ash was impressed with that goal of the trust. She'd never heard of the phrase food sovereignty but supposed that was just the fancy name for the way villages used to run, before big business took over.

His own fishing had never been a big part of her dad's business—there just weren't enough residents to make it viable. James relied on the private bookings by serious sport fisherman to make ends meet. But with Fox's encouragement, James now caught a small haul of fish and crabs to sell in the shop and in the next closest village. It brought a bit more money to their household.

After the meeting broke up, Ash went over to Blake and Eliska. "Eli, did you want to volunteer for the beekeeping role?"

"Yes, she did," Blake answered for her. "She was just too shy to volunteer."

"Blake," Eliska said sharply.

"Well, you did."

"Eli, would you be interested?"

Eliska wrung her hands together nervously. "Yes, I would find it interesting taking care of the little bees, but I don't know if I'd be good at it."

"Of course you would," Blake said.

"Blake, would you stop answering for me?"

Blake sighed. "Fine, you talk to Ash. I'll leave you to it." She walked over to talk to Kay, Casper, and the children.

"She means well," Eliska said. "Blake gets frustrated when I don't believe in myself."

"Well, she's right. You should believe in yourself more. Would you like me to tell Archie?"

"But Kay's already volunteered," Eliska said.

"Only because no one else did. If she's still interested, then you could both take the course," Ash said.

"It would be good to learn a new skill."

Ash smiled. "Leave it to me."

She left Eliska and hurried over to Archie, who was packing things away in her case.

"Archie, I spotted Blake trying to encourage Eliska to volunteer for the beekeeping role—"

"But I never saw her put her hand up," Archie interrupted.

"If you'd let me finish. She didn't have enough confidence, but I asked her just now, and she'd like to do it."

"Really? I never noticed Blake encouraging her, or I would have asked. Lucky I've got my co-chair to notice these things."

Ash grinned. "I'm useful for some things then?"

Archie looked her straight in the eye and said, "You're useful for lots of things, Ashling O'Rourke."

CHAPTER SIX

It had been a quiet weekend for Archie so far. Since she'd split up with Naomi, she had no date for Saturday night. Her usual routine was to go out for dinner on a Saturday night, then spend the night and breakfast with her date.

Archie could have called a few women who had given her their number, but she didn't feel like it. The drama she'd had with Naomi had put her off starting another casual dating relationship.

So she had a quiet night with Netflix and a takeaway. No drama, but also no one to talk to about the latest show she was binge-watching. The next morning, Archie followed her Sunday morning routine and walked along to the coffee shop a few minutes' walk from her flat in the trendy Notting Hill area of London.

She picked up a large coffee and a breakfast pastry, flirted a little with the barista, then went to buy the Sunday papers and her favourite magazine, *Eco World*. Normally she'd read the news online, but Sundays were for a slower pace, and she enjoyed slowly making her way through the papers in a more traditional way, while sipping her coffee.

She picked up *Eco World*. The cover story drew her in immediately. It was about something she'd dreamed about—a new eco city being built in Japan, called Takada. To be involved with something like that from the start would be a dream come true. Her loyalty was to Evan and to making Rosebrook work, but maybe one day when the community was working well, she could pursue that dream.

After a while Archie began to notice how quiet things were. She wasn't one for loud music or noise at the best of times, but this was different. It was an empty quiet. Strange, she'd never noticed it before. As she looked around the large room of her Victorian-built flat, the emptiness was uncomfortable.

She quickly started playing some music on her iPhone. The emptiness was a strange sensation—Archie had always had a full life, both professionally and privately. She had never wanted for the company of women, and she loved women.

Although she never had or wanted serious relationships, she'd always tried to be upfront about not getting serious, but something Naomi had said hit home with her, when she mentioned that at thirty-seven she was too old to waste time on a relationship going nowhere.

She'd gotten that impression from the last few women she'd dated. Somewhere deep inside she realized life was changing. She was entering a stage in life where the women she dated had different wants and priorities.

Archie took a big drink of her coffee and remembered that the weekend would be longer than usual, as Monday was a holiday. Maybe Dad would like to have lunch.

Quite often they would meet for Sunday lunch at a local gastro pub and talk about their week. She quickly dialled his number. "Hi, Dad."

"Hi, Arch. How are you?"

Archie tapped her fingers on the table. "I'm okay. I just wondered if you wanted to meet for lunch?"

He hesitated. "I'm sorry. Stuart's taking me to meet his sister's family today. We're having lunch at her house."

Archie tried not to sound too disappointed. "That's great. It really is getting serious then, Dad."

"It sure is. No lady to occupy your attention this weekend?"

When he said that, an image of Ashling O'Rourke entered her head. "No, I'm a pig, remember?"

He laughed. "That's right. Let's make plans for next weekend. I'd like you to come over to dinner with me and Stuart."

"I'd love that, Dad. I'll give you a call during the week."

"Okay, bye then."

Archie put the phone down, and the room felt even more empty. Everyone around her was settling down. Fox, her dad, the dates she had seen recently. She did admit that on nights like last night, sharing a meal with someone and binge-watching her favourite show with someone she cared about would be fun, but the screams, shouting, and pain from her childhood returned to her mind in an instant.

The enjoyment wasn't worth the feeling of being trapped in a long-term relationship. After suffering the ill effects of her parents' toxic marriage, she wasn't going down that road. She flicked through her phone's contact list, thinking of inviting someone for dinner.

She hovered over the name of a woman named Dior, who had come on to her at a party a few months ago and given her her number. Archie had only just met Naomi, so she'd declined, but perhaps now?

She was just about to press on her number when she changed her mind and sighed. She couldn't be bothered with the whole dating experience with someone who never even set her pulse racing.

It had been so long since anyone had set her pulse racing, since she'd felt that unquenchable need for someone. She was better off with her own company.

Archie swallowed the last of her coffee and got up to put the cup and the pastry bag in the bin. As she passed the bookcase in her living room, she saw the magazine Naomi had thrown at her across the wine bar table.

It was open to the picture of everyone dancing together at the Rosebrook party. She put down her empty cup, picked up the magazine, and gazed at the picture of Ash and her dancing. They were gazing into each other's eyes, and Archie recalled how they had bickered with each other and chuckled.

"You are the closest thing to making my pulse race recently, Ash."

She felt her stomach tighten at the memory. Wait—no. Archie hadn't meant that passionate, stomach-twisting feeling when you hungered for someone, but her body didn't get that memo.

"Passionate anger," she told herself.

Ash was beautiful, but she was thirteen years younger than her. Too big a gap for anything other than passionate anger.

Then she had a thought. She went back to get her phone and didn't hesitate to press on Ash's number.

When Ash answered, she said, "Hi, Ash, sorry to disturb you on a Sunday."

"Don't worry," Ash said. "Dad and I are doing a stock take of the boat shop. Nothing exciting."

Archie could see Ash in her mind's eye down on the beach, at the boat shop, and she couldn't help but smile.

"I know it's a holiday tomorrow, but I wondered if you wanted to meet up and go over our list of responsibilities, and splitting them up?"

"You want to come to Rosebrook on a non-workday?" Ash asked.

"Yes, why?" Archie said a bit more sharply than she'd meant to.

"Calm down, Archie. Okay then. Two o'clock okay?"

Archie tried to conceal her annoyance. In fact, she couldn't understand why she was annoyed anyway. "Two o'clock is fine. See you tomorrow."

When she ended the call, Archie said to herself, "What's so strange about going to Rosebrook on a day off?"

Then she noticed her heart was pumping hard and her pulse was racing.

❖

Ash was enjoying a lovely warm morning in Rosebrook. It was probably going to be a scorcher later on in the day.

She was walking to meet Alanna at her home—they had made arrangements to go down to the beach this morning. She'd packed sandwiches and snacks for lunch. After, she'd have plenty of time to get ready to meet Archie in the afternoon.

It was a strange turn of events, Archie coming to the village on a day off. She always gave the impression that she couldn't wait to get back to the bright lights of the big city. Ash would have thought Archie would have some gorgeous woman who spoke three languages or something to occupy her time on a day off.

Archie didn't give much away, but Clementine said that she didn't do long-term girlfriends. That was confirmed by the disdain that Archie had for Ash's romance novels.

She waved to Mr. Fergus as he passed on the other side of the road, out on his morning walk.

Ash wondered if someone had broken Archie's heart to make her so disdainful of love. If her books taught her nothing else, then they showed that there was always a psychological reason as to why people steered clear of love and relationships.

Everyone had their backstory, but what was Archie's? It would be exciting to find out.

Ash was jolted from her thoughts by her name being called. She looked up and saw Alanna waiting for her in her cottage garden.

"Hi, Al, ready for some sand, sea, and surf?" Ash asked.

"I can't wait," Alanna said.

Ash opened the gate and held it while Alanna came out in her wheelchair.

"What a lovely day it is, isn't it?" Ash said.

"Yeah, the weatherman said it's going to be super hot later."

Ash walked along beside Alanna. "I've got sandwiches and lots of snacks."

Alanna pointed to the cool bag hanging on her wheelchair. "And I've got the drinks."

"We're all set then," Ash said.

"You know, I still can't believe I've got a gorgeous beach on my doorstep, and that I'm actually able to use it."

One of the duchess's many ideas for Rosebrook was to make the beach accessible for wheelchair users. If they truly wanted a community that was open to all, then the beach had to be accessible to all.

After some research, Fox found the ideal system used on beaches around the world. The first was a wheelchair lift that ran down the beach stairs on the far side of the beach, because the other set was too steep.

They arrived at the stairs next to Ash's cottage, and Ash pressed the button on the lift. Alanna wheeled herself in, Ash shut the gate, and Alanna pressed the button inside. The lift slowly started to move, and Ash kept pace with it on the stairs.

"You know something?" Alanna said.

"What?"

"Since I've had to use this chair, I've watched people using beaches, and I was so sad that I'd never experience that again. I'm so lucky to be living here."

"I think we all feel lucky. Before Evan came here, the village was sad and neglected. It was quite depressing, to be honest," Ash said.

"I definitely feel lucky," Alanna replied. "I never even knew wheelchair access was possible on a beach."

If Evan was here, she'd say, *If you can dream it, anything is possible.*

At the bottom of the stairs, the door to the lift opened automatically and led out onto a hard pathway.

"Do you want a hand, Al?"

"Yes, thanks. Give me your bags and I'll hold them."

Next to the end of the line of beach huts were five water wheelchairs that allowed the users to go into the sea. But for now, she and Al wanted to sunbathe.

Ash pushed the chair down the access path until they reached a larger square area. "Shall I go and get some deckchairs?" Ash asked.

"Yeah, that would be more comfortable."

Ash returned with the chairs, and she and Alanna settled in.

"It's amazing to be on the beach. Thank you for coming with me," Alanna said.

"I'm always happy to be on the beach. I come down here every night to read my book. It's so relaxing."

"I brought my book. What are you into, Ash? I've got Stan Freeman's latest thriller."

"I'm a romance girl myself. A pompous prince, a dastardly duke, you know the kind of thing?"

Alanna smiled. "I do. I don't mind romance, but I really need a couple of bodies and a serial killer to keep me going."

At least Alanna hadn't made her feel bad about her love of romance. Not like Archie.

Ash unbuttoned her little denim shorts and pulled off her tiny T-shirt to reveal a white bikini.

"Wow, you look beautiful," Alanna said.

Ash suddenly felt bashful. She'd never bought anything like this before. She'd always worn a swimsuit, but since gaining confidence, she had started to express herself more in her clothes. When this bikini arrived from the online shop, she'd lost her nerve a bit. Could she really wear something like this?

But this morning she decided to be brave and wear it. It was only going to be herself and Alanna, and the beach would be quiet.

"Are you sure it's not too revealing?" Ash asked.

"Not at all, you have a great figure."

"Thanks, I'm a little nervous. I don't normally wear this kind of thing."

Alanna shook her head. "You've nothing to be nervous about. If you've got it, flaunt it, that's what I say. Life's too short to care about what other people think."

Ash smiled. "Thanks, I won't. Let's get the food out. I'm starving."

Ash gave Alanna some sandwiches, and they each took a drink.

"This is the life," Alanna said as she munched down on a sandwich.

"It's just perfect and getting hotter. I think the heat will be too much this afternoon," Ash replied.

"You're meeting Archie this afternoon, aren't you?"

"Yes, to sort out some work stuff. I was so surprised she wanted to come down here on a day off."

"What's Archie like? I haven't spent much time with her since I arrived," Alanna said.

Ash sighed. "Pompous, arrogant, bossy, a bit domineering, driven, but I think she has a kind streak hidden under the surface. She'd never intentionally hurt anyone, and she really cares about the project we're undertaking here, even if she doesn't want to live here."

"Well, that's quite a combination," Alanna said.

"Yes, so you can see why we butt heads a lot. She's coming to talk to me about our *responsibilities* this afternoon."

"Why, did something happen?"

Ash dug her toes into the warm sand. "The duchess and Evan gave us the exact same list of responsibilities for while they were away, so we've been bumping into each other all week, causing a lot of immature arguments."

Alanna smiled. "Are you going to fight it out this afternoon, then?"

Ash rolled her eyes. "I hope not. No, Friday she seemed more ready to share…I think."

❖

Archie didn't have to meet Ash till this afternoon, but she had nothing better to do, so she just got in her car and headed down to Rosebrook. She could always open up the office and get ahead of some work for the week.

She looked at her reflection in the driver's mirror and said, "You're sad."

Thinking of getting work done on a holiday showed how little she had in her life, but that was of her own choosing. She could have been spending time with Naomi this weekend, if she hadn't been honest about her feelings.

Archie's time alone yesterday had given her the chance to

reflect on her life and think about where it was going. She concluded that she was tired, tired of going through the motions with women that she had no intention of spending more than a few months with. She thought it was time to be single for a while, probably a long while. She'd had enough of the dating game. Maybe it was her age or the glass of wine thrown in her face that had woken her up. As for sex, no one had lit her on fire for a while, so going without didn't feel like a hardship.

Archie had hesitated to admit it to herself, but for some time, sex had become something she had to get in the right frame of mind for, which had never been the case in her life before.

Maybe she was getting too old? What a depressing thought.

As she drove into the village, Archie decided to stop at Ash's cottage, just to let her know she was there, and that they could meet in the office whenever Ash was ready.

She parked outside and made her way to the door. When she knocked, James O'Rourke answered.

"Archie?"

"Sorry, James. I'm supposed to be meeting Ash this afternoon, but I've come down early to catch up on work. I just wanted her to know I'm ready when she is."

"Sorry, Archie, she went to the beach with Alanna. Took a picnic, so they'll be a while."

"Okay, then, I'll see her when I see her. Thanks, James."

She was just about to walk away when James touched her arm. "Archie, do you have a minute?"

"Sure, how can I help?" Archie asked.

"I just wanted to thank you for helping Ash settle in with her job at the trust. She's like a changed girl since she started working there."

Archie immediately felt guilty because she hadn't made it easy for Ash. "You don't need to thank me. It's Fox and the duchess who deserve any thanks. She finds me annoying most of the time."

James laughed, and that was a strange sight. She didn't think she'd seen James smile once since she arrived.

"Not at all. Every time she complains about you, it makes me smile, because she's never been as animated about anything since her mum died. I don't know if the duchess told you about my wife..."

"Yes, yes she did. I'm sorry for your loss, James."

James nodded, his smile having long left his face. "The grief we both felt has been overwhelming, and I know Ashling has given up her chances in life to stay with me, and it's not fair. She's young, and she should have a life. Working at the trust has totally changed her. She's more confident, smiling more, and optimistic for the future. I'll mourn for the rest of my life, but it's time for my darling girl to live."

Being reminded of the pain Ash had been through made her feel even more guilty. She had been playing at a power game and fighting to be the one who opened up the office, and it felt pathetic now.

"Ash is a bright young woman, and we're lucky to have her."

"You'll keep an eye on her, won't you?"

"Of course I will."

Archie made a promise to herself to take Ash under her wing, help her as best she could, and protect her. Ash might annoy her sometimes, but she had to remember she was younger than her and had been through hell.

Archie said goodbye to James and drove towards the office, but as she got closer she had an urge to go to the lookout point to see Ash. She pulled in and walked to the coin operated tourist telescope the trust had put in place.

She searched for a coin in her jeans pocket and popped it in the slot. Archie didn't understand her compulsion to see Ash now when she would see her later, but she gave in to it anyway.

Archie turned the telescope toward the shore front and spotted two figures in the surf. She increased the magnification and saw Alanna in one of the beach wheelchairs, and Ash beside her. The wheelchair with its large yellow buoyant wheels had Alanna up to her knees in the sea, while Ash was a little further away, up to her neck in the water.

Both women were laughing and smiling, which made Archie smile. It was so nice to see Ash so carefree. *This must be what Ash was like when Archie wasn't annoying her.*

Then Ash started to wade into the shallower water. As she did, Archie's jaw dropped. Ash emerged from the surf wearing a skimpy white bikini, like Aphrodite rising from the sea. Water dripped down her breasts, and her wet hair cascaded down her shoulders.

Archie's body lit up with raging fiery passion, heat and fire that she hadn't felt for a woman in a very long time. She forced herself away from the telescope and wished she had some cold water to throw on herself.

It was wrong to look at Ash without her knowledge, and objectify her body. Archie slapped herself on the face.

"Now you decide to wake up? For Ash? She's too young for you. Get a grip."

As well as being thirteen years her junior, she was a workmate, and she had just promised her dad she would look out for her. Archie stomped back to her car and got in. She slammed the door shut and gazed at the driver's mirror.

"Whatever you're thinking, don't. She's too young, and you're supposed to be looking out for her."

Then she remembered the magazine Naomi had thrown at her. She'd suspected Archie was cheating on her because of the way both she and Ash were looking at each other. Had her warm feelings of attraction actually started a long time ago?

If they had, and these feelings of attraction were real, then their working relationship was going to be difficult.

Ash made her way down to the office after escorting Alanna home and getting showered and changed. She was surprised when her dad said Archie had arrived earlier when she was at the beach.

It was weird enough that Archie wanted to be in the village on a bank holiday, far less come early. When Ash imagined Archie's life in Notting Hill in London, as she had quite often, she saw her surrounded by a group of sophisticated friends, eating at fancy restaurants, frequenting wine bars and other places where Ash would feel like a country bumpkin, and of course with many beautiful women.

Ash was certain of that because despite being annoying, Archie was a gorgeous, masculine-presenting butch. She loved her undercut hair with that tiny precise topknot at the back.

She'd meditate on that hair often at her desk while gazing at Archie with a mixture of annoyance and fascination. That hair was never out of place, and she'd had the secret urge, more than once, to run her fingers up the nape of her neck, over the short shaved hair, then grasp the topknot, and let the hair loose. Ash would grasp the longer strands of hair, now loose, and pull Archie close and—

"Wait. What are you thinking?"

Ash realized that she was concentrating on the thoughts in her head so much that she'd walked past the office and arrived at Rosebrook House's front door.

"Wake up, Ash."

She made her way back to the office. When she opened the door and walked in, she found Archie at her desk, looking off into the distance, seemingly in a world of her own. Archie didn't break out of her daydream as Ash walked further into the office.

So she said, "Archie?" Then again, more loudly, "Archie?"

Archie jumped out of her seat and dropped her pen to the floor. "Shit. Where did you come from?"

"Sorry," Ash said, "I didn't sneak. What were you thinking about so intently?"

Archie rubbed her hands together nervously. "Nothing, nothing really. Can I get you a tea? Coffee?"

"Bottle of water, please," Ash said.

Archie shook her head and chuckled. "Of course."

Even when they weren't getting on each other's nerves, it was fun to keep Archie on her toes. She took a seat at her desk and waited till Archie returned.

"Dad said you came to the house earlier."

"Yes, I thought I would drive down early, so I just wanted to let you know I was here. Did you and Alanna have a nice time at the beach?"

"Yes, we did. Those beach wheelchairs Fox got are great. It was the first time Alanna's been able to go into the sea in years."

Archie smiled. "That's wonderful. It really makes you feel good about the community we're building here, doesn't it?"

"But *you* won't become part of the community. Why don't you live here with us?" Ash asked.

"I have my reasons." Archie's light-hearted attitude fell away.

Ash couldn't keep up. One minute Archie was being grumpy, having secret meetings, and couldn't wait to get back to London, and the next she was coming here on a holiday, being nice, and then annoyed again. Who did Archie remind her of?

It was in the back of her mind, but she just couldn't place it.

"Fine, grumpy. So why aren't you enjoying your long weekend in London?"

Archie furrowed her eyebrows. "I said I'd come here, so we could work things out."

"But why did you offer that? You normally race to get back to the city after work. Didn't you have friends to meet at the local wine bar or something?"

Ash couldn't help but say *wine bar* with a little disdain.

"No, that's why I said I could come down here."

"And what about Saturday, and last night?"

"What is it you're getting at?" Archie asked.

Why had she started with this line of questioning? Ash wondered. It was only making her look over-interested. Which, let's face it, she was. She wanted to know who and what kind of woman Archie liked.

"I just assumed you had a girlfriend, partner, someone you'd be spending your time with, not meeting me to plan our work schedule."

"No, I don't have any woman I'm spending my time with, apart from you, that is. I spent Saturday and Sunday night binge-watching a Netflix show I love. Sundays I usually have lunch with my dad, but he was busy. That enough information for you?"

Ash felt totally embarrassed by Archie's answer. Honestly, why would she care? She didn't know what to say next, so she tried to change the subject.

"What were you binge-watching?"

"*The Gatekeeper*, have you seen it?" Archie said.

"No, I don't have Netflix."

"No? You have so many amazing things to catch up with, then. I have a family package. Download the app on your work iPad, and use my account," Archie said excitedly.

"Wow, I would have never have put you down as a Netflix kind of person," Ash said.

"Too old and serious?"

"Serious, yes, but you're not old."

Archie snorted. "Compared to you, I am. Honestly, use my account and try watching *The Gatekeeper*. You'll love it."

"What's it about?"

"It's sci-fi, but in a weird way. I don't want to give too much away. There's a central romance you'd love. A will they, won't they kind of thing."

"Well, I know romance isn't your thing, and I wouldn't have pictured you as a sci-fi fan either," Ash said.

"There's a lot you don't know about me, so probably best not to make assumptions. I was a sci-fi fantasy geek as a teenager."

"A nerd who grew up to be a hipster butch?"

"I suppose. So will you watch it?" Archie asked.

A smile grew on Ash's face. "I'll watch if you read my favourite book."

Archie's face fell. "One of your cheesy romance books?"

"Yes, it won't kill you. I'd like you to see that you've got it all wrong about romance novels."

Archie sighed. "You're really going to make me do this?"

"If you want me to watch your precious bookkeeper thingy."

"Gatekeeper, it's called *The Gatekeeper*."

"Whatever. Do we have a deal?"

Archie shook her head. "Why did I open my big mouth? Okay, which book?"

"Give me your iPad."

Ash searched for the ebook and handed it back to Archie.

"You're kidding me. *The Dastardly Duke?*" Archie moaned.

"It's my favourite, and it was my mum's fave too."

"Okay, fine. *The Dastardly Duke* it is, but you'll start watching *Gatekeeper*? I've no one else to talk to about it."

Ash decided to probe a little further. "What about your last girlfriend?"

"Hardly," Archie said with disdain. "Naomi liked reality shows about people with too much money who worry about all sorts of drama, and besides, I wouldn't have shared the fact that I'm a sci-fi geek with her."

Naomi. Now she had a real woman with a real name to picture being with Archie. "But you'll share it with me?"

"I suppose so." Archie typed out her account details and sent them to Ash as a text message. "Now, get watching."

"Okay, I will. Don't worry."

"Can we get on with sorting out this list now?"

"Yes, grumpy," Ash joked.

❖

It didn't take long for them to split up Fox and Clementine's list between them. Archie had been annoyed at Fox for doing this, at first, but she supposed it was right to make them find a way of working together properly, and after talking to James, she was even more inspired to make Ash's job more comfortable.

With Archie's new relaxed attitude, they were able to go down the list quite easily.

"So, you're sure you want me to liaise between our resident farmers and Christian and Casper at the community garden?"

"Yeah," Ash said, "it feels weird dealing with Mr. Murdoch and Mr. Mason in a business way. To them I'll always be little Ash, a slip of a girl, as they would put it. They treat you differently."

"Well, if you're sure, that's no problem."

"Why are you being so accommodating?" This newfound flexibility didn't sit well with Ash.

"What do you mean?"

"You've gone from sharing some of the responsibilities with me, to handing anything I want to me," Ash said.

"I'm not. I just want us to work together without the need to argue every few minutes."

Wait—she spoke to Dad before she came here.

"Did my dad say something to you?"

"What? What could your dad say?" Archie said defensively.

"Something about my mum, probably. He thinks I'm some little girl who needs to be protected, but I'm a strong woman."

"I know that. I've been arguing with that strong woman since she arrived." Archie sat back in her chair. "I'm trying to change my behaviour and be less...domineering."

That brought a smile to Ash's face. Archie was trying to learn, but to be super honest, she liked that alpha personality, as well as Archie's being older than her. It was sexy in its way.

"Just be yourself, okay?" Ash said.

"Well, maybe a me that's more open to ideas. Last on the list is The Big Idea. Fox wants to publicize Rosebrook. I could come up with all sorts of environmental ideas, but does it need to be more than that?"

Ash doodled *The Big Idea* on her notebook. "I think so. Something or a series of things that will draw people to Rosebrook as tourists, and then while they are here, they can learn about our environmental projects."

"Hmm..." Archie tapped her pen on her notebook.

"Of course," Ash said, "it'll be easier once we have the students join us. Fox's plan was to have them get involved with the community outreach part of our project."

"Oh, by the way, Griffin called me. She won't arrive for another week or so."

"I can't wait to meet her. She sounds like a very interesting person," Ash said.

"Interesting is the word. A one-off, certainly. So are we ready to work in harmony together?"

"Here's hoping," Ash replied with a smile.

CHAPTER SEVEN

The next week went much better. Both Ash and Archie worked on their respective duties. Archie was actually enjoying coming to the village for work every day, now that the office was running smoothly and without the tension between her and Ash.

What was worrying was how much she was enjoying being here every day, and the excited feeling Archie got every morning when she came to work, and she knew why. The beautiful Ashling O'Rourke.

It felt so wrong to be attracted to her. She was a work colleague, much too young for her, and she'd promised her dad to look out for her, not lust after her. If only it was just lust—but it wasn't. Ash intrigued her.

Intrigued her by filling her thoughts. Archie could hear her laugh in her head and see the way she bit her lip when she was thinking hard. All the small things about her, Archie had swirling in her head.

She couldn't remember that giddy, excited feeling with Naomi or any of her more recent dates, but maybe that was because she knew Ash was off limits to her?

Archie reached into the drawer and brought out the magazine with the picture of the two of them dancing. She had been doing that a lot, trying to work out if it was just a random moment the photographer had caught, in between bouts of sniping.

She traced her finger over Ash's face and jumped when she heard Ash say, "What's that?"

"It's...ugh...the magazine article on the village—from the press evening, remember?"

Ash took the magazine from her and looked at it. "We're smiling at each other."

"Yes, I know. Unusual, eh?"

Ash looked up from the magazine and gave her a shy smile. "Weird."

That shy smile set Archie's heart off at a canter. "Yeah, who would have thought?"

Ash held her gaze for a few seconds then joked, "It's my turn to pick up the sandwiches from the pub. You can be in charge while I'm away."

Before Archie could think straight, she stood up quickly. "I'll come with you."

"You will?" Ash said with surprise.

"Yes, I could do with some fresh air."

"Okay then."

Archie walked around her desk and said to Rupert, "We're going out for the sandwiches. Can you hold the fort?"

"No problem."

Archie looked to Jenna and Claire sitting behind him. "Don't let Rupert work you too hard."

"As if," Rupert said. "We're going to have a dance break while you're away, boss."

Archie rolled her eyes. "Fox's influence still lingers on."

Once she and Ash walked outside the office, an awkward silence descended, and Archie wondered why she'd volunteered to do this. She searched for something to say. "Have you watched any of *The Gatekeeper* yet?"

"No. Not yet," Ash replied.

Archie sighed dramatically. "You said you would so I could talk about the series with you."

Ash looked at her and said, "Have you started *The Dastardly Duke* yet?"

She hadn't. She had picked up her iPad a few times but didn't get past the first page.

"No, I haven't quite gotten around to it."

"Thought not, but if you start it tonight, I'll watch the first episode after I've been to the beach," Ash suggested.

"That's a deal. Wait? You're going to the beach at night?"

"I go to the beach every night to read my book. I sit in my deckchair, with my feet in the waves, and live vicariously through the two people in love in my book. It helps me relax," Ash said.

Archie could just picture it, and it gave her a warm feeling inside. "It sounds idyllic. What book are you reading now?"

"*The Laird and the Lady.*"

"Laird? What's that?" Archie asked.

"Like a Scottish lord of the manor. It's set in the Highlands, it's so windswept and romantic."

"Like Clementine in Thistleburn? She would be the equivalent of a laird."

"I suppose she would. That's true. Anyway, I'll start your bookkeeper thing when I get home," Ash said.

"Gatekeeper. You know it's gatekeeper."

Ash laughed and put her arm through the crook of Archie's. "Okay, grumpy."

Archie had stiffened at first when she put her arm through hers but then relaxed more as they walked uphill to the shop to pick up the drinks and snacks, before heading back to the pub for the sandwiches.

"Have you had any more thoughts about our big project?" Archie said.

"Not specifically, but I think it has to be something that's going to reach a different crowd. So far we've reached out to the LGBTQ+ community and the eco community, but I think we need to get the tourists in. That'll give us a more diverse group of people to educate with our ideas."

"True, but how?" Archie asked.

Ash had a few different thoughts running around her head in the last few days but couldn't quite pull them together.

"Before we go into the shop, can I show you something?"

"Sure, lead the way."

Across from Ash's house there was the start of a wooded area. She walked into the trees and reached back with her hand. To her delight Archie took her hand and allowed herself to be guided through the woods.

They soon emerged into a clearing, and a decaying stone building lay in front of them.

"What's this?" Archie asked. "I thought I knew every building in this area."

"Oh, there's lots you still don't know about Rosebrook. Believe me, it still has its secrets."

Archie was led into the stone building and found a big room with rows of desks, covered in dust, stone, and falling wood.

"A school?" Archie asked.

Ash smiled. "Yeah, isn't it so amazing? I used to play in here as a child, but when Mum found out, she told me I couldn't because it was too dangerous."

Archie looked up and saw a thick tree branch sticking through a hole in the roof. "I can see that. It's a bit creepy too. When was this built? Do you know?"

"Eighteen ninety, I think. The number is carved in one of the stones outside. There's so much history here in Rosebrook. This school, the World War II defence structures on the beach, I don't think we're doing enough with all these things."

Archie walked to the nearest desk and lifted up its lid. Inside was carved *Elijah 1889.* "Elijah."

"There's boys names carved in most of the desks, and do you know something? They mostly all have gravestones in the churchyard. Elijah does."

"There definitely has to be more made of this site, as well as the other historical places," Archie said.

Ash walked up to her and said, "It doesn't just have to be historical. I think we can link it back to our environmental cause."

"How?" Archie asked.

"These boys lived and died in this village. That means they

were either farmers, fisherman, or worked in Rosebrook House. The original house, then the rebuilt one. I thought we could check the parish records, find out about these names, and make them part of some exhibits. If Elijah here is a farmer, talk about traditional farming methods and how we need to learn from the people of the past."

Archie's mind started to whirl with possibilities. "That is a fantastic idea, and I know Fox will love it."

Ash put her hand on her heart and said, "Archie? Are you saying I actually have good ideas?"

Archie laughed. "You have amazing ideas. The local knowledge you have will be invaluable."

Ash blushed. "I don't know about that. It's still not quite right for The Big Idea, but it gets us started. Oh, and wait until I show you this."

Ash hurried to the front of the classroom and brought back something behind her back.

"Hands out, Archie."

Archie frowned. "What for?"

"Just trust me."

Archie held out her hands, and Ash got a gleam in her eye. "I've been dreaming about doing this since you first asked me to make the tea."

Ash brought out a teacher's leather strap and smacked it softly onto Archie's hands.

Archie felt a ripple of excitement. "Is that an original?"

"Yes, it's always hung on a hook on the wall. It's barbaric— imagine what poor Elijah and his friends went through."

Archie shook her head. "It's awful to think of these poor kids being whacked with that."

"Do you want a go? I'm sure you've thought of giving me a whack before now."

Archie smiled. "Don't be silly."

Ash took a step towards her and put the belt in her hand. "Go on, just to say you've tried it."

Archie gulped. Ash's voice was laced with sexual tension. Did

Ash realize she was teasing, or was she innocent enough not to know that her words had started a heavy beat and a longing inside of her?

Archie took the belt and squeezed the handle tightly, never taking her eyes off Ash. It got even worse when Ash held out her hands and gave her such an innocent look. The mantra kept repeating inside her mind: *She's too young for you. You shouldn't be feeling this.*

But it had no effect. She brought the strap down a couple of times on Ash's hands with a thwack. She saw Ash shiver and her wet lips part. Archie couldn't think of anything other than kissing those soft wet lips.

Archie forcefully held herself back and held out the strap for Ash to take it. When she did, Ash's fingers lingered on hers.

"Archie—"

"We better get back," Archie interrupted her before she could say any more.

"I suppose. Back to the real world." Ash took the strap and walked back to put it on the wall.

Archie had nearly lost control, and what's more, she'd detected want in Ash's voice and touch. Was she interested in her? Did that picture capture the truth?

❖

"What a prick," Archie said out loud.

After returning home, having dinner, and dealing with some emails, Archie settled on the couch to keep her promise to Ash and read her book.

The first few chapters revealed an extremely disagreeable male lead. Ash idolized this hero?

"It should be called *The Dick of a Duke*, not *dastardly.*"

So far the heroine, who had no money and no prospects, came to work as a governess to his two children, two years after his wife died. Rather than be grateful for the help of this lovely young woman, the duke was making each day miserable for her.

If it wasn't for the promise she had made to Ash, Archie would have shut the book and never opened it again, but she couldn't.

Archie sighed and picked up her glass of red wine. Better get back to this. Then she had a thought. Ash had chosen this book out of all her collection for Archie to read. Did Ash think of her as the Dastardly Duke? They had been at loggerheads daily since she arrived in Rosebrook.

But surely that had changed in the last week? She thought back to this lunchtime in the derelict school room. Something changed between them. Archie's feelings for Ash had been changing slowly for some time, but today was the first time she felt that Ash had changing feelings too.

If so, why did she? Apart from being out of her age group, if Ash knew her history with women, she wouldn't be so attracted. Ash had lived a pretty sheltered life in Rosebrook, and Archie would hate to think of her being attracted to someone who dated someone for a month or two and moved on. Ash deserved better than that. Plus, Ash had never actually come out and said she was gay, or bi, or whatever. Archie just assumed.

Just then Archie's phone lit up and rang out, alerting her to a video call. It was Ash.

She answered straight away and saw tears rolling down Ash's face. Her eyes were puffed up from prolonged crying, and she was clearly distressed.

"My God, Ash. What's happened?"

"How could you, Archie?" Ash said through tears.

Archie's heart sank, and she felt guilty for something—she didn't even know that she'd done. "What did I do? I wouldn't do anything to hurt you, Ash."

"You made me watch this stupid bookkeeper thing. You said it has a romance in it, a romance between two women."

"It does." Archie was really confused.

"These two people are soulmates. I'm falling in love with them all through the first episode. Then they get killed at end of the episode? They died together. How could you, Archie?"

Archie slapped her forehead. "You're in convulsive tears over the characters dying? Are you serious? I thought something had happened to your dad or something."

"No, two soulmates are killed in the first episode of a series. You know how much I love love stories, how sentimental I am, and you don't warn me at least?"

"Oh my God, Ash," Archie said with exasperation.

In a way it was sweet how affected Ash was by this. No wonder she liked these sickly sweet love stories, like *The Dastardly Duke*.

"Don't panic. They are the lead characters. Why do you think they would be killed in the first episode?"

Ash calmed her tears and blew her nose with a hanky. Then a smile slowly crept upon her face. "So they can find each other through time and space?"

Archie snapped her fingers. "Give the girl a medal, yes. You have it all before you to watch. All three seasons so far, and the new one starts next month."

"Still, you should have warned me. I'm going to have a headache now because I've been crying. I try to avoid anything I know will make me cry. TV shows, songs, and don't get me started on the YouTube videos where they save dogs from the streets."

Archie chuckled. "You are adorable." As soon as she said the word *adorable*, she regretted it. She'd said too much.

Ash stopped sniffing and crying and said, "I am?"

"Yes, well. You're very emotional. I promise I'll warn you about any future episodes. Did you like the story, though?"

"I think so. I've never really watched sci-fi stuff before, but the two lead women are great. I loved the scene where that one with the muscles, the tough butch one, goes to rescue her girl and beats up the bar of bad guys."

Archie thought for a moment before asking this question. "Do you think she's good-looking? The tough butch one?"

"Yeah, who wouldn't?" Ash replied.

"You've never actually said if you were interested in women."

"Do I have to make an announcement? I thought our Rosebrook community was about being a safe, open place, where these questions don't matter?"

Ash was right. It shouldn't matter, and it was wrong to ask, but Archie longed to know, even though she knew her attraction could come to nothing.

"I'm sorry—you're right. Ignore me."

Ash wiped the final tears from her eyes and said, "I'm gay. I like women."

Archie had to stop the smile creeping up on her face. "You didn't have to tell me."

"I wanted you to know," Ash said.

Archie could feel the sexual tension from this afternoon again. The way Ash had said that was as if she was giving her a signal.

As much as Archie was beginning to feel for Ash, she was all types of wrong for her. Too young, and she lived in the village, a place Archie could never make her life. She needed to send her own signal.

"You should always be yourself, Ash, and if that's who you are, then I'm sure you'll find someone nice, and your own age, soon."

Ash's face fell, and an awkwardness came between them. The silence was killing Archie, so she held up the book and said, "Look, I'm reading your book."

Ash's smile returned. "How is it so far?"

"I don't know why you like this duke. He's a bloody dick to this girl."

Ash laughed softly. "That's the point. It's what makes it such a triumphant love story. His backstory is what makes him who he is, and the only person in the world who he can work out his pain with is Diana the governess."

Ash spoke with such passion that her face lit up, and it made Archie's heart ache.

"In all the love stories, there's that one person and one person alone who can help the other character deal with their pain, and make them a better, happier person."

"Well, I'll give him another chance. But he better start being nice soon," Archie said.

"He will. Love always wins."

"You won't think that when you're a bit older."

"Why are you so against love, Archie? Your favourite TV show is about love being the most powerful force in the universe."

"That's TV, not real life, Ash," Archie said.

"You go into every relationship you have not expecting to fall in love?"

"I never have, and I don't have long-term relationships. I date," Archie said.

"That's sad. Surely you want to spend your life with someone who loves you beyond reason?" Ash said.

"I have a very full life, believe me. I don't need a wife at home to make it any more fulfilled," Archie said with sharpness in her voice.

"I'm sure," Ash said. "I'll see you at work, then."

When Ash hung up, Archie threw her phone and the book down. "Fuck."

The look of disappointment on Ash's face made Archie feel terrible.

❖

On Tuesday the office was quiet as everyone got on with their work. Ash couldn't help but look up and watch Archie as she typed away on her computer. Something had changed in the way she looked at Archie. She used to revel in annoying her, and it made her feel excited—she couldn't deny that—but Archie had mellowed since Fox and Clementine went away.

She was kind and considerate, and was sharing parts of herself that she hadn't before, like the TV show Archie enjoyed. Ash was enjoying it too. It wasn't something she would have thought she'd like, but it was surprisingly good, and she loved the central love story.

The excited annoyance had morphed into excited attraction—Ash couldn't deny that. When she closed her eyes last night in bed, she'd imagined Archie as her dastardly duke, as the story played out in her head.

There was one scene in particular that kept playing over and over in her dreams. It was when the governess, Diana, got upset and ran away, while the rain pelted down. The duke ran after her, and they shared their first passionate kiss, in the rain.

It was so hot, so passionate. She could see, in her mind's eye, the rain rolling down their cheeks, and Archie's hair so wet and sexy.

She let out a sigh. Her thoughts had been so hot that she felt embarrassed this morning when she came into the office. The other night when they'd talked on the phone, Archie said Ash would find someone her own age. It had blown the wind from her sails and disappointed her.

Was Archie trying to say she wasn't interested, by trying to frighten her off? Ash was sure Archie had felt something when they were together in the schoolroom. She'd pushed it, playing around with the strap, and she could almost feel an invisible energy pulling them together, but Archie had stopped it.

The duke in her book was much older than the governess. Why couldn't it work for her and Archie? Wait. Was she actually thinking about Archie and her being together? Archie didn't even want to spend one night in the village while Fox was away. Why would she be interested in a country bumpkin whose life was in this village? That was depressing.

"Knock knock?" Ash looked up—Kay had come into the office. "I hope I'm not interrupting?"

"Come in. Of course you're not interrupting—isn't she not, Archie?"

"No, come in," Archie said.

"Clem emailed some pictures and videos from their honeymoon. I thought you'd like to see them."

Rupert piped up, "Are they X-rated?"

Kay laughed. "No, you're out of luck, Rupert."

"Let's put them on the screen in the conference room," Archie said.

"You can do that?" Kay asked.

"Yes, give me your phone, and I'll do it for you."

Archie led everyone into the conference room and cast it to the screen. All of them huddled around the table, and Archie let Kay flick through the pictures.

The first few were from their drive in the camper van, and in one video, taken by Clementine from the passenger seat, Fox sang along to a Celine Dion song in her usual exuberant way.

Ash laughed along with everyone else, and then Archie, who was standing behind her, leaned down and whispered in her ear. "Typical Fox."

Ash shivered from her neck all the way down to her toes. She couldn't help but follow her instincts and take a step back into Archie's space. Her breathing hitched when she felt her bottom touch Archie.

She was struggling to get enough air in her lungs, being this close to Archie. She wanted Archie to be her dastardly duke, but would a sophisticated woman like her ever want a bumpkin like her?

Archie had hinted that she was too young for her, but Ash didn't accept that. She found the thought of an older woman so exciting. Ash didn't have much experience with women, in fact she'd only had one girlfriend in her life, a girl she fell for in her school, but the heat she'd felt with that girl had been nothing compared to being close to Archie.

Ash shut her eyes briefly and imagined Archie putting her hands on her waist from behind. An experienced older woman like Archie would know just what to do with her hands when she touched her.

But Ash didn't feel Archie's hands hold on to her waist. She felt a nudge from Rupert. "Look at Clementine and Fox."

Before she looked at the screen, Ash looked behind to Archie. Her jaw was clenched, and she was looking down at the space between them. Then Archie closed her eyes briefly and took a step back from Ash.

Archie did feel attracted to her—Ash knew it. If Archie thought the age difference was too much, then she'd just have to change her mind.

I'm going to tease the life out of you, Archie.

But did she even know where to start? It was easy to say but not easy to do. She had little experience in this area. With her first girlfriend, they'd had no experience between them, so they just bumbled through together.

Archie was a different proposition altogether.

Everyone started to laugh at the next video. Clementine explained before she left for Scotland that her Scottish earldom came with its own private army, the only private army left in the UK. Now merely ceremonial, Clementine's role as clan chief was to take the salute of her army foot soldiers, every year in the summer months.

Clementine looked elegant in a skirt of the clan tartan and a simple jacket, but Fox was wearing the clansman's ceremonial dress.

Rupert laughed and said, "Trust Fox to wear the local garb."

"She looks super handsome," Ash said.

❖

Everyone had left for the day, leaving Archie to work alone. There was nothing that she was doing that she couldn't do at home, but something was keeping her here, and she didn't want to face going home to her empty flat.

It wasn't something that usually bothered her, but Archie's thoughts were a maelstrom of new and unsettling feelings this week. Her thoughts were filled with Ash and this afternoon when they'd looked at the pictures Kay had brought.

She had seen Ash break out in goosebumps when she spoke softly in her ear, and then it seemed like Ash purposefully stepped back into her space. Archie had been an inch from Ash's hips. She could feel how close they were, and it made her so hot. That was all she could think about the rest of the day.

Archie tapped her pen repeatedly on her notepad. She was achieving nothing sitting here, so she packed up her briefcase and closed the office up. She got into her car and drove off through the village.

She slowed as she approached the beach staircase nearest Ash's house. Archie remembered Ash said she came down to the beach to read every evening. She felt the urge to find out if she was down there just now.

Archie pulled over and got out of her car, then walked up to the top of the stairs. She was there. Archie's heart soared when she saw the figure of a woman, sitting in a deckchair, with a wide-brimmed hat on. It was the height of the summer, and the sun wouldn't set for another hour or so.

As idyllic as the setting appeared and how much Ash said she enjoyed this part of her day, Archie was struck by how isolated Ash looked. She had no friends in the village her own age—the closest was Alanna, but she was still older, and they'd only met recently.

Ash had such a sheltered life here—she needed to feel the love that only a partner could bring. Maybe someone would move to Rosebrook who would fit her age profile. But Ash had no experience, as far as she knew. Ash wouldn't know if someone was using her or bullshitting her, and she wouldn't recognize any other kind of relationship hazards out there.

She'd be like a lamb to the slaughter.

Before her mind could countermand her decision, Archie found herself walking down the steps to the beach. When she got to the bottom of the steps, she nearly turned around, but she wanted to say hi to Ash. She started to walk across the beach, and as she did she promised herself she would keep an eye on Ash, and try to make sure that didn't happen. After all, she knew about all the bullshit, the broken promises—she could recognize that in others because she herself had behaved like that. But Archie couldn't countenance Ash being treated that way.

As she got closer, Ash must have heard her footsteps because she turned and said with surprise, "Archie? Hi."

"Hi, I worked on longer than I planned, but I saw you down here, and I wanted to say goodbye before I left."

"Why don't you sit down for a minute? I can get you a deckchair—"

Ash went to stand but Archie shook her head. "It's okay. The sand is good enough."

Archie flopped down onto the sand beside her.

Ash put her bookmark in and closed her book. She couldn't have been more surprised to see Archie walking down the beach, especially since her face had been bouncing around her head. No matter how hard she tried to picture the main character in her books, Archie's face infiltrated her thoughts instead. She had become the hero from *The Laird and the Lady* and, more fittingly, *The Dastardly Duke*.

A silence hung between them, and Ash wondered if Archie was thinking about this afternoon, as they looked at the pictures. The electricity between them had been crackling. She was starting to feel for Archie, in many ways, but Ash realized she hardly knew anything about her.

"This is beautiful," Archie said. "You're lucky to have this beach on your doorstep."

"It is. The beach, the sand, the water, it's all part of me. Do you know what my favourite thing about living next to the sea is?"

Archie shook her head.

"Lying in bed at night with the window open, and listening to the sound of the waves. Especially if it's a little stormy."

Archie smiled. "It sounds so relaxing. I listen to the sound of car alarms and people shouting in the streets."

"Well, why don't you ever take Fox up on her offer of a cottage in the village?" Ash asked.

Archie's smile disappeared. "I'm a city person. Country life isn't something that appeals to me."

Ash couldn't help but feel disappointed. "I can understand if it's not something you're used to if you've grown up in a city, but maybe if you gave it a try—"

"I was born and brought up in a village. I know all about them," Archie said with some sharpness in her voice.

Ash was surprised. She just assumed London was Archie's home. She wanted to know more but felt that she would push Archie away if she did at this moment.

"Nobody's saying you should live here, but while Fox and Clem are away, you could have stayed at Rosebrook. You've got such a long commute back and forth."

Archie was silent for a second, then said, "It's the way I prefer it."

In other words, shut up, Ash said to herself. She just let it go. It sounded like there was a reason behind Archie's dislike of the country, but she wasn't going to learn anything tonight.

"Are you still reading your Laird book?" Archie said.

She was quite clearly changing the subject.

"No, I finished it at break time. I've started a new one."

Ash held up the book for Archie to see. Archie read the title on the cover. "*The Saint and the Sinner.* Another historical?"

"No, it's a lesbian contemporary romance. A bad girl kind of thing. You know the sort?" Ash said.

Archie squinted. "Not really."

Ash sighed. "You really have no idea about romance, do you?"

"I've never needed to."

"Well, bad girl characters are the ones that are really no good for you in the long run, but women are attracted to them, even though they know the relationship will probably hurt them."

"So that's what your book is about?" Archie asked.

"Yes, sometimes in romances, the bad girl can be redeemed, but mostly the heroine has a choice between suitors, like in my book. She has to choose between her saint and her sinner. The saint originally seems very boring and bland, but the heroine comes to see that the less flashy woman is the one who will love her the best."

"Life is rarely as clear-cut as that, Ash."

"I don't know—my books have always given me an insight into the new people I meet," Ash said.

"Did you do that with me?"

"Oh yes, but I won't tell who or what."

That brought a sexy smile from Archie. "I hope whoever I remind you of, good or ill, that I'm at least dashing. I do know these romances have characters described as dashing, do they not?"

"Yes, and of course you are. Who could doubt it, with your hipster hair and waistcoat," Ash said.

Archie scratched the shaved part of her undercut hair, as if unsure whether Ash liked her hair or was mocking it.

"There's Dad," Ash said. James's fishing boat was heading into shore. Ash continued, "I always read until Dad comes back. I better get this chair packed away."

They both stood and Archie brushed sand off her jeans. "Let me get that chair for you."

"How gallant," Ash said with a smile.

Archie laughed. "I'll walk you along to the pier afterwards."

After the deckchair was packed away, they started to make their way along the beach. Ash didn't hesitate to loop her arm through Archie's as they walked.

"How's your reading getting on?" she asked.

"I'm about halfway through it now." Archie paused for quite a few seconds then continued, "The duke is starting to have feelings for the governess, but he thinks it's wrong. He's much older and in a position of power."

Ash had the feeling Archie was trying to admit to what was going on in her head, through the duke. Did she really feel something for her?

She gripped Archie's arm tighter. "Who cares about age, as long as both the people are adults."

"It feels wrong to me," Archie replied.

Was Archie talking openly about them now?

"My mum was older than my dad," Ash said.

"Really?"

"Yes, ten years' difference. His fishing boat stopped over in Rosebrook, he fell in love at first sight with my mum, and he never left. It was all very romantic. I know you're not interested in love, Archie, but some people would turn their world upside down for it."

Archie looked at her, nervously it seemed. "It's not something I've ever looked for before, but what about you? I don't suppose there were many opportunities in a small village like this."

"I told you I've been in love," Ash said.

"Oh yes."

"Yeah, I met her at high school. I had to get the bus to school in the next town. She sat next to me on my first day, and I was dreaming about her that night," Ash said.

"What was she like?" Archie asked.

A smile came to Ash's face remembering her first love. "She was a baby butch, with lots of attitude, but she was kind to me."

They reached the wooden pier, and Archie helped her up the steps. Her father's boat wasn't quite in yet, so they waited.

"What happened to break you up? If you don't mind me asking."

"We had our future all planned, we'd go to university together, but then Mum got ill. I had to stay with Mum and Dad, and she went off to uni and started a new life."

Ash had a crack of emotion in her voice, and without prompting Archie pulled her into a hug. It was a great surprise being in Archie's arms. But she wasn't complaining. She rested her head on Archie's chest and breathed in the comforting smell of her cologne.

She clutched at Archie's chest tightly. When she fantasized about her duke, her older, more experienced woman, she imagined being held tightly in Archie's arms.

Archie held her in silence until she whispered, "Your dad's boat is here."

That whisper sent shivers down Ash's spine. She could only imagine what a kiss from Archie would make her feel.

Archie pulled away and looked uncomfortable. "I better get going then."

"Okay, drive safe, won't you?"

Archie smiled. "Of course I'll be safe."

"But it's a long drive and you'll be tired," Ash added.

"I'll be fine, I promise. See you tomorrow."

Ash said goodbye, then watched as Archie walked away up the steps. "I want you, Archie."

CHAPTER EIGHT

A rchie was late. Extremely late for work. There had been a major car crash on the motorway this morning that had shut it for two hours. She had phoned Ash to let her know what was happening, and it wasn't a major issue, but Archie prided herself on never being late.

As she drove into the village, she saw Ash, Blake, Eliska, and Prisha, with baby Rohan in his pram, standing around talking. They waved to her as she passed, and Archie noticed a new closeness between Blake and Eliska.

They stood very close with their hands clasped, and Eliska looked much freer and happier than she had seen her before. Archie parked at the office and quickly made her way back out to the road.

Blake spotted her, then whispered to Eliska, who smiled and blushed. Archie stayed where she was, and Blake walked over to join her. After Blake left the group, Archie spotted Ash giving Eliska a couple of books and then a hug.

"Good morning, Archie. Ash was telling us about your nightmare morning."

Archie sighed. "Yes, the commute is awful when there's an accident, or roadworks."

"Could you not stay in the village?" Blake asked.

She must look so ridiculous to everyone, staying in London, and driving here every day. The truth was, Archie had less and less tying her to London. All she did was eat, sleep, and read Ash's book on the sofa, while having a running commentary via text from Ash watching *The Gatekeeper*.

Since she split up with Naomi, the only person she'd met up with was her dad. Village life here in Rosebrook was so different to what she'd experienced as a child with her mum and dad, and yet when she closed her eyes and thought about moving here, she started to feel an irrational panic.

"Village life isn't really my scene, Blake. How's things with you?"

A big smiled erupted on Blake's face. "Perfect. Eli told me she has feelings for me, and our relationship is progressing. It's as if she's let go of some of her fears and is opening up her heart."

"That's fantastic, Blake. I'm so happy for you. What changed?"

"She's been reading these books Ash gave her, and it's as if she's been learning what love could be. She's been abused most of her life, physically and mentally, and I don't think she understood how to articulate how she felt, and that it was okay to touch and build up intimacy slowly. It's going to take time and patience, but those books have given us a place to start."

Archie was astonished. She had reprimanded Ash for giving Eliska what she thought was a silly book, and it turned out it was exactly what Eliska had needed.

She looked over at Ash, who was laughing and joking with her friends, and her heart ached, and her chest went tight. She had to ball up her fist to stop herself from reaching out for Ash. For someone who was young and had very little experience with women, Ash was wise beyond her years when it came to love.

Ash looked at her, smiled, and waved her over. She started moving at Ash's command. Archie could do nothing else. Blake followed and went straight to her wife's side. Eliska grasped Blake's hand and pulled her close.

Archie had the urge to do the same with Ash but resisted. "Good morning, everyone."

They all replied with hellos and smiles.

"You manged to get here, then?" Ash said.

"Eventually. I hate being late."

Archie nearly jumped when Ash put her hand on the small of her back and rubbed softly.

"Don't worry. I held the fort."

Almost as soon as it started, the touch was over, but the sensations in her body were far from over. She inhaled and exhaled slowly.

They chatted amongst themselves for about five minutes, and then Prisha said, "Wow, who is that?"

Everyone followed Prisha's gaze to a tall, slender butch, loping down the road in combat trousers, a sleeveless T-shirt, a back-to-front baseball cap on her short dark blond hair, and a worn rucksack on her back. She looked every inch of what she was, a travelling nomad.

Ash nudged her. "Do you know who it is?"

The traveller stopped briefly, took off her hat, and ran her hand through her floppy hair. Ash, Prisha, and Eliska sighed at the sight, which annoyed Archie.

"Yes, that's Griffin, our new brewery manager."

❖

"Archie, wait," Ash said.

She ran down the road to try to catch up with her. She hadn't noticed Archie leaving the office as she was gossiping with Rupert about their new resident, Griffin.

Everyone had been charmed by the nomadic looking Griffin. She had an open warm personality, quite a contrast to Archie, who had been in a foul mood this morning. Archie had taken Griffin to her new cottage to settle in and made arrangements to meet at the brewery after lunch.

Ash wanted to chat with Griffin and help with the brewery set-up. It really was wonderful having so many of her own LGBTQ+ community living in the village now. She and the duchess used to be the only ones.

Archie wasn't slowing down, so Ash shouted again, "Archie—will you wait for me?"

Archie finally stopped and turned around. "What are you doing? There's no need for you to come."

Ash was out of breath by the time she'd caught up with Archie. "I want to come. I'd like to help."

Archie snorted in derision. "You don't—you just want to gawk at her some more."

They started to walk again and Ash had to make a fast pace to keep up with Archie. "What's got into you? You really are in a bad mood. I thought she was your friend."

"She is—well, I met her through Fox."

"Then why do you seem annoyed by her arriving?" Ash asked.

"I'm not. I've just had a bad day so far, okay?"

"I'm so sorry," Ash said sarcastically.

They walked on in silence before Ash said, "I've been working on getting the schoolchildren's information this morning. It's so interesting."

"What did you find?" Archie asked.

"I've gotten young Elijah's birth and death certificates from the General Register Office online. He's unusual in that he didn't get married."

"That was highly unusual in those days," Archie agreed.

"I checked every census until he died, and he lived with a man. His whole life? That's even more suspicious. I think he could be gay."

"It could be, I suppose, but it would have been really hard to live with a man in those days."

"But if it was as companions, maybe nobody even considered their being gay a possibility. I have to try to find out more, because Elijah could be perfect for our social history project."

"How can you find out more? I mean, about his social life."

"I texted Clem to ask if she had any old papers or photographs of the village. She said her grandmother's papers are in her office. I thought Agatha and Ada might remember something—maybe their parents talked about him or something."

Archie's face softened, and she even got a small smile. "Good thinking."

"See? We don't need grumpy Archie."

Archie didn't say anything, so Ash felt obliged to fill the gap in the conversation.

"So, tell me about Griffin. She's an unusual character."

"She is. You wouldn't think it by her appearance, but she owns half of Hampshire."

That kind of annoyed Ash. She tried never to judge people by their appearance. "Why wouldn't you think it?"

Archie looked at her quickly and turned away again. She obviously didn't think she'd be caught out by those comments.

"I—I simply mean she looks a little scruffy, you know, a backpacker type," Archie tried to explain.

"Very judgy, aren't you?"

Archie sighed. "I didn't mean…I just meant she doesn't present as someone who's very rich."

"I'll let you off—so, tell me more."

"Well it's really her story to tell, but her father died unexpectedly, and she inherited his fortune. She was born and brought up on a council estate with her mum and never had any contact with her dad. When she got his fortune and land, she was embarrassed by her wealth, I think. She'd always been very socially conscious—that's why she gets on so well with Fox. She has always lived as simply as she could and pledged to do as much charity work as she could."

"Sounds so interesting. I can't wait to get to know her better."

Archie opened up the brewery building's doors and let Ash go in first. Griffin was sitting cross-legged, in the middle of the large floor space, writing on a notepad.

Typical, thought Archie. Could she be any more laid back?

When Ash saw her, she hurried over and greeted Griffin in an even more girly voice than she normally had.

"Griffin? Hi."

Griffin jumped up with her annoyingly charming smile. "Ashling, call me Griff, only my lawyer calls me Griffin."

Ash giggled like a schoolgirl, and Archie's mood deteriorated further.

"Call me Ash. I thought I'd come along with Archie and hear about your plans. I hope you don't mind."

Archie shook her head. Griff was her friend. She shouldn't be feeling annoyed by the attention Ash was giving her, but she was.

"The more the merrier." Griff winked at Ash, then turned to Archie. "Archie, this is a great space. You can almost feel the history here. Lady Clementine's grandmother opened this brewery?"

"Yes," Archie said, "Isadora planned for the brewery and the factory just outside the village to be the main employers for the area, but the brewery manager embezzled the company's funds. It was the start of her downfall."

"It's a fantastic opportunity. I've always dreamed of building a brewery from the ground up."

Griffin held up her hands and twirled in a circle excitedly. Archie had forgotten how much she was like Fox.

"Let's use all of this social history for our new beers. Do either of you have the original brewery logo, images of the bottled beer?" Griffin said.

"Lady Clementine may have some information in her records. We can check when she returns."

Ash butted in, "I can look for you, Griff. I've got access to her papers."

"Fantastic, Ash. What a woman you are," Griffin said.

Ash giggled like a twelve-year-old girl again, and it was really pissing Archie off. Ash was giving Griffin so much more attention than she'd gotten when she arrived in the village. In fact, all she'd asked for when she arrived was a cup of tea, and for that she was cold-shouldered for months.

"Can you give me a list of everything you'll need, Griff?" Archie asked.

"Yeah, I'm making a list now. I'm thinking we'll start off with an IPA and a lager, use citrus hops," Griff said.

"There's no rush. The population of the village isn't big yet, so the jobs aren't needed quite yet. As with the toy factory, Fox wants to build up the new workplaces slowly."

"Breweries aren't workplaces, Archie. They are laboratories, and brewers are more like scientists."

"We better get back to work, Ash," Archie said.

"Are you sure you'll be okay, Griff?" Ash said. "You've only just arrived, and we're abandoning you."

"More than fine. I'll head up to the pub and introduce myself to the bar manager, then work on my plans with a nice cool pint."

Ash smiled, then said, "Oh, before I forget. Some of the villagers and I are having a barbecue on the beach on Sunday. Will you come along? It's a good chance for you to meet everyone."

"You never told me about that," Archie said sharply.

"Didn't I? Well, I meant to. I probably forgot because I knew you wouldn't come anyway." Ash then turned to Griffin and said, "Archie doesn't grace us with her presence at the weekend. I think she'd miss her soy lattes too much."

Both Ash and Griffin laughed, and Archie felt fury touch every part of her. A fury fuelled by jealousy. She had to get out of there.

❖

Later that afternoon, Ash went up to Rosebrook to try to find the information she needed for the social history project. She unlocked the door and walked into the big entrance hallway.

The door creaked as she walked in, and she immediately got a creepy vibe. The hallway was large and echoey. She hadn't been in the house before with no one in it. There was usually house staff, Clem, or Fox making it feel more lived in.

She tried to shake off the feeling and walked over to the staircase. By the standard of English country estates, Rosebrook wasn't that old, with the old castle having been knocked down and the house rebuilt in the 1920s, but Ash still found it creepy.

As long as she could remember, Rosebrook had been a run-down, dilapidated house. She used to walk around the overgrown garden as a young girl. Ash had heard stories growing up of spirits that walked the grounds, spirits who didn't approve of the new house that was built over their former home.

At the top of the stairs, Ash walked along the corridor, the floorboards creaking, until she reached Clementine's office. She took hold of the handle and opened it slowly. Again, she had been here many times, but on her own it was much more daunting.

She half expected some ghoul to be sitting at Clementine's desk. Instead the room was empty, and the only sound was the ticking of the clock.

"Okay, get a grip," Ash said to herself.

The walls around the office were lined with bookshelves, filled with books, photo albums, and files. Clementine said that her grandmother's wife, Louisa, was an avid village and family historian. She collected and catalogued pictures, documents, anything she could get hold of to build up a picture of the past. It would be invaluable.

She found photo albums labelled *The 1800s* and took them over to the desk.

Before Ash opened the first one, she thought, *I wish Archie was here.*

Why was Archie acting all angry and strained with her friend Griffin? Archie had said goodbye to Griffin and walked out of the brewery, without looking back.

She'd run after her.

"Archie, wait!" Archie didn't wait, and Ash had to break into a slight jog. "What is your problem?"

"I've got no problem." Archie slowed her pace.

"Of course you do. Ever since Griffin arrived, you've been like a bear with a sore head. She's your friend."

Archie stopped and turned to talk to Ash. "You're behaving like a schoolgirl around her. I promised your father I'd look out for you—"

"Wait, you told him what?"

"He asked if I'd look out for you because you'd had a really

difficult time of it, but now he sees you're happy and wants it to continue. Griff is a good person, and a friend, but not someone you want to be romantically involved with."

"Why not?" Ash asked.

"She's a nomad, a wanderer, a girl in every port. She doesn't like to be tied down, but still, women fall for her."

"Who said anything about falling for her? I just about said hello, and that's it."

Archie looked frustrated and clearly wasn't listening. "She's like…" Then Archie snapped her fingers. "Yes, that's it. She's the bad girl—you know, the kind from your romance books you were telling me about? Griff is a good person, but she isn't serious about women."

"Oh, listen to you, throwing out the romance tropes. You have listened. So she's like you then?"

Archie hadn't replied, and they'd walked back to Rosebrook in silence, before Ash left the office to come up here. It felt like Archie was jealous, but maybe she was reading too much into it. After all, at every turn Archie reminded her of why a relationship between them would be impossible.

She wasn't best pleased that her dad had asked Archie to keep an eye on her like some older sibling. Ash didn't want a sibling—she wanted Archie to see she was a woman and not a girl.

A small part of her own brain was warning her off trying to get any closer to Archie. Archie had made it clear that she didn't do relationships, even though most women her age were eager to settle down.

Ash's knowledge of romance novels taught her two things. One was that it was usually folly to think you were the one who could change someone's attitude to love, which was what Ash had been thinking, and two, there was always a reason, a backstory, why characters shied away from love.

"I need to find out your backstory, Archie."

Ash opened the photo album and found a little notebook sitting inside, referencing every photograph with a short description and important notes. Louisa had taken great care in her research.

She'd started to search the notebook for the name *Elijah,* when she heard footsteps slowly coming up the hall. Ash's heart started to pound. A ghost?

As the footsteps got nearer to the office door, she could hear the creaking of floorboards. There was nothing creepier. The footsteps stopped outside the office, and the door handle began to turn, and Ash's hands started to shake.

The door opened, and Archie walked into the room.

"My God, Archie. I thought you were a creepy ghost!" Ash clutched her heart.

"Sorry, I didn't mean to scare you."

"Just give me a second to get my breath back," Ash said.

Archie lifted a chair from near one of the bookcases and brought it over to the desk.

"Are you okay now?" Archie asked.

"Yeah I'm fine, kind of."

Archie smiled and said, "You're too sweet. Afraid of ghosts and ghouls?"

Ash stuck her tongue out at Archie. "Did you want something, or did you just come to annoy me?"

"No, I did. Fox called to say they are cutting short their honeymoon. I thought you'd want to know."

Ash was worried. "What's wrong? Are they okay?"

"They're fine. Remember Lucy? Lady Clementine's heir and god-daughter?"

"Yeah, we met her at Clem's mum's funeral. She was so sweet, but her dad was obnoxious."

"That's them. Lucy's dad Peter had a heart attack and died yesterday," Archie said.

"Poor girl, I know he wasn't the nicest of men, but she's only fifteen."

"Fox and Clementine are traveling down to her home right now." Archie placed her hand on the desk near Ash's. Her impulse was to take Ash's hand, but instead she balled her fist. One of the things she loved about Ash was her compassion and kindness. Ash really made her heart ache in a way it never had before in her life. "Lucy has no other family to look after her or her father's affairs, but she's staying with a neighbour until they get there."

"Where do they live?"

"Hastings, just along the coast. Fox thinks they might be there for a good few weeks or more. Peter had very little money apparently, and the family house is very run-down, so there will probably be a lot to take care of."

"I remember Clem telling me that her cousin Peter was not a very nice man. He was bitter about Clem inheriting the title and the estate, and since he was much older than Clem, he would probably never inherit from her. He was a bachelor all his life, then married a woman later in life and had Lucy. He was determined someone in his family would get their hands on the estate one way or another," Ash said.

"You mean he had Lucy just to have her inherit?" Archie couldn't imagine anyone being that cold.

"That's what Clem suspected. He and his wife divorced soon after their marriage, and she died a short time later. But luckily Lucy turned out to be lovely, and Clem says she couldn't leave her title to a nicer girl."

"Well, all she's got are Fox and Clementine now," Archie said.

"Did they say what was going to happen with Lucy?" Ash asked.

"Fox thought Clementine would be declared her guardian, but whatever happens, I think they'd want her to come back here with them."

Ash looked down at the desk and said, with emotion in her voice, "Losing a parent at any age is—"

Archie didn't hesitate this time. She grasped Ash's hand and squeezed. "I know. Listen, about earlier. I'm sorry I was in a bad mood. I shouldn't have taken it out on you, or Griff."

Ash wiped her eyes. "That's okay. Everyone has bad days."

Archie wanted to distract Ash from her sad thoughts. "So, how are you getting on with your research?"

"I've just scratched the surface, really, but it's going to be great, I think. Isadora's wife has done a great job. She's got photo albums and folders of documents, and they all have notes on them. It's going to be fun. I was just trying to find Elijah's name when this big ghost came walking up the hall."

Archie laughed. "I can't believe you're frightened of ghosts."

Ash play-slapped Archie on the arm. "Stop it. Listen, do you think Fox and Clem would mind if I took some of these albums and documents home, so I can study them?"

"Of course not. I think we can say you are completely trustworthy."

❖

Ash spent the next few evenings working her way through some of Louisa's research. Every night after dinner, her dad would do the dishes while she studied the documents at the kitchen table. She was thoroughly enjoying this unexpected part of her new job.

"Here's a cup of tea for you," he said.

"Thanks, Dad."

He set it down in front of her and walked over to his armchair in front of the fire. "You really are enjoying this project, aren't you?"

Ash grinned. "I'm loving it. I'm not even reading my books so much as I was. I think I would have liked to have studied history at university."

Almost as soon as she said it, Ash wished she had kept her mouth shut when she saw her dad's head droop. She knew her dad felt a lot of guilt for her having given up her dream of going to university.

"Dad, don't. I chose to stay here with you. This was my choice, and look where it's led me—into an amazing job—and gotten me some fantastic friends."

"It's true that I've never seen you happier," he said.

Ash smiled brightly. "You see? Wait till I show you what I've found."

She gathered the photos, Louisa's notes, and her own notebook and walked over to the couch.

"Look, this is a picture of one of the children's names, carved into the desk at the school. This little boy, Elijah, led me to local births, marriages, and deaths. The family name was Winters. And in Louisa Fitzroy's photo collection, I found him."

Ash handed him a photograph of a group of children. "This is a class photograph. You can see all their names are marked."

James pointed to a little boy sitting in a regimented fashion. "This one?"

"That's him. Do you see he's got no shoes on? Imagine little children having to live like that."

"People were often very poor back then, Ash. My own father remembered children at his school who couldn't afford shoes. You don't have to go back too far to find awful poverty," he said.

"According to Louisa's notes, those children were ten years old. Elijah was one of five children, and the son of a Mary Winters. Her husband was long dead, but he got a job at Rosebrook as a stable boy."

"Lady Louisa's research is really good, then? It doesn't surprise me," he said.

Ash went to take a breath to speak, but then something her dad said made her pause. "*Lady* Louisa? You all called her that?"

He nodded. "Being gay wasn't talked about as freely, but we all knew and understood they were in a relationship."

Now Ash was interested. She'd never really talked that much about this subject before, and she'd never said she was gay, so it was interesting to find out her dad's reaction to others who were gay.

"What was Louisa like?"

He took a sip of his tea and thought for a few seconds. "One of the kindest people I ever met. She tempered Lady Dora's loud, sometimes overenthusiastic personality. A bit like Fox and Lady Clementine."

Ash leaned her head on her hand and sighed. "It's funny and

so lovely how history has repeated itself. Did anyone in the village have any problem with them being a gay couple?"

"Some, but they ended up leaving or keeping their opinions to themselves. Remember, Dora owned everything around here, so it didn't do well to antagonize her. Lady Louisa did charity work in the village, visiting the old and new mothers, taking people who were sick food. Your mum was very fond of her. Louisa'd known her since she was a little girl, of course."

"It's nice to think of Mum knowing Dora and Louisa. You didn't have a problem with them being gay, did you, Dad?" Ash decided to test the waters.

He gave her an incredulous look. "Do you think I would?"

Ash shook her head hopefully.

"That's right. Live and let live, I say. Remember, I know what it feels like to be different in this village. I was a foreigner, even if I was just from across the sea in Ireland. It takes a long time to be accepted in places like this. I became a local only after twenty-five years," he joked.

Coming out to her dad suddenly became all she could think of. Ash's heart thudded, and she fiddled with the hem of her skirt so she didn't have to look him in the eye.

"You know Fox has made this a village open to all, gay, trans, all backgrounds—"

"A safe place for people who feel *other*. Yes, I know," he finished for her.

Ash had never had such an open conversation with her dad, and there was no going back now.

"You know Fox, Lady Clem, and Archie are lesbians?"

"Ash, look at me." She looked up at her dad's loving, open face, and he said, "I know, and it's okay. You don't have to worry about saying it to me."

Even though he was paving her way to her truth, it was still hard to say the words out loud. She took a breath and said, "I'm a lesbian."

"I know that, my darling girl, and I'm sorry if you've not felt able to talk about it to me before." Her dad grasped her hand.

The relief at saying the words and being accepted made the tears spill from her eyes. "You knew? How could you?"

He smiled and said, "Your mammy told me. She knew you weren't interested in boys and told me about your school romance."

Ash was gobsmacked. "Mum knew about Sammy?"

"Yes, and I was sad for you when she left to go to university without you, but I'm sorry. I was selfish and wrapped up in my own grief."

Ash wiped her tears away with the back of her hand. "There is not a selfish bone in your body, Dad."

She placed the documents and pictures carefully on the couch and then went to give her dad a hug. He stood up and gave her the bear hug she so needed.

"Nothing left unsaid between us, okay?"

"Yes, thank you for loving me, Daddy."

Archie felt such a sense of pride watching Ash give her presentation in the conference room. She was passionate, clever, and even more beautiful when talking about something that inspired her.

Ash was presenting what she had found out about the schoolchildren from so long ago, and all the office staff were hanging on her every word.

"And this is where it gets interesting. Elijah then goes to live with a Mr. Gavin Burton at his farmhouse. It's the derelict farmhouse near Mr. Murdoch's. You know the one I mean?"

Rupert looked to Jenna, Claire, and Archie. "I don't think I do."

"It's just off the road, but there are a few trees covering it from view," Ash said.

"What happened then?"

"He lived there, never married, and Mr. Burton never married. Two bachelors in those days? It made me suspicious. According to Louisa's notes, there were rumours around the village that they were *unnatural*, as they called it then. She interviewed some of the elderly residents of Rosebrook, and they said they knew they were different."

"If that's true, then they were exceptionally brave men. Homosexuality was still illegal then," Archie said.

"Brave men they were. Especially Elijah. The First World War came, and Elijah was called up. Gavin was older than Elijah and wasn't conscripted. This is where we get confirmation of their relationship. I don't know where she got it, but in Louisa's papers was a letter from Elijah to Gavin." She put up a slide, showing the letter.

My beloved G,

Every time I close my eyes, I see you sitting in our garden on a beautiful summer's day. When I open them I see, smell, and taste death in the air. Without the thought of you waiting for me, I think I would walk out into no man's land and end it all. But I don't—because of you. I want you to know if I am killed, it will not be without the want of trying to stay alive for you, and the dream of walking down our path when this godforsaken war is over.

If I'm called to our Lord's side, I'll wait for you for eternity. I love you, G.

Your beloved Elijah

"That's beautiful," Rupert said with tears in his eyes.

Archie heard sniffles from Jenna and Claire and saw a tear run down Ash's face. She quickly handed around a box of tissues because she could sense what was coming next.

"Elijah was killed in France the day the war ended."

Everyone's tears were flowing now, apart from Archie's. She felt the same empathy and sadness, but she had learned a long time ago not to show how hurt she was over anything.

Ash wiped her tears away, and her voice was wobbly as she said, "I think Elijah's story is powerful. It's a love story at a time when love between two men was unthinkable. It touches on the poverty that the working class had to endure. He was of the first generation to have compulsory schooling, and also the generation decimated by the First World War and the tragedy of that. I think Elijah Winters should be the lead character in our social history project. We can follow him from birth to death in the graveyard. His legacy is everywhere if you look hard enough."

After Ash finished her presentation, everyone except Archie filed out of the room. Ash looked nervous but Archie could only smile at her.

"What did you think?" Ash asked.

"I think you are amazing, Ash, and I seriously underestimated you."

Ash seemed to gain a few inches in height at that comment, and her face was wreathed in smiles.

"Really? You liked my ideas? I have more that I didn't say in front of everyone in case you thought it was silly."

"I'd never think you were silly. Come sit down and tell me."

Ash sat beside her and started to lay out her ideas. "I think the social history project can lead our visitors and tourists towards our ecological message. They follow Elijah's history to the farmhouse, and we introduce them to the farming methods of the time, and how far away from traditional, organic farming we have come. Talk about the environmental consequences, things like that."

Archie felt excitement immediately. "That's a fantastic idea. And we can find other former members of the village to highlight different aspects of animal conservation and things like that. What would I do without you?"

As soon as she said it, Archie realized she had said too much, but Ash made it hard for her to hide her feelings.

"I don't know," Ash joked. "Make your own tea?"

"Very funny."

"I'll work on it more at the weekend."

Archie's excited feeling was replaced by the churning of anxiety and, she had to admit, jealousy.

"But you have your beach party on Sunday."

"It's hardly partying in Ibiza. We're just having a barbecue and a few drinks in the evening," Ash said. "Besides, you could come if you weren't so stubborn. You could stay for the weekend at Rosebrook, and you wouldn't need to worry about driving the next day, so you could have a drink."

"I have plans for Sunday," Archie said flatly.

Ash tapped her pen on the table repeatedly. "Who's the lucky lady?" Ash said with great annoyance.

"No lady, I'm having dinner with my dad and his partner."

"How long have they been together?" Ash asked. Partner could mean anything these days, so this was a good chance to find out more about grumpy Archie's backstory.

"He's been dating Stuart for around six months."

"Your dad's gay?" Ash was surprised and happy that Archie was sharing this with her.

"They've just moved in together."

Archie sounded...not sad, but maybe more worried. "Do you not like Stuart?" Ash asked.

"No, I do. He's a nice man, and he makes my dad happy. That's all that matters. It's just—well, it's complicated, but I suppose I'm worried I'll lose my dad somehow. Sounds ridiculous for a thirty-six-year-old woman to say, isn't it?"

Ash took Archie's hand. This was a different Archie she was seeing in this moment. She looked and sounded vulnerable, like someone who had been through an awful lot and struggled to handle those hurt emotions.

"It's not ridiculous. It's only natural. I would say, though, that if Stuart is the nice man you say he is, then you're gaining someone in your family, not losing them. What about your mum?"

The emotional look was gone, and Archie shut down. "We're not on speaking terms. I haven't been in contact with her since I was a teenager."

"Did something—"

Archie cut her off straight away. "I think Prisha would like to help with this kind of thing."

There it was. That was the backstory she was looking for, the reason Archie had little faith in love and relationships. She had to find out more about her mum, but she could tell Archie was about to flee, so she said, "I told my dad I was gay."

Archie did a double take. "You did?"

"Yeah, I was telling him about Elijah likely being gay. He seemed understanding, and I just couldn't hold it in any longer. But…"

"But what? Was he angry?"

Ash shook her head. "No, he already knew. My mum told him. She even knew about my girlfriend, Sammy."

"Really?"

"I suppose Sammy was around a lot, and Mum was quite ill at that point, so I didn't like to go into town. She must have seen us together. I wish I would have had the chance to talk to her about it."

Ash's voice cracked with emotion, and she found herself being pulled into Archie's safe, strong arms. She pressed her nose and lips against Archie's neck and inhaled her scent.

She had never felt so safe, so warm.

"You're lucky to have such understanding parents. Your dad is a good man."

More than anything in the world, Ash wanted to reach up and scratch her nails down Archie's undercut hair. She felt Archie's hands slip from her back down to her hips, then stroke the sides of her thighs.

Ash ached to touch Archie and to feel her lips. She pulled back and looked into Archie's eyes. Ash's lips parted, and Archie inched her lips closer. It was going to happen. Archie was going to kiss her—

Then a knock came to the conference room door, and Archie jumped away from her like she'd been burned.

"Archie—"

Rupert popped his head around the door and said, "Archie? The brewing supplier is on the phone."

"I'm coming."

CHAPTER NINE

When the end of the week came around, Archie decided to break the habit of a lifetime and finish up early. Ash and Rupert were still there, tidying up some work before the weekend. The group was usually in an excitable mood, but even more so that they were looking forward to the beach barbecue this weekend. She knew it would be even worse if Fox had been there.

While everyone else was excited, Archie grew more melancholy as the day went on. She wanted to sit on the beach with Ash, paddle in the water, and cook burgers for them on the barbecue.

This was a new feeling for Archie. Dating women had always been a physical thing, but with Ash all she kept thinking about all day was walking barefoot along the shoreline, holding her hand, talking about her silly romance books and her Netflix series.

Of course she wanted to kiss her, to make love to her, and the thoughts fuelled her dreams, but just spending some simple time on a sunny beach sounded like heaven. If only she was ten years younger, and more emotionally ready for a relationship.

But she wasn't, so she had to internalize her longing, bad luck, and jealousy. Although she hadn't made a very good job of internalizing it the other day in the conference room. They'd come so close to kissing, and she had been thinking about it ever since.

She picked up her case and walked over to Ash's desk. "I'm off, Ash."

Ash looked surprised. "You don't usually leave this early."

Archie shrugged. "Everything's done, and I've got a long commute home."

"Well, you could be staying at Rosebrook and having fun with your friends. Having fun with me."

Ash winked when she said that last sentence, and Archie felt the heat rising inside.

"I'm happy with my city life—you know that."

Ash's smile faltered. "Whatever. Have you finished the book yet?"

"No."

Another sigh from Ash. In truth, she had finished it days ago, but she didn't want to let Ash know she'd raced through to the end and had downloaded a list of similar books from the same author and publisher. Ash would be too triumphant.

She felt closer to Ash through the love stories and had to admit she enjoyed the vicarious excitement of watching the two leads fall in love, and of course she always pictured Ashling as her beautiful heroine.

"You did promise, Archie. I'm watching your stupid bookkeeper thing," Ash said with an annoyed tone.

Archie secretly loved the way Ash purposely called her show The Bookkeeper just to annoy her. Instead she found it endearing.

"I will. I just haven't had time."

"I certainly won't have time to watch The Bookkeeper this weekend. I'll be busy prepping the barbecue food tomorrow. Griff is picking me up." Ash looked over to the office door and said, "Talk of the devil."

"Knock knock." Griffin came through the door. "Hi, everyone."

Ash made a big show of walking over to Griffin and putting her arm through hers.

"Griffin was kind enough to offer to come with me to the wholesaler to pick up some food and drinks for Sunday. Wasn't that kind of her?"

Ash had a smug look on her face. Was she trying to make her jealous?

"Very kind," Archie said through gritted teeth.

Griff looked a little bemused as to what was going on. Archie decided to get out of the situation and not act like a jealous teenager. "Well, good luck food shopping Friday night, Griff."

It seemed to then dawn on Griff what she was in for, but Archie—satisfied she'd struck a blow—said goodnight to Rupert and headed out of the office. She could hear someone come after her. It was Griff.

"Hey, Archie. Is there something wrong? Are you and Ash... you know?"

"What? Of course not. I'm hardly in her age bracket, am I?"

Griff furrowed her eyebrows. "You're not—"

"She's all yours." Archie opened up her car door and slipped in the driver's seat.

Griff looked really confused. "But I'm—"

Ash came out of the office and shouted, "I'll send you some photos of the barbecue on Sunday."

"I'm sure you will."

❖

Ash couldn't remember the beach being filled with such noise and laughter before. It had definitely woken from its long slumber.

They set up the seating area and barbecue next to the wheelchair-friendly beach pathway, so that Alanna wouldn't have to worry about getting down to the water and back.

Blake, Griffin, Casper, and Rupert were playing with the children near the shoreline. Casper had Prisha's little Rohan up in his arms, giving his mum a break.

Jonah and Jay were cooking the food, and Prisha, Whitney, and Alanna were chatting amongst themselves while Eliska and Ash sat watching the kids play, while enjoying a cool drink.

"Ola looks really happy playing with Blake, doesn't she?" Ash said.

"I don't have the words to say how grateful I am to Blake for bringing us here. It's like a paradise," Eliska said.

"Blake would do anything for you. I know that."

"I love her with all my heart. I never knew my heart could love any more, with everything we've been through. Ola saw a lot of bad things, but not as much as I did. Now she gets to be just a child."

"I'm so happy we can give you both a safe place to live," Ash said.

Prisha got up and filled everyone's disposable wine cup. She stopped for a second and looked down at the shore.

"Griffin's bloody gorgeous, isn't she?" Prisha said.

"Absolutely," Whitney said, "I'm straight, and even I can see that she has some kind of, I don't know, sensuality that makes you want to growl."

Alanna laughed. "Do you like her, Ash?"

"Yes, she's lovely. Really nice."

"Nice isn't really how I would describe Griffin. Sexy, dangerous, edible, maybe," Alanna joked.

All that was true, but as gorgeous as she was, and as much fun as this all was—all Ash could think of was Archie.

The others continued to chat as Ash wished that Archie was here. Rupert plonked down on the sand beside her. "You seem distracted. Are you okay?"

"Yeah, I'm fine," Ash said a little too brightly.

"You're missing one person who didn't come, aren't you?" Rupert said.

"What do you mean?"

"I see the way you look at each other every day at work. Some days I'm not sure whether you want to devour each other or wrestle on the ground."

"It's complicated. My feelings aren't like anything I'm used to, and she…I don't know what she thinks or feels. She pushes me away, makes constant references to my age. I mean, it's not like she's sixty and I'm twenty-one."

"It's probably a convenient excuse to not face what she feels," Rupert said. "You know, when I was getting to know Jonah, *I* told *him* he was in love with me."

Ash laughed. "What did he say?"

"Um...yeah, I do. Love you, I mean...a lot." Ash smiled at Rupert's imitation of his partner's voice. "Then we spent the rest of the day in bed."

"I would never have the confidence to say that to Archie. I mean, am I even in love? I don't know."

"How does it feel when you think about her right now," Rupert asked.

Ash sighed and searched her feelings. "I miss her, I wish she was here and we were talking about her favourite TV show, and I'm dreading the thought that she met someone new last night."

"What's her favourite show?"

"The book—sorry, *The Gatekeeper*."

Rupert's eyes went wide with surprise. "Really? I would never have guessed that was her kind of thing. Jonah and I love that show."

"She's a secret sci-fi geek."

"See? Already she's shared things with you I bet no one else knows." Rupert looked over to the shore and said, "Here comes our sexy brewer. Why don't we concentrate Archie's mind?"

He stood up, got his phone out, and said, "Okay, everyone. Time for pictures."

❖

Archie looked at the clock in her dad's dining room. They would be eating now.

Even though she had been at her dad's for the last few hours, her mind was on Rosebrook beach. It was killing her not to be there. Archie had never felt territorial or jealous about any woman before. It just wasn't her. She was never with anyone long enough—or cared enough about anyone—to feel emotions like that. Ash was different. Her emotions were so strong and so confusing that Archie felt like a teenager again.

Her father came through with two bottles of wine. One white, one red.

"I think you're going to like these ones, Arch."

"Hmm?" Archie was distracted.

"Are you okay?" he asked. "You've been quiet since you arrived."

Just then Stuart came in with the starter course.

"I'm fine, Dad."

Not only did she have to cope with her confusing feelings for Ash, but she had to deal with her dad's new situation. She'd met Stuart many times before. She'd met a few of her dad's boyfriends over the years, but like her relationships, they never became serious. Stuart was different. He'd been with her dad the longest and now he was living with him.

It was harder than she'd expected, seeing her dad being domestic with Stuart. Making and preparing dinner together, setting the dining table, joking and sharing intimate glances between them.

Did her dad not remember how much domesticity had hurt them both?

"Are you sure you're okay?" he asked.

"I'm fine, okay?" Archie said sharply.

Her dad and Stuart exchanged a look, and she immediately felt bad.

"Why don't we eat," Stuart said diplomatically.

They ate the first course and exchanged small talk about the wine and Stuart's job at Christie's auction house, but Archie was struggling to cope with the tumultuous emotions being stirred inside her.

When her dad and Stuart went to get the main course, Archie's phone beeped. Her heart thumped when she saw it was from Ash, but then dropped when she saw the pictures. There were group shots with everyone having fun on the beach, and two of Ash and Griff. She should be there.

How could she make sure Ash was okay, like James had asked her to do, when she was not there?

They started to eat the main course, and Archie's frustration built and built.

Then her father said, "Archie, we wanted to tell you something."

Archie looked up from her meal and saw her dad and Stuart

smiling and holding hands. And something she hadn't spotted before—a ring on Stuart's wedding finger.

No. It couldn't be.

"I wanted you to be the first to know—I asked Stuart to marry me, and he said yes."

Her dad's excited smile faltered when Archie went silent. Archie couldn't believe what she was hearing. How could her dad want to marry again?

"Archie, are you okay with this?" Stuart asked.

Archie felt like she couldn't breathe. She had to get out of there. "This is absurd." Archie threw her napkin down and stormed out of the dining room.

She needed air and went out the french doors and into the garden. Archie stood against a stone balustrade that went around the perimeter of her dad's garden. She took a deep breath and scrubbed her face with her hands.

How could this be happening again?

She heard footsteps coming out to the garden. Archie expected it to be her dad, but it wasn't—it was Stuart who stood beside her.

"This was all a bit of a shock for you, Archie."

Why was he being so reasonable? She'd expected both of them to be angry at her, because deep down she knew she was being childish. "I—I don't know what to say."

"Your dad has told me about his first marriage and the effect it had on you and him. I promise you, I love your dad, and our relationship is nothing like that."

"I didn't ever expect him to marry again. I didn't think he had it in him to open up his heart again. I know I never have," Archie said.

"It must be hard seeing your dad in a couple again too. I get that," Stuart said.

That fact that Stuart was being so understanding was making her feel worse.

"Domesticity is arguments and pain. Marriage destroyed my dad, made him feel ashamed of who he was."

"I love Adam, Archie. I could never purposely hurt him, and if our relationship started to break down, we would be amicable, but I know that will never happen."

Archie sighed. "I know you're different, and I'm sorry about how I reacted."

Stuart put a comforting hand on her shoulder. "Don't worry about it. We're going to be family. See you inside."

Her dad replaced Stuart at her side.

"I'm sorry, Dad. I shouldn't have reacted like that. I suppose I'm jealous of you."

"Jealous? Why?" he said.

"You went through a horrendous marriage, you even lost who you were for a while, but now after all these years you have the courage to open up your heart again."

Her dad sighed. "Arch, you were a child and were witness to a toxic relationship. It's no wonder you're protective of me and of your heart, but that was our fault. Your mum and I didn't set an example of how a normal relationship can work."

"I've never been strong enough to open myself up to that potential pain," Archie said.

"Does that make you unhappy?" he asked.

"As I've gotten older? Yes."

"Arch, to exorcise the past, I had to move on, I had to take that chance with Stuart. It might be my last chance for happiness."

"I know." Archie turned to face her dad. "Stuart is a good man, Dad. I'm sorry for how I reacted."

He pulled her into a hug. "Don't worry about it. We can have a good meal, some good wine and brandy, and it'll be all forgotten."

"I have feelings for someone, and I'm struggling to cope with them."

"The woman from the magazine picture?"

Archie nodded. "Ashling O'Rourke, and I've pushed her away so much that I might have pushed her into someone else's arms."

Archie showed him the picture of Ash and Griff.

"Why are you not there, Archie? If the villagers are having a celebration, you should be there. We could have had dinner another time."

"I didn't want to be part of a small insular village again. They were the unhappiest years of my life."

"Rosebrook is not Haverswood. People make a village community, and Rosebrook is full of a diverse group of people determined to make the world a better place. Quite different from Haverswood."

"You're right, but I don't know. I just have this fear of being trapped. My home has always been in the city."

"Arch, home is where the heart is, and by the sounds of it, you may be living in Notting Hill, but your heart is in Rosebrook."

That made total sense. She'd never thought of it that way, but her fears were still there. "I think I'm too old for her. Ash is thirteen years younger than me."

"That's your fears trying to make excuses. You always have to take a chance on love, and I know it's frightening, but I also know you're a strong person, and you can be brave."

Archie ran her hand over the back of her neck. She was tense, but a bubble of excitement was starting.

"Fox did say I could stay at Rosebrook while they were away. Every Friday it's getting harder and harder to leave the village."

Adam put his arm around her. "Go and pack your bags, stay at Fox's house, and prove to yourself you can handle everything that you've always feared. And woo this young lady."

"I don't know if I'd know how. I've never had to work hard to get a woman's attention before," Archie said.

"Tell me what she likes, her interests, hobbies."

"She loves reading on the beach, and she's obsessed with romance novels."

He slapped her on the back. "Then what better person to woo and romance? She'll love it."

Archie thought about Ash's favourite book, *The Dastardly Duke*, and remembered there was a part of the book where a rival comes on the scene. The duke realizes how much he loves his children's governess, and just like her dad said, the duke learned to woo his love.

Could she learn to open her heart and prove to Ash that she

could love her—and prove to herself that she could too? But would it all be too late?

❖

The sun was setting, and many people had gone home. All the parents had left mid-evening with completely tired-out kids. Only Jonah, Rupert, Ash, and Griff were left.

Ash was sitting around a small fire Griff had built on the sand, and the only sounds she could hear were the rolling waves splashing onto shore and the pops and crackles from the fire.

Griff took a bottle of beer from the cool box and popped it open. "Do you want one?"

"No thanks, I think I've had enough for today."

Griff took a swig of her lager and said, "You know, I've been on beaches all over the world, and this is as beautiful as any of the best."

"I'm glad you think so. I feel very lucky to have been born here. So you think you'll be able to settle in the village?" Ash asked.

"Yeah, for as long as it takes to get the brewery up and running. That's what I promised Fox. I'm not used to being settled in one place very long, so it will be an experience." She gave Ash a charming smile and nudged her. "Plus, I'll have some beautiful company."

"Archie said you were a bit of a traveller."

Griff nodded. "Yeah, wherever I lay my hat is my home kind of thing. I have a travel vlog, and I've visited South America, Asia, Australia, New Zealand, but I've never charted any time I spent in the UK, so it'll be a different experience for my subscribers."

"Archie says you do a lot of charity in the places you visit."

"Yeah, I feel I have to." Griff's gaze fell to her bare feet in the sand, and she tapped her fingers on the neck of the glass bottle. "Did Archie tell you any more about me?"

It was clear Griff felt awkward about her wealth. It was strange—most people wouldn't feel that at all.

"She said that you owned a lot of land in Hampshire but that it was your story to tell."

"I suppose it is," Griff said.

"You don't need to tell me. It's none of my business," Ash said.

"Don't be silly—I have nothing to hide, especially from you. I like you."

Again, Griff gave her that sexy smile. Was she flirting? Or was it just Griff's natural personality?

"I like you too."

"Good. Well, my sordid story is I never knew my dad. My mum had a very short relationship with him. He knew my mum had me, but he suffered from drug addiction and didn't care, as far as I know, so I never had a relationship with him. My mum brought me up in a council estate—she worked two jobs and had very little money. I didn't know who he was."

"Who was he?" Ash asked.

"The Right Honourable Gyles de Beaufort. His family had lived in and owned most of Hampshire for three hundred years."

"Wow," Ash replied.

"When he died, the lawyers came to see me and Mum, asked if I'd take a DNA test. Lo and behold, I was his closest heir. One day Mum and I were budgeting our weekly shop, and the next day we didn't have to ever budget again."

"What an amazing story, Griff."

"I was never into monetary things, consumption, all that stuff, so I used my inheritance to live my dream of travelling and promised to make a contribution to every community I visited."

Ash could see just how easy it would be to fall for that kind heart and rumpled, good-looking persona. "That's a great thing to do with it. Helping others is the best thing in life. It's funny—I've known you for a week, and I know more about you than Archie."

"I'm an open book, but not everyone is the same. Can I ask you something?"

"Uh-huh."

Griff looked as if she was choosing her words carefully. "Are you and Archie…have you got something going on, because she's been a bit strange with me since I arrived. It's completely normal when we're alone, but when you're there, she gets pissed off and weird."

Griff had noticed. She wasn't imagining it. Archie was jealous.

"No, there's nothing. Archie is complicated, and I don't think she knows what she wants or has the nerve to take it."

"But you'd like there to be something?" Griff asked.

"It doesn't matter. She has her own life elsewhere, and nothing's going to change that," Ash said sadly.

Chapter Ten

A rchie brought her last case out the door and left it on the bottom step. There were just her suit carriers to come. After leaving her dad's last night, she had packed her things up, ready to live, for the time being, in the village, at Rosebrook House.

It was strange. Since talking with her dad about it last night, she felt lighter, like the emotional baggage she carried around was lessened. If her dad could emotionally close that chapter in his life, maybe she could too.

In fact Archie actually felt excited. She couldn't wait to get to Rosebrook, and to try to romance Ashling O'Rourke. Although it might already be too late. After all, Ash'd spent the weekend with the charismatic Griffin, who tended to charm and bed any woman that she fancied.

But as the dastardly duke did in Ash's favourite novel, she was going to show Ash that she wasn't always grumpy Archie. She could be loving—she could be romantic—if she tried.

Archie hadn't experienced love before, but she was sure her heart was pulling her to Rosebrook, and she was ready to push herself.

She went back into the living room and picked up her suit carriers. Archie hesitated before leaving the living room and looked around the space. The only noise was the clock ticking on the wall, and she got the overwhelming feeling of emptiness and loneliness.

This wasn't a home, and she wouldn't miss it, but could she find a home somewhere else?

Time to find out. Once the car was packed, she set off for Rosebrook, eager to see if that home for her was there. She'd left so early that the drive to Rosebrook was quick and hassle free. When she entered the village, Archie stopped at the shop to pick up a couple of energy drinks, then made her way to the house.

She had an hour before the office opened. All she would have time to do was put her bags in the house, and she could deal with them after work. As she was unloading her things, she heard the crunch of gravel behind her.

Archie turned around and saw Ash walking towards her.

"You're up early," Archie said.

"Dad had an early fishing booking, so I thought I'd just get some more of my village research done. Why are you parked up by the house?"

Archie smiled and opened the boot of her car. "I thought I'd take everyone's advice and stay at Rosebrook."

Ash looked gobsmacked. "Really?"

"Yes, well, it looks like Fox and Lady Clementine are going to be away for longer than they thought, so I better keep an eye on the place."

Much to Archie's surprise, Ash threw her arms around her. "Yay, it'll be so much nicer for you, and you can get to know everyone better."

"You can show me all the great things about village life," Archie said.

"That'll be fun," Ash said, then seemed to realize maybe she had been a bit overenthusiastic, because then she tried to look disinterested. "Um, it'll save you a lot of stress on the commute."

Archie had her first indication that this was where she was meant to be. Just by coming here, she had made Ash happy. She felt wanted for the first time in her life, and it was a really good feeling.

"Yes, it'll be good. I'll be less tired, anyway. I'm just going to put some bags in the hall, and then I can sort them out later."

"I'll help you get settled after work. You'll need some food from the shop too."

"I suppose I will."

Archie was desperate to talk about the barbecue beach day with Griff. Had Griff's charms worked on Ash?

"How was your beach day?"

"It was great fun. The villagers really bonded," Ash said.

Archie wanted to know about Griff, but Ash wasn't giving much away.

"And the charming Griff, did you bond with her?"

"Oh yeah, she told me all about herself. Her life story is amazing. Then she built a fire on the sand, and we talked and talked into the night."

Typical. Griff always appeared to have a natural way with women. Not that Archie struggled to chat and flirt with women who took her interest. And she'd never had much trouble trying to talk a woman into bed, but Ash was different.

She didn't want anyone to talk Ash into bed, far less herself. Ash deserved so much more than that.

Archie got the impression Ash was trying to make her jealous, so she tried her best not to show it. If there was truly anything between Ash and Griff, then it was Archie's job to show Ash that she could romance her too.

"Lovely, I got your pictures. Everyone appeared to be having a good time."

Ash narrowed her eyes.

Ha! Ash definitely wasn't expecting that response. Archie lifted out two of the suitcases.

"Can I help with the bags?" Ash asked.

"You could get a couple of the small holdalls. Don't lift anything heavy."

"Why? You think I'm a weak little girl?" Ash snapped.

Archie turned on her best charm and leaned in to Ash. "No, but when you've got a tall, strong person like me to do the heavy lifting, then why do it yourself?"

She could see Ash shiver slightly, and that gave Archie a burst of energy and excitement. Ash had been teasing her, so maybe it was time to have some fun with her.

❖

Archie had one thing she needed to do. Talk to Griff. She felt guilty that she had taken her jealousy out on Griff. It wasn't her fault that Archie had been incapable of facing what she felt for Ash.

Just as she walked through the garden gate of Griff's cottage, she saw Ash and Kay pushing Agatha and Ada in their wheelchairs. The ladies were having their yearly medical with Blake at the surgery, and they needed support.

Everyone was used to seeing them whizz through the village on their mobility scooters, but both were recovering from the flu and not at their strongest.

Archie waved and they all waved back. She saw Ash whisper something into Ada's ear and they all laughed. It was probably some wisecrack about her, but that only made her smile.

The door opened unexpectedly, and Griff was there. "Archie, hi."

"Hi, I thought I'd pop over and have a chat. Is that okay?"

"In you come. I'll put the kettle on," Griff said.

Archie followed her into the living room. It was a nice room. Clementine made sure the cottages were decorated to a really high standard. The TV and couch area was at the far end of the room, and in front of the bay window there was a small round table, where a laptop and a notebook lay open.

When Griff came back in, Archie sat at the table. "I'm not disturbing you, am I?"

Griff put cups of tea and a packet of biscuits down on the table and sat down.

"Nah. I was due a break. I've been doing some planning for the brewery. It'll be a small operation until I get the recipes down. Jonah's keen to help in his spare time."

"However long it takes, it takes. Fox is in no hurry to rush anything, though I do have a new staff member for you, if you don't mind," Archie said.

"Sure, I'll need someone full-time to help me in the beginning. Jonah can only give me a few hours here and there. Who are they?"

"Patrick Doyle. He's arriving this week. He's only twenty, and Fox and I hoped he might apprentice with you as a brewer."

"Sounds like a great idea. I can't wait to meet him," Griff said.

Archie took a sip of tea and said, "I think being around a confident person like you would help him too. Patrick's been through a lot."

"I suppose his story's confidential?" Griff said.

"No, he's given Fox permission to tell you. He wanted everything out in the open since you're going to be working together so closely. He applied to the trust for a house and job here in Rosebrook. Patrick has been homeless for a year. His dad beat him so badly that he had to go to the hospital."

"My God. Why would he do that?" Griff asked.

"Patrick is a trans man. He told his mum and dad, and that's what happened. He's been living on the streets and in shelters for a year. Fox wanted his application fast-tracked because he really needed Rosebrook. This is what our community is all about, an accepting, caring community."

"If Patrick is happy to work with me, I'd be really happy to have an apprentice. I've been taught about brewing from the best local brewers around the world, and I'm happy to pass on that knowledge."

"Great. I know Fox and Lady Clementine feel really strongly about giving him a chance for a safe, happy life."

Griff shook her head. "You know, I've seen the physical and mental abuse inflicted on all parts of the LGBTQ+ community, and to come back here and see the great work you've all done, it shows me how much it's needed."

"Yes, it really is."

Archie cleared her throat. This was the difficult bit. She tapped her fingers against the teacup. She hated awkward conversations like this.

"Did you have a good time at the barbecue?"

"Yeah, it was really good. Everyone is so nice and welcoming."

"Ash sent me pictures. The two of you looked like you were getting on well," Archie said.

"Ash is a sweetheart. So beautiful too."

There it was. Archie's worst fear. Had she missed her chance to woo? Archie had to do the right thing and apologize over her behaviour even if Griff had jumped ahead of her.

"Griff, I—"

Before she could finish her sentence Griff said, "So sweet and so beautiful, so why are you not sweeping her off her feet?"

"What?"

"I spent all day being charming, and my charm is top-notch, but she spent her time talking about you, sending you pictures, and wishing you were there. I'm not the one she's interested in, bearing in mind who's talking here—the king of charm."

Archie didn't know what to say. Even though she had pushed Ash away, Ash still felt something for her.

"Thanks for telling me that, Griff. I really came here to apologize. I've acted like a jealous idiot around you and Ash. I just have never felt this way, and I didn't think it was right for so many reasons. I thought I was too old for her, for a start."

"Oh, come on! That stuff doesn't matter any more. You're both adults."

"I think it was an excuse not to face my feelings."

"But you're no stranger to women, Archie. I've seen you charm more than one woman at Fox's parties, over the years," Griff said.

Archie looked up at Griff and said seriously, "I can't hurt this one, Griff. She's too important."

Griff leaned forward and said, "If that's the case, then don't hurt her—make her happy."

Easier said than done.

CHAPTER ELEVEN

Later that day Ash hurried down to see her dad at the boat shop. She walked in but didn't see him. "Dad?"

"I'm just out back. Give me a second."

A moment later he came out and gave Ash a kiss on the cheek. "How was your day at work?"

"Really good, and Kay and I took the Tucker twins for their yearly medical. But that's not what I wanted to tell you." Ash was full of excitement, like all her nerves were sparking at the same time, and her heart was pounding. "Archie brought her bags this morning. She's going to stay at Rosebrook while Fox and Clem are away."

Her dad raised an eyebrow. "Well, that's nice."

Ash felt silly. She was obviously not hiding her feelings and being too excitable. "I mean, it's nice for her, I suppose. Um...I'll be late back—I said I'd pick up some food at the shop while she gets unpacked and settled in. Is that all right?"

"Of course it is. Why don't you have dinner with her? I can knock up some bacon and eggs for myself."

Ash loved that idea. "Are you sure, Dad?"

"I'm sure. Go and enjoy yourself for a change."

Ash hugged him. "See you later then."

She then hurried up the beach steps and made her way to the shop. Jay was behind the counter, and his wife Erica was stocking some shelves.

"Afternoon Jay, Erica."

"Hi there, sweetie," Erica said

"What can we do for you today?" Jay asked.

"I need to get some supplies for Rosebrook. Archie is moving in till Fox and Clementine come home," Ash said happily.

"Oh lovely," Erica said. "I told her she was going to exhaust herself with that long commute."

"I need the vegan stuff," Ash said

"All along the back row you can find the chilled items, and the rest Erica can point you to," Jay said.

"Thanks."

A large part of the chilled and frozen section at the back was dedicated to the vegan and vegetarian items. Fox made sure when the shop was planned that it would carry a large selection of vegan goods, not just for herself, but also to encourage others to try new things.

She chose a selection of items and paid for them. Carrying four bags of shopping, Ash made her way back to Rosebrook. The door was open, and as she went in, out of breath, she heard Archie coming down the stairs.

"You didn't have to get that much, Ash. I would have come with you and carried the bags," Archie said.

Ash let the bags drop the last few inches to the floor. "Oh God."

She looked at the deep indents in her hands and then shook them to try to relieve the sting. Archie caught her hands and looked carefully at them. "Don't carry heavy things like that now that I'm around. I'll be your packhorse."

"How gallant."

"That's me. Always ready to help a damsel"—Archie started to massage her left hand between hers—"in distress."

Ash gazed at her much smaller hand in Archie's bigger ones and imagined how those hands would feel touching her body. Heat spread up her arm, and she prayed for Archie to pull her into her arms and kiss her.

Instead, they looked at each other for a long few seconds,

and for some stupid reason Ash's brain had to ruin the moment by saying, "There's frozen things in the bags."

"Oh, okay, better get them down to the kitchen."

Archie picked up the bags and started to walk off towards the stairs to the kitchen, and Ash could have kicked herself.

She'd ruined the moment with concern about frozen goods. Idiot.

When she got down to the kitchen, Archie was already unpacking the bags.

"Are those things okay? I've never done shopping for a vegan before," Ash said.

"Perfect—burgers, sausages, bacon, pizza—all the food groups covered. I'm not as healthy as Fox. Thanks for getting these things for me."

"No problem. I'm happy to help."

"Take a seat. Would you like a drink? I could open one of Fox's disgustingly expensive bottles of wine. Or do you have to get back for your dad?"

"No, I said I'd be late, so he's going to make bacon and egg for himself."

Archie lifted up one of the pizzas from the bag and looked at it intently. "Would you like to have a new experience and share a vegan pizza too?"

Archie had hardly finished speaking and Ash replied, "Yes, that would be nice."

"Great, take a seat, and I'll get everything organized."

It didn't take long before Archie was walking over to the couch with a bottle and two glasses.

"It's a nice room, isn't it? Cosier than the rest of the house."

Archie poured a glass of chilled white wine and gave it to Ash. She glanced around the room with the original kitchen brickwork painted white, a very comfortable couch, a TV mounted on the wall, and a door leading to a bathroom.

"Yes, it's kind of like a large open-plan flat in itself. Fox said they spend a lot of time down here."

Archie sat down next to Ash and took a sip of Fox's wine. "Hmm...nice choice, Fox."

"Have you heard how they are?" Ash asked.

"Yes, Fox said Lucy will definitely be coming back to live with them here, but they aren't sure when they're coming home," Archie said.

"It's wonderful that she has Fox and Clem. I can't imagine what it would have been like if I didn't have Dad when Mum passed away."

"Will you tell me about your mum?" Archie asked.

Ash nodded. "She was a beautiful, warm, loving woman. A selfless woman, my dad always said, and he worshipped the ground she walked on."

Archie smiled. If Ash was anything to go by, her mother Kate must have been beautiful and kind.

Ash continued, "She had already beaten cancer once, but then it came back and spread."

Archie saw tears welling in Ash's eyes, and without thinking, she took her hand and squeezed.

"My dad was devastated, and I took care of them both, because he was in pieces. Near the end it was a heart attack that took her. I found her in the morning."

Tears now rolled freely down Ash's cheeks. Archie pulled her into a hug and said, "You were so strong, so brave."

Ash grasped Archie's shirt and buried her face in her neck. Archie was acutely aware of Ash's lips and cheek. All she wanted to do was kiss Ash and make it better.

Ash pulled away from Archie and said with a sniffly voice, "That's why I can't leave him here in the village. He needs me."

It was yet another red flag that would have sent the old Archie running for the hills. If she wanted Ash, she had to accept village life, but since talking with her dad she realized she had to try.

Archie looked into Ash's eyes, cupped her head with her hands, then wiped her tears with her thumbs. "You are such a good, kind, and beautiful soul, Ash."

Ash sniffled and reached up to the sides of Archie's head and scratched her fingernails over her short, shaved undercut.

Archie had to kiss her, she just had to. She leaned in and saw Ash lick her lips, but just as they were about to kiss, a loud alarm blared in the room, making them jump in fright.

Archie got up quickly and smelled smoke. "It's the smoke alarm."

"The pizza, Archie," Ash said with her hands over her ears.

Archie hurried over to the kitchen area and saw smoke billowing from the oven. "Shit! Open the kitchen door, Ash."

Archie grabbed the kitchen towel and carefully opened up the oven. She crouched and spluttered as smoke rushed out. "Ash, stay outside, till I try to get rid of some of this smoke."

Ash hurried over and picked up a tea towel. "No, I'll help."

They both waved their towels, and the thick smoke cleared to reveal an extremely burnt pizza.

"I think I had the temperature too high."

They coughed and coughed, so Archie took Ash's hand and said, "Let's both go out until it clears."

❖

"I love a good sandwich," Ash said as they left Rosebrook.

Archie insisted on walking Ash home, and Ash was secretly pleased. There appeared to be a change in Archie since she came back from London, which delighted Ash.

"Well, that's lucky, since I incinerated dinner."

They managed to get the smoke to clear and disposed of the ashes of the pizza. Then Ash made them some sandwiches.

"It wasn't your fault. You weren't used to the new oven," Ash said.

"You're too kind. I think we both know I messed up." Archie offered her arm, and Ash gratefully took it.

"It's a beautiful night."

Archie looked up. "The stars are so clear. That's amazing."

"I don't suppose it's as easy to see the stars in the city. Too much street lighting."

"And the rest. There's light coming from everything. You know, when I was young we had an outbuilding with a flat roof, and when things got too bad in the house, I used to go out, lie on the flat roof, and stare up at the night sky."

"What was your village called?" Ash asked.

"Haverswood in Canterbury. A very insular village."

"Like Rosebrook?"

"No, not like Rosebrook. Rosebrook might be small, but it's open-minded. The people of Haverswood were the opposite of open-minded," Archie said.

Ash could hear anger in Archie's voice. She still had a lot of resentment to whatever had happened when she was younger.

They passed the gates of Rosebrook in silence, but Ash was eager to learn more about Archie. "Were your parents both from Haverswood?"

"Yes, born, bred, and indoctrinated. It was and is conservative in the extreme."

She could feel Archie tense up. Maybe this line of questioning would make Archie close down, so Ash kept quiet and let Archie move the conversation on.

"I don't know how my dad stuck it out for so long, especially with the relationship between him and my mum."

"It wasn't good, I take it?"

"No. She and I weren't close, and I think she resented my close relationship with my dad," Archie said.

"You said your dad is gay. How did he end up marrying her?"

"He told me he was always scared of telling his parents. My grandfather was handy with his fists, and that's why I'm so determined Patrick Doyle gets a safe supportive home with us here."

"Yeah, you're right."

"My dad says that his mum and dad suggested he get together with Mum, because he'd never shown any interest in women, for obvious reasons."

Ash sighed. "That doesn't sound like a recipe for a happy marriage."

"Not at all. At the time I thought my mum was in the wrong, the bad one, but looking back, I can see it wasn't quite like that."

"How so?"

"She genuinely loved him, I think, and was crying out for affection, for all the things a wife would expect but Dad couldn't give her because he was gay. He pushed her away, and her love became resentment and hurt. She was the victim of the family's homophobia, just as Dad was. But all I remember was arguing. I think Mum always knew about Dad but maybe thought he could learn to love her, especially after I came along. Dad told me that when I was born, he finally had sunshine in his life."

"He sounds like a nice man," Ash said.

"He is, really nice, and as soon as I was big enough, I got between them in their arguments and tried to stand up for my dad. I didn't understand the pain and hurt that my mum was dealing with back then. All I saw was my dad, my hero, unhappy, and I wanted to help him. We used to go on long walks, just to get away from home, and when I was older, I asked him if we could just run away."

"Did he never think about leaving?" Ash asked.

"He was frightened of losing me. Especially if Mum and her family found out about him being gay. His mental health suffered— hiding who he was and living with mum was killing him. In the meantime, I was growing up and being my butch, boyish self, further infuriating my mum. She tried at every turn to make me more *ladylike*, as she put it."

"Nothing could make you more ladylike, Archie," Ash joked.

Archie smiled at her. "That's what made her angrier. I couldn't be changed."

They started to walk up the hill towards Ash's house. Ash didn't want the house to come too soon as she was loving learning about Archie, so she slowed her walk.

"But he did eventually leave. How did that happen?"

"I was fourteen and coming to terms with the fact that I was gay.

I mean, looking back, I'd always liked girls, but I finally understood it, and I was going to burst if I didn't tell my dad. So the next time we went on a long hike alone, I was ready to tell him. But he had other ideas."

"What did he say?"

"That he was gay and couldn't live this lie any more. He had to leave Haverswood, but he would do everything he could to take me too."

"He couldn't, I take it?" Ash asked.

"No, my mum won custody. I learned later they used history of depression against him."

Frustratingly they were already at Ash's house. Ash sat down on a bench set below the window of the front room and patted it.

"Did you still get to see your dad?"

"Every other weekend and school holidays. I lived for the holidays because the rest of the time I was suffocated in the village. My dad was living this free, cosmopolitan life in London. His new wine business was going well. We'd go to museums, restaurants, shopping—it was amazing. I could express myself the way I wanted."

She took Archie's hand, and Archie didn't pull away. "I suppose London was the only place you could be yourself."

"You're not kidding." Archie turned on the bench so she was facing Ash.

"You know that part in *The Lion, the Witch and the Wardrobe* where they go through the wardrobe to Narnia?"

Ash nodded.

"That's what going to visit my dad in London was like."

Ash laughed. "I can just imagine."

"Going back home from there was just horrific. Mum had remarried, a minister of all things, who hated how his stepdaughter acted and dressed. I was being suffocated more and more by them and the village. I hatched a plan to run away to my dad's, and I did it, but Dad was forced by the court to bring me back."

Ash's heart ached for Archie. She placed her free hand on top of their clasped hands and started to soothingly stroke Archie's.

"I can't imagine how that must have felt. I'm sorry you had to go through that."

"It wasn't forever. I just kept running away, and eventually the court allowed me to choose where I wanted to go, and I moved full-time to my dad's. I hurt Mum, and I know it. So she shut me out of her life after that, and I vowed I'd never live in a small community like that again. I thought all villages were the same."

"Until you came to Rosebrook?" Ash smiled.

"Until I came to Rosebrook."

"I'm sorry you had to go through that, Archie."

"It's nothing to what you've been through, Ash."

"I'm just glad you're here now."

Ash's heart started to beat as fast as it had in the kitchen when they nearly kissed. If it hadn't been for that stupid pizza, Archie would have kissed her. She tried to pluck up the courage to initiate a kiss herself, but what if Archie rejected her? The fear stopped her in her tracks.

Instead she said, "Have you read any more of the book?"

Archie surprised her and said, "Yes, I have."

"Oh, really? Well, what did you think of my so-called trashy romance book?"

"It was a nice story. I liked it." Archie was full of surprises today.

"You're kidding me."

"No, seriously. It was a nice change of pace, and the dastardly duke turned out not to be so much of a prick as I thought."

"See, I told you, didn't I?" Ash stabbed a finger at Archie.

"You did, and you were right," Archie said.

Ash clutched her heart dramatically. "Wait, I was right? Could you say that in front of everyone at the office?"

"Maybe. Have you watched any more of *The Gatekeeper*?"

"No, I got sidetracked," Ash said, "but I'll watch one tonight just because you finished my book."

"Deal," Archie said. "I better let you get inside."

"Yeah, I suppose I should."

Archie leaned in and kissed her cheek. There was a moment

when Archie pulled away from her a few inches, and she thought Archie might kiss her on the lips, but the outside light went on and she heard her dad's voice.

"Ashling? Is that you?"

She stood up and said, "Yes, it's me." She turned to Archie. "I better say goodnight then."

Archie got up and walked her over to her dad. "Goodnight."

When she walked away, Ash hated it. She longed to be with her. "I'll text you later after I watch the episode."

Archie turned as she walked and smiled at her. "I can't wait."

With that smile, Ash's heart was finally gone.

Archie slipped into bed and lifted her iPad. She was going to read another one of Ash's books. She was racing through them. It felt like she was experiencing each one of the aspects of falling in love, in a safe way.

She'd had a good first day living in the village. It was great to find out that Griff wasn't after Ash. Archie just prayed she was capable of staying here and of being in a relationship, and that Ash still wanted her.

Archie pulled the covers up and over and began to look through social media apps. She followed lots of environmental groups and activists. An article about the new Japanese eco city about to begin the land clearing and building process had gone viral.

Archie found it amazing and imagined how exciting it would be to work on a project like that from scratch. You could go even further than they had in Rosebrook, without any established locals to be accounted for.

She continued to read the article until she got a text beep from her phone. When she saw it was Ash, her heart began to get faster.

Are you all settled in now?

She replied, *Yes, all tucked up in bed. I'm about to start another one of your trashy novels.*

Great, but I thought we agreed my romance novels were really good.

Archie smiled. *Maybe. So what are you doing?*

I'm in bed watching your bookkeeper thing.

Archie imagined what the really serious fanbase of the show would make of Ash calling it bookkeeper and laughed.

What episode are you on?

I'm just starting the one where they make love for the first time since they were separated.

Archie remembered that episode clearly. It was so hot, so fevered. She grabbed the remote control and switched on Netflix.

She quickly typed, *I'm going to watch along with you.*

Great!

It was exciting, watching at the same time. The characters were having an intense conversation, laden with sexual tension.

The older butch character is so sexy, Ash texted.

You think?

Yes, I have a thing for older women.

Was Ash trying to test the water and find out if she really was interested?

Really? Why? Archie asked.

As Archie was waiting for a reply, she watched as the butch character couldn't take any more of their intense conversation and pulled the femme character into a deep kiss, then walked her back against the wall. Archie loved this scene. It was so hot and passionate, and it was even more so knowing that Ash was lying in bed, watching the same scene.

Ash's reply finally came through. *I love older women because they are usually so confident in their sexuality and know what they're doing. Can you keep a secret?*

"Jesus," Archie said out loud.

A heavy beat started inside that matched her heart. This text was turning into something...different.

Yes, of course. You're safe with me.

Meanwhile, on TV, the characters were grasping at each other's clothes, desperately needing to touch each other, and it was making Archie more wound up by the second.

Ash replied, *That's my fantasy. An older butch woman making love to me.*

Archie dropped the phone on the bed and put a pillow over her face. "I can't take this. This is torture."

Ash must have thought there was something wrong when she didn't reply, because her next text was, *Archie? Have I said too much?*

She quickly typed out, *No, never.*

It was probably a bad idea to get into this any deeper, but she couldn't help herself.

You'd like experienced hands to touch you?

Yes, just like this scene we're watching. It's so like my fantasy.

"Fuck." Archie closed her eyes and pictured Ash touching herself. She wanted her so much.

Then Ash texted, *I'm tired. I better go and get some sleep.*

Get some sleep? Archie was on fire. How could she sleep, aching for Ash? The two characters on TV were happily making love, and Archie didn't want to listen to them any more, when she was left frustrated.

CHAPTER TWELVE

The next morning Archie felt awkward in the office, as clearly Ash did too. Ash was trying to avoid talking to her. As well as feeling awkward, Archie was frustrated and tired. She'd hardly slept a wink last night after their late-night texting.

By the afternoon, it felt like a cloud of sexual tension filled the office, and Rupert, Jenna, and Claire had no idea. It had been building all day. Every time Archie looked up, Ash was gazing back at her.

Archie had never wanted anyone the way she wanted Ash. Every nerve ending was agitated inside her. She tapped her fingers against the desk repeatedly. Wanting and being near to Ash was all she could think about.

An instant message popped up on her computer. It was from Ash.

Could you not tap your fingers so loudly please? You're very annoying.

She looked up and Ash was giving her a look that matched her message. A ball of anger and frustration rolled inside her.

She marched over to Ash's desk. "Can I see you in the conference room, now."

She didn't want the rest of the office to see her vent her anger. Archie walked into the room, and luckily all the blinds on the glass windows were closed, so they wouldn't see their probably heated conversation.

Ash followed her in and closed the door. "What's your problem?"

Archie spun round and pointed a finger at herself. "What's my problem? You've been avoiding me all morning, then you send me a message that I'm annoying you, and you scowl at me."

Ash stepped up closer to her and said with anger, "You're one to talk. Every time I look over at you, you put your head down. Is this because of last night? You think I'm weird..."

Ash continued on rambling, but Archie's frustrations were just becoming unbearable. She wanted Ash and wanted to shut her up, so she pulled her close and kissed her hard. Ash made a high-pitched noise of discontent, but then a millisecond later threw her arms around Archie's neck and pulled her closer and moaned.

Archie became more frantic by the second. Ash's lips were so soft that she just melted into them. Just like the scene last night, Archie walked Ash back against the wall and then ran her hand down her side and her hip.

Archie slipped her tongue into Ash's wet mouth, and Ash pulled Archie's hips as close to her as she could. Pulling away from the kiss, Archie moved her lips to Ash's neck.

Ash ran her fingers up the shaved part of her hair and dug her fingernails in enough to make Archie groan and graze her neck with her teeth.

"Archie?" This was what she dreamed of, fantasized of, and here she was, feeling every moment.

Archie looked deeply into Ash's eyes, ran her hand under her skirt, and grasped her thigh.

"Is this what you wanted in your fantasy?" Archie asked.

Ash nodded, and Archie rested her forehead against hers and said, "You turned me on so much last night that I couldn't sleep. You are driving me crazy. What were you thinking last night?"

"I was thinking about you touching me, leading me, and whispering in my ear what you were going to do."

Archie kneaded Ash's thigh and then lifted it so she could press her groin closer, between Ash's legs, and whispered in her ear, "Are you wet?"

Ash could have melted down the wall. "Yes, I was last night too."

Archie moved her hand and squeezed her buttock. "You have no idea how much I want you, Ash, how much I've been holding back from you."

"Kiss me," Ash said.

Archie kissed her slow at first, taking her time to run her tongue inside Ash's mouth, teasing her, but then their passion picked up the pace. Their kisses became frantic. Archie picked Ash up and carried her over to the conference table and set her on the edge.

"Our friends are out there," Ash said. "What if someone comes in?"

"They'll knock."

Ash thought about it, and it actually made her feel hotter, the threat of someone catching them. She grabbed for Archie's belt and struggled to open it. She really had no idea what she was doing. Her relationship with her first girlfriend was really just fumbles and discovering their own bodies, but Ash knew she wanted to touch Archie and pull her close.

Archie suddenly put her hand over Ash's on her belt, stopping her. "No, not like this."

Ash didn't understand. "What?"

Archie closed her eyes for a second and looked as if she was getting her breath and a bit of control back.

Then she cupped Ash's face with her hands. "Your romance story shouldn't start with sex and losing control. Did the dastardly duke make love to his sweetheart the first time they kissed?"

Ash let out a breath of tension. "No, he didn't."

"I took everything in about your favourite story and how you've always dreamed your romance would be, and starting like this isn't what you want it to be."

"But you'd like to start...whatever this is?" Ash asked nervously.

Archie brushed her fingers tenderly across Ash's cheek. "You are why I wanted to stay in Fox's house while they were away. I'd like to romance you, woo you, the way you deserve and see where this goes. I might be experienced with women, but not with someone like you, someone I care about."

"You care about me?" Ash said.

Archie kissed her nose. "Of course I do, but we need to take things slow. I don't ever want to hurt you, and with the extensive baggage I carry around, I'm worried I would."

Ash placed her head on Archie's chest and said, "You wouldn't, but slow sounds right."

The one thing Ash didn't want was for Archie to panic and run. She knew that village life might make her feel suffocated. Add to that an intense relationship, and it could make her panic.

She would take everything as slow as Archie wanted, because she knew she was falling in love and would be devastated if she lost Archie.

There was a knock at the conference room door, and Ash jumped down off the table and tried to straighten her clothes. Archie did the same.

"Come in," Archie said.

Rupert popped in the door and said, "I hope I'm not interrupting?"

"No, not at all," Archie replied.

But Ash could feel the hot blush on her face and see the small grin Rupert gave her, that showed he knew what they had been doing.

"Andrew Jones from Fox Toys' head office on the phone for you, Archie."

Since Archie was working with the Rosebrook Trust on secondment, her deputy Andrew Jones was doing her role back at the head office.

"Okay, tell him I'll phone him back shortly," Archie said, trying to sound normal and not as if they were nearly making love on the conference room table.

"Okay," Rupert said.

Once he left, Ash let out a breath. "Well, that was awkward."

"Do you think he suspected anything?"

"Since you have my lipstick smudged on your lips, I'd guess so, but Rupert wouldn't mind if we were overcome with attraction to each other," Ash said.

Archie rubbed her lips and looked at the lipstick now on her fingers. "Hmm, I suppose we are rumpled."

Ash was going to be brave in case things got tense between them again after this.

"Would you like to come to dinner with me and Dad tonight?"

"Your dad wouldn't mind, would he?" Archie asked.

"No, he likes you—I told you. Then we could watch a few bookkeeper episodes."

"Sounds perfect."

Ash had been highly suspicious when Archie had said she wanted to go and meet her dad down at the pier, but she wanted to speak to James on his own. So while Ash started to prepare dinner, she wandered down the beach steps.

Archie saw James tying off his boat and started to feel nervous. This was a week of firsts—moving down here to stay, albeit temporarily, beginning to show Ash how she felt, and now going to talk to her dad about their relationship.

It reminded her of the scene in *The Dastardly Duke* where the duke goes to the governess's father to ask for her hand in marriage. Although if she thought about that for too long, her bravery might waver.

No, she wanted to ask Ash out for a romantic picnic on Saturday, and she wanted to show some imagination and not just have it on the beach. But Ash knew every inch of Rosebrook, so she needed to find somewhere a little different and thought James could help.

To do that, she'd need to admit she was interested in Ash, and Archie didn't know what his reaction would be. Ash had only just come out to her dad, and now she, an older, more worldly woman, was coming and swooping in—well, that's how Archie feared it might look.

Archie walked up the steps from the beach to the pier and shouted, "James, busy day?"

James looked up and smiled. "Archie, how are you?"

"I'm fine, thanks."

When Archie reached the boat, she shook James's hand. "How was your day?"

"Good. I had a fishing party out first thing, but I was just out checking my lobster pots."

"Great, I hope you don't mind, but Ash invited me to dinner." Archie thought that would be a good opening.

"Ah, I see. That's fine by me."

The big *ah* at the beginning of his reply was worrying her. "Are you sure?"

Then he smiled. "Yes, of course."

Archie hadn't felt so nervous in a long time. This was harder than she thought.

"I wanted to talk to you while Ash wasn't here. I was going to ask her to have a picnic with me on Saturday. We've become closer and—"

"Well, I did ask you to keep an eye on her. Maybe you've taken that too literally?"

Archie's stomach dropped. "You don't think I took advantage, do you? I care about Ash, and I know I'm older than her, that's what's held me back from showing her I cared, but—"

James held up his hands. "Hold on, hold on. Relax, Archie, I was just kidding. I know you're a good person who cares about the world, about the animals we farm and fish. And as for being older, I was my wife's toy boy. Did Ashling tell you that?"

James had a smile and a glint in his eye when he said *toy boy*, and Archie was relieved.

"Yes, she did. But I thought you might look on me differently. I mean, I've lived in the world, and Ash's had quite a sheltered life here."

"She's wiser than most her age, but I will be keeping my eye on you. Remember, I can get rid of bodies at the bottom on the sea, and no one would ever find out."

Archie's eyes went wide because James was looking deadly serious, but he burst into laughter and smacked her on the shoulder.

"Just joking. You should see the look on your face," James said.

"I bet." Archie laughed nervously.

James finished tying off the boat rope and said, "So, a picnic?"

"Uh, yes, I don't just want to go to the beach. Is there anywhere special or unusual I could take her?"

James stood back in the boat and put his hands on his hips. "Well, there is somewhere, but—"

"Where?"

"The secret cove."

"Secret cove? Where's that?" Archie asked.

James pointed to the cliffs at the far side of the beach. "It's just around the cliffs there. It's called the secret cove because you can only reach it by boat. All the courting couples in the old days used to go there. I took my wife there often. Ash hasn't been, so it would be something new for her, something special."

"It sounds perfect. You said there was a *but*?"

"But I'll only let you borrow a boat to go there if you can show me you can handle it safely and take all the safety equipment I'll give you. The beach disappears when the tide comes in, so you can get into all sorts of trouble."

"I've used rowing boats before, but not in the sea," Archie said.

"I'll give you one of mine with a motor on it. Come by on Friday afternoon, and I'll take you out. Make sure you can control it well."

"I will. Thanks very much for this, James."

Archie nodded. "I just want to see my little girl living a life at last. She deserves some fun. We better get up to the cottage. I'll just be a second."

James walked back into the cab of his boat. Archie had an excited buzz inside her. She'd been worried she wouldn't be able to find somewhere different to take Ash. She was by no means an expert in romance, despite racing through Ash's romance novels, but a picnic in a secluded cove was really romantic—she was sure of it.

James came back from the cab of his boat with two large hessian sacks.

"Can I take one of those for you?" He handed her a bag, full of plastic bottles, plastic bags, and all sorts of other rubbish. "Where did you get all this rubbish?"

"Out there." James pointed out to the sea. "I take these sacks out with me and pick up anything I see out there. I know in the grand scheme of things it isn't much help, but I can't just pass it and know it might hurt or damage the wildlife. Follow me."

Archie followed him to the side of the boat shop. There she saw baskets filled with bottles and other rubbish.

"When the bags are full, I bring them back here, sort them into plastic, metal, and cans in the baskets. When they're full, I recycle them. I used to have to drive into the next town, but now Fox has built a recycling centre here, so it's perfect."

"That's a great thing to do, James, and don't think you're not making a difference. Every piece of this plastic is one that could hurt a sea creature. Let me tell you about some of the ideas Fox and I are talking about for the coast around Rosebrook."

❖

Ash couldn't help but smile. She poured out a glass of water from the jug on the dining table and took a sip. The first meal she, her dad, and Archie had together couldn't be going better. Ever since they returned to the cottage for dinner, Archie and her dad had been locked in deep discussion about the ocean, fish stocks, and pollution.

"You're kidding? Like a vacuum?" James said.

Archie's ideas were bringing out the passion her dad had for the sea, so much so he hadn't even noticed Archie and her vegan version of the chicken dish she had made. She had been sure the lifelong meat and seafood eater would have a few things to say.

"Yes," Archie said, "all you see on the surface is a long series of buoys, and underneath the machine, powered by solar energy, sucks up any plastic or rubbish in its path."

"You say Fox is interested in bringing something like that here?" James asked.

"Those machines are run by a huge corporation, for large ocean-going projects. We'd like to have something around the Rosebrook coastline that we could maintain. On a smaller scale we've found a company that sells sea bins to collect the rubbish."

Ash nearly spat out her water. "Sea bins? Seriously? Is that for the seagulls to pop their rubbish in as they fly over?"

Archie rummaged in her pocket and brought out her phone. "I'll show you."

Archie searched YouTube and started to play a video. She held it up so both Ash and her dad could see.

"So, you see the lip of the bin in the water? It uses the sea's currents to draw the water in with the debris we're trying to get rid of, while filtering the water out the bottom."

"Good God in heaven," James said. "What will they think of next?"

Ash smiled at Archie. "So is Fox going to buy some of these?"

"We hope to. Fox and I were going to move forward with it when she got back from her honeymoon, but her plans will be delayed now."

"Poor little girl," James said. "Losing her dad so young."

Ash nodded. "But she'll have no better guardians than Lady Clem and Fox."

"Very true," Archie added.

After dinner James retreated to his bedroom to read so that Ash and Archie could watch their TV show in the living room.

Ash made them each a cup of tea and brought them over. "Here you go."

Archie took the cup carefully and placed it on the coffee table in front of the couch.

"Are you sure dinner was okay? I'm not used to vegan cooking."

"It was perfect, and I really enjoyed talking with your dad. He's a great man."

Ash held the hot teacup between her hands. She couldn't believe Archie had actually had dinner with them and didn't run at the domesticity of it all.

"I told you. He likes you. It was nice having you here. There hasn't been lively conversation around our dining table in a long time," Ash said.

"I like your dad as well."

Archie looked around the room and indicated the photos on the wall. "Is that your mum, Ash?"

"Yeah, Dad likes to keep lots of pictures of her around. It makes him sad to see them but, at the same time, comforted to see her everywhere. Does that make sense?"

Archie nodded. "You look a lot like her."

"I suppose I do." Ash hesitated then asked, "Will you tell me more about your mum?"

Archie's head dropped and she went silent.

"I'm sorry. I shouldn't have asked," Ash said.

"No." Archie looked up at her. "I need to open some of this baggage if I ever want to be free of it. She was so hurt that my dad didn't love her the way he should. Looking back, I can see it really cut her deeply. So she lashed out at him, and Dad became more distant. Even when my dad got custody of me, I still had to go to stay with her in the holidays."

"What was that like?" Ash asked.

"I dreaded it. Living with my dad, I was able to express myself the way I wanted, just like he did. For me, that meant wearing traditionally male clothes, and my mum just couldn't deal with that, and even less so her new husband."

"The minister?"

"Oh yes. One who found my masculine side incompatible with their family values. They tried to change me when I stayed with them, but when I resisted, they sent me home to Dad, and eventually they stopped welcoming me to their home. She has a new family now. They adopted two children. I have two stepbrothers I haven't met."

"I'm sorry, Arch."

Archie smiled. "My dad calls me that."

"I'm sorry your relationship with your mum is difficult," Ash said.

"Don't worry about me. I have my dad and you—that's all I need."

Ash wasn't convinced. There was pain deep inside Archie that she hadn't processed yet, she was sure.

"Let's get on with this bookkeeper thing," Ash said.

"I know you're just trying to annoy me, calling it that."

"Does it work?" Ash asked.

"Yes."

Ash laughed. "Then mission accomplished." She used the remote and got Netflix going.

"What episode are you on?" Archie asked.

"Episode nine."

Archie sighed dramatically. "Oh no."

"What? What is it?"

"Remember you made me promise I'd let you know if it was going to be a difficult episode?" Archie said.

"Uh-huh."

"This is a difficult episode."

Archie's fears were realized, and as the credits rolled, Ash was cuddled under her arm, head on her chest, and snuffling and crying.

"Shh…it's okay. It's finished now. I don't think we should binge-watch tonight. You're too upset."

"I…couldn't. Can't take any more. She's alive, but she can't remember that she loves her?"

"Sit up and take some breaths, okay?" Archie said.

Ash sat up and wiped her eyes. "I blame you for getting me into this show. I'm going to be a nervous wreck before it ends."

"You'll be fine, and anyway, you can always cry on my shoulder."

Ash took a few deep breaths, and she started to calm. "I must look a mess, with puffy eyes and everything."

Archie cupped her cheek and said, "You've never looked lovelier."

"Oh, shut up." Ash laughed.

"I wanted to ask you if…"

"What?"

"Would you like to come on a picnic with me on Saturday?" Archie asked.

"A picnic? Where? On the beach?"

Archie smiled. "No, our destination is a surprise."

"But you don't know anywhere around here."

Archie was so glad she'd asked James's advice on where to go. This was going to be special.

"I know more than you think." Archie looked at her watch. "I better get back to Rosebrook. We've got a busy day tomorrow. Patrick's arriving, and we have our village meeting in the evening."

Ash yawned. "I suppose so."

"At the meeting tomorrow, I'd like you to lead it."

"Wait, what? You fought tooth and nail to lead the meetings at The Meeting Place."

"I reflected on it, and you were right. Leadership should be shared, and you are very good with the villagers," Archie said.

"Well, if you think so, that would be good."

They got up and walked to the door. Ash opened the door and they stepped outside.

Archie felt an awkwardness descend between them. She felt like a teenager worrying about whether she should kiss her girlfriend goodbye or not.

"Thanks for dinner."

Ash smiled warmly. "I loved cooking for you. You'll need to let me cook in Clem's lovely big kitchen one time."

"I'd like that." *Have some courage*, Archie told herself. She stepped forward and cradled Ash's face in her hands. "Goodnight, Ash."

Archie kissed her softly, gently, until she heard Ash moan. She pulled back and brushed her nose against Ash's.

"Sweet dreams," Ash said.

"They are never sweet when I dream about you."

CHAPTER THIRTEEN

The next morning, Archie went to pick up Patrick Doyle at the bus station in the next town over, while Ash and Kay got his cottage set for him.

Archie parked her car and walked to the bus arrivals area. Ash had made her a card with Patrick's name on, so he would know who she was. Unfortunately, she had also drawn a smiley face on the card, which would embarrass the life out of her, but she had little choice.

She stood at the number seven bus stop and waited for the bus to appear. She looked down at the sign and Ash's little smiley face and shook her head.

Ash was such a girl. A girl who made her heart flutter in a way Archie never knew possible.

She used to mock friends who felt like this—in fact, she had warned Fox as strongly as possible about falling too quickly for Lady Clementine. If Fox had listened to her, she would be single and lonely, but now she was married and happy. Even her dad had been able to love after all he had been through.

What did she know? Before Rosebrook came into her life, she was happy living her metropolitan life and having lots of short-term relationships. Now she was planning a secret romantic picnic for a woman thirteen years her junior and reading romance novels.

She should feel worried or suffocated, but truly all she thought about was when was the next time she could see Ashling.

The sound of a bus engine made Archie look up. This must be Patrick's bus.

She held up her slightly embarrassing sign, while the bus occupants got off and waited for their luggage. After a few minutes, Archie saw a young man walking towards her, looking unsure. He was a little shorter than her, with short dark hair. He had very worn jeans and shoes, plus a vintage rock band T-shirt on. He was pulling a case and had a rucksack on his back.

"Patrick?" Archie said.

He smiled and said nervously, "Yeah, that's me."

Archie held her hand out. "Pleased to meet you, Patrick. I'm Archie. We spoke on the phone. I'm looking after things while Fox is on honeymoon."

"Oh yeah, hi. Thanks for coming to meet me," Patrick said.

Archie lifted the sign and said jokingly, "Don't judge my sign. That was my—" What could she say? Ash wasn't a girlfriend, was she? They hadn't even gone on a date yet, yet Archie felt some invisible bond to Ashling already. She decided to play it safe. "My friend at the trust made it. Let me take a bag for you." Archie took the wheeled suitcase.

"Thanks," Patrick said.

"Let's get these back to the car. I'm parked not too far away."

As they walked to the car, Archie could feel the nerves coming from Patrick. She tried to make small talk. "How was the journey?"

"It was okay. Went by pretty quick."

"Good, it won't take us long to get back to Rosebrook."

Archie pressed the button for the car to unlock and opened the boot. "Okay, suitcase first, I think."

She packed the case and rucksack in the boot, and then they both got into the front seat. Archie turned on the engine and checked to see if Patrick had put on his seat belt.

"Okay, let's get you going to your new life," Archie said.

Patrick gave her a strained smile. He looked so nervous and tense. Archie pulled out of the car park, and they were on their way.

"It must be very overwhelming, all of this."

"Yeah, uh…it's a big step, but I know it's the right one."

"We hope you think so. Rosebrook is a special place."

"It'll be a dream compared to living on the streets or at home," Patrick said.

"It must have been so hard for you. I can't imagine."

Patrick sighed. "Homeless shelters were difficult, especially when I started to transition."

"I'm hopeful now you'll see a brighter future. Rosebrook is set up to be inclusive to everyone, right down to the most everyday details. For example, all our public toilets are unisex, so there's no uncomfortable choices to be made when you don't conform to gender norms."

"Wow, yeah. People don't understand how small, everyday things like that make our lives harder."

"Don't get me wrong—some of our older residents found it a bit strange going into the same bathroom at the pub, but they got used to it. We try to think of everything, but if there's an issue we haven't thought of, just let us know."

Patrick went silent.

"Are you okay?" Archie asked.

"Yeah, it's just a bit overwhelming, like you said. Have you told anyone about me?"

"Just your new boss, as you allowed us to do. Apart from that, your story is yours to tell, no one else's."

"Cheers. Was the brewery boss okay about it?"

"Griff is delighted to have you working for her. You'll get on like a house on fire."

"I thought I'd no chance of getting a place in Rosebrook. I'd heard there was a long waiting list," Patrick said.

"There is. We want to build the village up slowly, so we aren't giving out many places just now. You were the perfect candidate. We've put you in one of the Woodlanders cottages. My colleague Ashling is back at the cottage now, making sure it's all ready for you."

Archie felt so bad calling Ash her colleague, but for just now it was the best she could do without getting too personal.

❖

The sound of the vacuum cleaner roared loudly in the living room, while Ash put away the shopping Jay had just delivered from the shop. Kay was in charge of vacuuming every inch of the cottage. Not that it was majorly untidy or dirty, but after the workmen had been in and out, the newly decorated cottage was dusty.

Ash lifted a tin of soup and placed it in the cupboard. She hoped Patrick wouldn't mind the food that she had chosen. She'd made sure that Patrick wasn't vegan or vegetarian and then tried to pick a wide range of different foods and household items when she phoned her order through to Jay and Erica at the shop.

The blaring of the vacuum stopped, and then a short time later Kay came into the kitchen.

"I think that's everything clean and tidy, Ash. Bathroom cleaned, floors vacuumed, and I dusted everywhere."

"Thanks for volunteering to help, Kay. It was great to have your help," Ash said.

Kay picked up some items from the bags and started to help putting them away.

"It's my pleasure. It's wonderful to have the village filling up at last. You said Patrick was homeless?"

"Yeah, his dad kicked him out," Ash said.

"How any parent could do that is beyond me. There's nothing my two boys could do that would make me want to throw them out. Do you know why they did?"

"I do, but I think it should be up to our residents to share their stories with others, when and if they feel comfortable."

"Quite right." Kay lifted dishwasher tablets out of the bag and took them over to the sink area. "So, care to share your story?" Kay grinned.

"What do you mean?"

"I hear Archie is staying at Rosebrook and becoming close to a certain PA of the duchess."

Ash felt her cheeks heat up. "Really? Who's been talking? Rupert?"

"Maybe." Kay nudged Ash. "So tell me—is romance brewing? Last I heard, you were at each other's throats."

"It's complicated," Ash said.

"Isn't everything? Tell your Aunty Kay."

Ash let out a breath and smiled. "I'm falling for her."

Kay clapped her hands together. "Oh, I knew it. I said to Clem, when you were dancing at their wedding, that the pair of you were either going to have a fist fight or rip each other's clothes off."

Ash laughed at the image in her head. "You saw that, then?"

Kay nodded. "Oh yes. I love a good romance."

"It's not completely straightforward. She's pushed me away for a while because she thought she was too old for me."

Kay folded her arms. "It's hardly a seventy-year-old with a twenty-year-old."

"I know. I've told her it's not an issue, and I think she's come around. She's asked me on a picnic on Saturday."

"Picnic? Nice, very romantic. What does your dad say?"

"Dad really likes her, and he seems happy for me. He was supportive when I told him I was gay."

"I told you he would be," Kay said.

"Yeah, I didn't give him enough credit."

"I know."

Ash looked at her watch. "Better get these things away. Patrick will be here soon."

❖

Patrick had been quiet on the journey to Rosebrook. But Archie could feel the nervousness pouring off him, as well as see it as he tapped his fingers incessantly on his leg.

She hadn't exactly been in Patrick's shoes, but she knew what it was like to have a parent reject you for what you were, and she was determined their new resident would have a safe, happy home here in Rosebrook.

As they got to the outskirts of the village, Archie pointed out the window. "That's the old factory building. We're going to be making toys and sensory items for children and adults with special needs, at affordable prices."

"That's a great thing to do. When is it starting up?"

"Once we get the brewery on its feet, we'll get started. There's a lot of work going on behind the scenes, coming up with environmentally friendly suppliers. That's part of my job."

They passed the Welcome to Rosebrook sign, and Archie started to point out all the places of interest.

"That's the shop, run by a lovely couple, Jay and Erica. The pub is run by Jonah, whose husband works with us at the Rosebrook Trust."

"This really is a different place," Patrick said.

Eventually they pulled up outside Patrick's cottage. Patrick looked out the window and said, "Is my room upstairs or down?"

Archie didn't quite know what he meant. "Your room?"

"Yeah, you know, my room. Is there a shared kitchen and bathroom?"

It finally dawned on Archie. Patrick thought he was only getting one room as his living quarters.

"Patrick, the whole cottage is yours. This is your new home."

He looked shocked, and then he gulped hard. "I—I don't believe it."

"Believe it. Come on. Let's get inside." Archie got out and shut the car door. "Leave your bags for now—we can get them later."

She opened the gate and invited Patrick to go into the garden. As they walked in, Alanna came around the side of her cottage with some gardening things on her lap.

"Good timing," Archie said. "Good morning, Alanna, this is your new neighbour. Patrick, this is Alanna."

Alanna beamed a warm smile and held out her hand, "Lovely to meet you, Patrick." Patrick appeared to be struck speechless, and Alanna said jokingly, "I would get up, but it's kind of difficult."

Archie gave him a small shove, which seemed to do the trick.

"Oh—sorry. Hi, good to meet you. I'm Patrick."

Alanna chuckled. "Yes, Archie said."

The red blush on Patrick's cheeks was unmistakable to Archie. A beautiful woman like Alanna clearly made Patrick feel like a teenager again.

"It'll be great to have neighbours both sides of me now. You're very welcome, Patrick."

"Cheers, uh, if you need anything, just yell or whatever," Patrick stammered.

"I will, thanks. I hope you're happy in your new home."

Archie guided Patrick to the door and opened it. "Welcome to your new home."

Handing over the refurbished cottages was always good. But to Ash, giving Patrick his cottage was the most rewarding so far. Knowing what he had been through made this moment all the more sweet and emotional.

Watching Patrick being shown around his new home, with wonder and amazement, brought tears to her eyes, but she managed not to let the others see her.

Archie led Patrick downstairs after showing him the rooms upstairs and rejoined Ash in the living room. Kay had left earlier, after welcoming Patrick, so the cottage wasn't crowded.

"And that's everything." Archie held out the bunch of keys to the cottage. "These are yours."

Patrick took them and then placed his hands over his eyes, covering tears that he was struggling to keep under control.

"I'm sorry," Patrick said.

Ash lost all hope of stopping her tears. She quickly wiped them away and tried to calm herself.

"You don't need to be sorry, Patrick. It's a lot to take in," Archie said.

"Honestly, I can't thank you and Fox enough," Patrick said. "This is more than I ever dreamed of."

Archie grasped him by the shoulder. "You may not have been

seen as who you truly are by your family and the world so far, Patrick, but you will be seen here in Rosebrook. I promise you that."

At that moment, Ash truly lost her heart and soul to Archie. Ash was aware of how Archie had been rejected by her mother for who she was, and she knew that those words had come straight from Archie's heart.

I love you, Archie.

Ash didn't know when she would have the courage to say those words out loud, but just saying them to herself and admitting her true feelings was freeing in itself. More than anything she wanted to connect with Archie, wanted to touch her and feel her lips on hers.

They both soon left Patrick to settle in himself. Once they got out of the garden, Archie beeped the car to open, but Ash said, "Can I show you something before we go back?"

"If you like. Where is it?"

Ash took Archie's hand and led her across the road to the trees.

"Where are we going?" Archie asked. "You haven't got another secret building tucked in there, do you?"

"Just follow me." Ash was single-minded and wanted Archie away from others' eyes.

They walked through the thick evergreen trees, until they were far enough away from the road and prying eyes. She spotted a big tree with a thick trunk and gently pushed Archie back against it.

"What is it?" Archie asked, looking perplexed.

Ash reached out to caress Archie's cheek. "What you said to Patrick in there. It was beautiful."

"I meant every word."

"I know you did, and I just wanted to show you how much I love your kindness"—Ash kissed Archie's lips extremely softly, moved only a few inches back—"and how much I love your kind heart."

Archie cupped Ash's cheek and then threaded her fingers though her hair.

"I just needed to touch you and kiss you," Ash said.

Ash kissed her more fully this time, and Archie moaned before reversing their positions and pinning her against the tree trunk.

Their kiss became passionate and hot. Ash pulled Archie's shirt out a little so she could touch and scratch her nails along her skin. Archie shivered and grasped her breast and squeezed.

Ash wanted to rip off her clothes so Archie could touch her breasts, skin to skin. Every time Archie squeezed, a jolt of electricity shot to her sex. She was wet, and all Ash wanted was Archie to touch her more intimately.

She grasped Archie's hand and pushed it to the hem of her dress. Archie ran her hand up and down her thigh.

"Do you know how much I want you, Ash?" Archie gently dug her fingernails into the flesh of Ash's thigh. "I dream of kissing and licking your thighs."

Ash wanted nothing more. She took Archie's hand and pushed towards her sex. Archie broke away from the kiss and said, "No, we're going to do things right."

"Archie," Ash moaned in frustration.

"No, the dastardly duke doesn't have his way with the governess in the forest."

Ash didn't care at this point, she was so frustrated. "He doesn't have his way till after they are married. If I have to wait that long, I might explode."

Realizing what she said just fully hit her, and she was frightened Archie would run.

"I'm sorry, I didn't mean that would be us, just that they didn't…that class of lady didn't till after marriage in those days."

Archie smiled. "It's okay, I knew what you meant. We better get back to the office."

And with that the moment was gone. She had obviously terrified Archie.

What an idiot.

❖

Archie was struggling to keep her eyes and her hands off Ash after earlier today. They seemed to have crossed some boundary that gave her no control over her wants or needs. Ash, on the other hand, had appeared nervous since.

Ash probably thought she'd scared her off with the marriage comment, and in times gone by, a woman mentioning marriage, even in jest, made Archie want to get away, but Ash wasn't any old woman. She was Ash.

They were at The Meeting Place for this week's community meeting. Archie had managed to leave Ash long enough to go and open up the doors, while Ash got the leaflets with the agenda out on the stage.

Archie hurried back. She probably had around five minutes before the villagers started to arrive, and she was determined to have some more time with Ash to show her she wasn't scared off.

She bounded up the steps of the stage and walked up behind Ash, as she bent over the table putting the leaflets in piles.

She grasped around her waist, making Ash jump.

"Arch, stop." Ash giggled when Archie nibbled at her neck.

"I can't, my hands are burning to touch you."

"Then how are you going to hold out and wait like the duke?"

Archie gave a dramatic sigh and slumped her head onto Ash's shoulder. "I don't know, because you are intoxicating."

Ash turned around in Archie's embrace and wrapped her arms around her neck. "No one has ever called me intoxicating before."

"Well, you are. You smell beautiful, you feel beautiful, and I want to know—" Archie hesitated and grinned. "No, I won't say that."

"You won't say what? Oh, tell me, please?"

Archie was having fun teasing her. She moved her lips to Ash's ear and whispered, "I want to know what you taste like."

Ash's knees went weak, but luckily Archie was holding her tightly. "Yes, yes. I can't wait, Arch."

She kissed her and teasingly bit Archie's bottom lip. Then they heard someone clear their throat behind them. Ash spun around to see Kay with a broad smile on her face.

"I'd put her down, Archie. Everyone's about to come in."

Ash felt so embarrassed. Before she could say anything, the sound of chatter and laughter wafted in the door. She smoothed her clothes down quickly.

Archie, on the other hand, appeared to find it funny. She had the biggest smile on her face and said, "I'll go and hand out the leaflets."

"You're a big tease, Archie," Ash whispered.

Archie whistled as she walked down the steps from the stage, and Ash couldn't help but smile. She'd never seen Archie as relaxed and happy since she arrived in the village. Ash supposed that made the frustration she felt worth it.

As the villagers came in she was so happy to see Patrick coming in with Alanna, and she was introducing Patrick to everyone.

Patrick had made a friend already. All was going well.

Chapter Fourteen

The rest of the week was filled with kisses but not much more, and despite the frustration, that was the way Archie wanted it. Because if she was learning anything from Ash's romance novels, then it was that taking the time to build a friendship made the best basis for a relationship.

She still got a slight shiver every time she even thought the word *relationship*, but it was soon replaced by the warm feelings that she had building up for Ash. Ash deserved so much more than she was usually prepared to give, and the fact that Archie was willing meant things were changing for Archie.

Today was a special day. It was her first official date with Ash and her chance to show how romantic she could be. Archie looked at herself in Fox's bedroom mirror. She had on long shorts and a crop-top style sports bra to wear for swimming. A T-shirt to cover up was lying on the bed.

These clothes weren't Archie's most comfortable choice, but this was for Ash, and giving her the romance she truly deserved.

"I'm as ready as I'll ever be."

Archie went downstairs to the kitchen. She had noticed a few nights ago that Fox had a wine cooler that she used sometimes on the beach with the duchess. She got two bottles of champagne from Fox's drinks fridge in the kitchen and put them in the cooler. Archie didn't know if champagne would be to Ash's taste, but it was a romantic gesture in any case.

Having picked up her rucksack with a blanket and a few towels, Archie set off for her next stop—The King's Arms.

She knocked at the door, knowing the pub would be shut at this time in the morning. Rupert's husband Jonah opened the doors.

"Archie, morning. I've got everything ready for you."

She'd asked Jonah to make up a picnic for her. Archie spotted a large cool box on the bar. "Thanks."

Jonah walked behind the bar. "There's just a couple of things I wanted to put in last thing."

As Jonah rummaged around in the drinks fridge, Archie thought of how this mirrored the chapter in *The Dastardly Duke* that her picnic inspiration came from.

The duke, to win his love's heart and prove that he wasn't the haughty man the governess thought he was, took her on a picnic to the river that passed through his land. He did so without servants, as was apparently the norm, and had his kitchen staff make him up a picnic basket.

Archie hoped Ash would appreciate this gesture, as in some senses Archie was Ash's dastardly duke, and she wanted to show Ash that she had been listening and changing just as the duke had.

Jonah placed a selection of small bottles of drinks into the large cool box. "Do you want some wine too?" Jonah asked.

Archie lifted up the drinks cooler and smiled. "I've got that part covered, thanks."

"Okay, well, that's everything," Jonah said. "You have all sorts of food and drinks to woo Ash. She's a beautiful girl—you're very lucky to be spending the day with her."

Jonah was right. She was lucky and intended to make the most of her luck. "I am. Thank you so much for this, Jonah."

"Not a problem."

Archie paid Jonah for the food and lifted the heavy picnic box. "Wish me luck."

She left the pub and started to walk up the slight incline to Ash's house. Halfway up she really started to feel the weight of the picnic box. She wasn't going to need an arm workout for the next few days. Jonah had offered to help carry it, but she was never going to turn up to Ash's door with a helper.

As she neared Ash's cottage, she saw Alanna and Patrick at the top of the beach stairs. When she got closer, Archie said, "Hi, Patrick—morning, Alanna."

"Hi, Archie," Alanna said brightly.

"Yeah, hi," Patrick said shyly.

Archie put down the heavy box. "Lovely warm day, isn't it?"

"Yes," Alanna replied. "I'm just showing Patrick around. The beach is the next and most beautiful stop."

"That's great. How are you settling in, Patrick?"

Patrick scratched the back of his short hair in a nervous gesture. "Good. Alanna's been really helpful, teaching me all about the village."

"It's the least I could do," Alanna said while beaming up at Patrick. "This big, strong guy helped me chop some of the bushes in the back garden and pitched in with the weeding."

Archie was sure she could see Patrick grow a few inches taller on the spot. This was probably the first time in his life that his masculinity had been properly recognized.

"That's what Rosebrook is all about—caring and helping. Did Griffin come by and introduce herself?" Archie asked Patrick.

"Yeah, she's great. I spent the day with her at the beer factory. She's so full of ideas. It's exciting to be a part of it."

Archie was falling in love with this village. Look at the effect it was having on people's lives already, and they hadn't even gotten all their plans in motion yet. It gave her such a strong sense of satisfaction knowing the difference the trust was making, and she couldn't wait to do more.

"I'm glad you're enjoying it. Any help or anything you need, just drop in at the trust office. I better get going. I promised Ash a picnic."

"Oh, she'll like that," Alanna said with a knowing smile.

Had Ash been talking about her to Alanna?

"Will she?"

"Oh yes. Have a nice time."

"I will, thanks."

Archie picked up her things again and walked to Ash's house. She wondered what Ash had said to Alanna. Was she complaining or excited by this new turn in their relationship?

She opened the gate and was about to walk up the cottage path when Ash opened her front door. Archie nearly dropped the picnic box when she saw Ash wearing an almost see-through blue sarong dress. She was absolutely gorgeous, and Archie was intoxicated by the glimpse of Ash's bikini underneath.

"Wow, you look wonderful, Ash."

Ash looked down at her dress and swept her hands over it. "I haven't really worn anything like this before. Is it really okay?"

Ash really had no idea how beautiful she was, and her innocence melted Archie's heart and reiterated how much Ash deserved her utmost respect, care, and attention. The thought of disappointing Ash or hurting her scared Archie, but breaking the habits of a lifetime, her determination was to go towards that fear and not run away.

Archie put down her bags and boxes and walked through the gate to Ash. She took Ash's hand and kissed it softly.

"You look wonderful."

She felt Ash shiver slightly, and the simple shiver gave her such a thrill. Romance truly had its rewards.

"Let's get going, shall we?"

Ash picked up her own beach bags and followed Archie out the gate. "Is that a picnic box I see? Did you make the sandwiches yourself?"

Archie laughed. "You know I didn't, but I'm excellent at delegating. Jonah organized the food for me, so don't worry. You won't get poisoned."

"Can I help you with anything?" Ash asked.

Archie picked up the box and her bags. "No, I am perfectly balanced." She then offered her arm. "May I escort you to our picnic?"

Ash giggled. "You're quite the gentleman."

"I hope so. Now let's get going."

"Where are we going, to the beach?" Ash asked.

Archie tutted dramatically. "Do you really think I have that little imagination?"

"Well, I know everywhere else, so…"

Archie steered them to the beach steps. "First stop, your dad's boat shop."

Ash looked confused. "What on earth for?"

"Just wait, okay? It's a surprise."

They walked down the stairs, and Archie picked up a rock outside the boat shop door. Underneath were the keys to the motorboat.

"Archie, tell me what we need keys for?"

"A boat. Follow me."

All of a sudden the penny dropped, and Ash squealed, "Are we going to the cove?"

"We might be," Archie replied with a smile.

"How did you know about it?" Ash asked.

"I was talking to your dad about us and asked if there was somewhere you didn't go to often in the village. He told me about this secret cove just around the bay."

"Oh, is that what you were talking about on the pier that night you came over for dinner?"

Archie nodded. "He said it was a special place for him and your mum."

"I've never been. I always wanted to, but Dad would never take me, too many bad memories, and I didn't want to go myself," Ash said sadly.

"Now you'll get to go and enjoy it with me, if that's okay with you."

Ash dropped her bags and threw her arms around Archie. "It's perfect. Thank you."

This gave Archie her first chance to run her hands over Ash in her sarong dress. She could feel the curves and contours of Ash's body and wanted more, but that would have to wait. Romance, Archie had learned, went at a much slower pace.

Ash pushed back from Archie and said, "Wait. Can you drive a motorboat?"

"I've handled a few boats on holiday over the years, and your dad took me out on the bay to test me. James wasn't about to put the safety of his little girl in the hands of a novice."

"Did you pass?" Ash asked.

"Just about. Let's get going."

❖

Ash couldn't have imagined a better plan for her and Archie's first date. Archie had gone to so much trouble and taken the time to research what would be the perfect date.

She sat back in the front seat of the boat, her sunglasses on and enjoying the heat of the sun and the smell of the briny sea water. Ash watched Archie carefully as she navigated at speed across the water.

Archie in shorts and T-shirt was a new thing, and Ash was enjoying seeing this new side of Archie. She only hoped that she would get a chance to see the tall, broad torso she was sure was under that T-shirt.

It occurred to Ash that their first date would be similar to the one in *The Dastardly Duke*. She wondered if Archie had taken inspiration from her favourite book.

In the book, the date was the first time the duke had organized something himself, and not relied on the servants. Ash supposed, in a way, Archie had done something similar, taking the time to research the local area and find a special place where Ash had never been.

Ash had always dreamed of this kind of romance, and life was starting to feel like a romance novel, only better, because real life was so much better, she was beginning to learn. She only hoped Archie's feelings for her were getting as deep as hers for Archie.

After a time, they went around the outcropping on the coastline that separated the main beach from the small cove behind it. Then Ash spotted it.

"There it is, Arch. Look." The small sandy cove was entirely private, with no access from the high cliffs above. "It's gorgeous," Ash said.

"Wow," Archie replied. "It's like a Caribbean beach. Totally unspoiled and beautiful. Much like yourself."

Ash laughed. "You think so?"

Archie just smiled and raised her eyebrows.

Archie slowed their speed incrementally as they got further into shore. As soon as it was shallow enough, Archie jumped out into the sea and guided the boat onto the sand.

When the water levels were at Archie's ankles she said, "I think it's safe to get out. Here, take my hand."

Ash took off her sandals and jumped into the cool water. The water was so refreshing after being baked by the sun in the boat.

"Leave your bags," Archie said. "I'll get them when I pull the boat in."

As Ash made her way up onto the hot sandy beach, she spotted the cave she'd heard so much about. It looked dark and just a bit spooky. She stopped halfway up the beach and watched Archie pull the boat some way up onto the sand, then gather all their bags.

"Your dad made me promise to pull the boat up quite far. It's our only way out."

"Time and tide wait for no man, my dad always says," Ash said.

"Quite true. Okay, here are your bags."

While Archie went to get the others, Ash got out the towels and laid two side by side.

When Archie returned with the rest of their things, Ash started to feel nervous. Nervous that she would need to disrobe soon and reveal more of herself to Archie than she had before. Maybe she shouldn't have gone for the bikini?

She told herself not to be so silly. Archie didn't judge women in that way, she knew from their many conversations. But even still, she hoped that Archie would like what she saw.

The moment came when Archie dropped to her knees and pulled her T-shirt off. She revealed a pair of solid shoulders and arms, and a toned stomach. Ash imagined throwing her arms around her neck and holding on tight.

Archie opened the cool box and asked, "Soft drink or…?"

"Just some water for just now, thanks."

Archie handed her what looked like a small milk carton. "That's water?"

"Yeah, it's a company that only uses recycled cardboard for their water. Fox asked the pub to stock this brand to cut down on the plastic being used."

"A simple but clever idea."

Next, Archie took out a glass bottle of lager. Archie looked up at her and said, "Don't worry. It's non-alcoholic. I won't be drunk in charge of a motorboat. Your dad would kill me."

It was getting really hot, so it was now or never for the sarong. She slipped it off and folded it neatly into her bag. When she sat down she saw Archie looking out of the corner of her eye.

She sat on the towel, and Archie was looking out towards the sea but, for some reason, tapping her fingers on the glass bottle incessantly.

"It's such a beautiful place, isn't it?" Ash said.

"Idyllic." Archie turned to her and said, "You look beautiful, by the way."

Ash lowered her head bashfully. "I'm sure you've seen lots of beautiful women."

"None like you."

Archie looked back to the shoreline. It was strange to Ash, but even though they had been close all week, and sharing kisses, now there was a nervousness that hung between them. It was truly like a first date.

"So?" Do you want to sunbathe or have a swim before lunch?" Archie asked.

"A swim." Ash reached into her beach bag and pulled out an inflatable. She threw it to Archie and said, "Get blowing."

❖

Ash couldn't have been more content. The sun was beating down from above while she floated on her lilo, her hands trailing in the cool water. She heard splashing nearby and then felt Archie lean on her inflatable, pooling cold water onto her stomach.

"Oh, that's cold. Be careful, Archie."

"Just trying to cool you down."

"You know what this is like?" Ash said.

"What?"

"That scene in *Titanic*," Ash said.

"I went to see that with my dad," Archie said with disdain. "He was crying by the end. I bet you were too."

"Of course I was. Everyone apart from you was upset. I don't think I'd find room on my escape raft, just like Rose."

"I'll just have to take it, then." Archie pushed the lilo into the water, knocking Ash off into the sea.

Ash squealed, "It's freezing. Why did you do that, Archie?"

Archie pulled Ash to her. "Because I want you to hold on to me."

Ash wrapped her arms around Archie's neck, and her legs around her waist. This was the closest Archie had gotten to her. Tantalizingly close in the revealing white bikini.

She kissed Ash and cupped her breast. Archie could feel Ash's nipple harden, and she could just imagine putting it in her mouth. But her racy thoughts were interrupted by Ash saying in panic, "My lilo, Archie."

Archie looked behind her and saw that the inflatable had floated away. She would have to enjoy Ash's kisses later.

"I'll go and get it."

She swam out and retrieved the inflatable, and they both went back to shore. It didn't take long for them to dry off in the hot sun. They were both more than ready to eat. Archie picked up a paper plate covered in foil. "It says sandwiches, pasta salad, spicy couscous."

"Lovely." Ash took off the foil to reveal a compartmented plate with little portions of food in all of them. "This is beautiful. Well done, Jonah. Wait, do you have cutlery?"

Archie rummaged in her rucksack and pulled out a packet of cutlery. She passed it to Ash and said, "Eco-friendly bamboo cutlery."

Ash smiled. "You think of everything."

"I tried," Archie said seriously.

Ash met her gaze. "You did."

"Oh, one more thing. It's very decadent," Archie said.

"What?"

Archie pulled a bottle of champagne out of the wine cooler.

"Champagne?" Ash said.

"Fox's champagne. It makes it taste even better, stealing hers," Archie joked.

Ash giggled. "You are terrible. I'm telling Fox."

Archie opened the bottle with ease and poured out some into a champagne flute. "You're a co-conspirator. Besides, she's very generous."

"True. I thought you weren't drinking."

"Just one glass to keep you company." Archie handed Ash the glass and thought about the inspiration for today, Ash's favourite book. "Do you remember a certain couple having champagne by the river?"

Ash smiled. "The duke and his true love, Diana."

"Exactly. I wanted to show you that I really did take in and appreciate your book," Archie said.

Ash gave her a little smile and said, "I appreciate that."

They started to eat, and Archie realized just how hungry she was. "Hmm, this is delicious."

"Jonah is a really good cook," Ash agreed.

"So, what book are you reading now?" Archie asked.

"*The Princess and the Pauper*. It's a classic. They adapted that one for TV."

"Really? I bet you loved that." Archie smiled.

"I did—I watch all the classics when I need a pick-me-up from the life," Ash said.

"These stories are a place for you to find calm in difficult times, aren't they?" Archie was beginning to realize why these books were so important to Ash.

"Exactly. They are a safe place to go. Everything follows a certain pattern, and the characters follow strict rules of social structure and language. That idea is very safe and comforting to me."

Archie took a bite of her sandwich. Ash had coped with grief from such a young age. It was no wonder she sought order and the knowledge that there is a happy ending every time.

"I think I understand," Archie said.

"A lot of other people feel the same ways as me. There are huge online communities of people that love my kind of books. There are even conventions where people meet, dress up as their favourite characters."

"Have you ever been?"

Ash shook her head. "They only have them in the big cities throughout the country."

"That's a shame. I know how much you would love that."

Ash shrugged. "Maybe one day, but this picnic is letting me experience my favourite part of my favourite book."

Archie smiled. Then her phone beeped with a text. She looked in her bag for her phone.

"Is everything all right?" Ash asked.

"It's my dad. He's set the date for his wedding. He wants me to be his best person, as it were."

"That's wonderful news. Are you happy?"

Archie had to be honest. "I'm happy for him—I just want *him* to be happy. Marriage really hurt both Mum and Dad the first time around."

"But he's older and wiser this time, Archie. Plus, he's not having to pretend he's straight. Hiding that part of himself must have been so hard."

"I know, and his fiancé is a really nice man. It's hard letting go of your fears, though."

"Tell me about your dad."

Archie smiled. "He's the most loving man you could imagine. He was mum *and* dad to me growing up a lot of the time."

"What does he do?"

"He owns his own online wine merchant. There's nothing he doesn't know about wine."

"When's the wedding?" Ash asked.

"Two months' time." Then Archie had a thought. "Would you like to come as my guest?"

"If it's okay with your dad, I'd love to."

"That's great. I'd like him to meet you before that."

Archie stabbed her fork in her food, worry starting to flow through her body.

She felt Ash's hand on her arm. "Archie, don't worry so much. I know you haven't seen a very good example of marriage, but it isn't always a prison with pain and hurt. Sometimes a marriage can be a safe place full of happiness."

"Real life isn't as safe and happy as your romance books, Ash."

"Archie, I have seen it in real life. My mum and dad adored each other. As I grew up, I watched two people who couldn't be more in love. Two people who shared a close intimacy. And that was why my dad was so badly affected when she died."

Archie tried to imagine Ash suddenly taken from her, and she felt a deep hurt in her chest.

"I can't imagine how he felt."

"He told me he would never love another woman in his life, because true love like that doesn't come along twice in a lifetime."

What Ash said resonated with her. She couldn't imagine feeling for anyone else the way she was beginning to feel for Ash. No one had ever come close to getting inside her heart before, and if she didn't take this chance on love, it might never come about again.

"You're right, Dad is right, to take a chance on love. Life is short."

"Good," Ash said. "I'm looking forward to meeting your dad and his partner."

Archie shook off her worry and tried to focus on Ash. Her insecurities weren't going to mess with this perfect date.

"After you've finished eating, do you want to explore the cave?" Archie asked.

"As long as you hold my hand. It's creepy."

Archie winked and said, "I'll keep a tight hold on you."

CHAPTER FIFTEEN

"Are you sure about this?" Ash asked as they walked towards the cave.

"You'll be safe enough with me. Come on."

Ash allowed herself to be pulled into the mouth of the cave. "I can't imagine my mum liking to come in here."

"She trusted your dad to keep her safe. I'll keep you safe," Archie said firmly.

They walked into the cave, and Ash shivered. It was much colder in here, and the sound of dripping water didn't make the place any more inviting.

"Are there any old stories about this cave?" Archie asked.

"Smugglers were supposed to have used it to hide their cargo, and when I was young, I was brought up on stories that this was a sea monster's lair."

Archie turned to her and grinned. "Oh, really?" She pushed Ash up against the cold stone of the cave and snapped her teeth. "Like that?"

Ash hit Archie softly. "Don't. It's creepy enough as it is."

"I can make you forget your fear." Archie placed her lips close to Ash's neck and growled like the fictional sea monster.

Ash gasped when she felt Archie's teeth graze her neck.

"You are so beautiful."

Ash placed her hands around Archie's neck and swept her

fingers in her loose hair. Archie licked and kissed her neck, and Ash felt her sex throb. She had fantasized about Archie touching her, and she needed it so badly.

"Archie? Let's go back to Rosebrook. Dad's not expecting me back tonight."

"What? Really?" Archie asked.

Ash smiled and nodded her head. "I told Dad I was staying with you."

"And he was all right with that?"

"Yes." Ash breathed while she caressed Archie's cheek.

Archie brought her lips close and said, "Well, he shouldn't, because I want to make love to you all night."

"Do you promise?"

Archie took her hand and pulled her out of the cave. "Let's go."

They made the return journey much more quickly than the trip out, both desperate to be together. Archie dumped the bags at the front door and pulled Ash over to the lift instead of the stairs. It was a nice little perk, allowing her to kiss Ash while disposing of her sarong.

She felt Ash shiver. "Are you okay? You're sure you want to do this?"

Ash stroked her cheek. "I've wanted this for so long."

The lift arrived upstairs, and the doors opened. Archie led them along to the bedroom she was staying in and felt her heart start to thud hard. This was really going to happen.

They walked in, and Ash stood with her back against the door. Ash looked even more sexy with her hair wet from her recent swim in the sea, but she appeared nervous.

Ash was a confident young woman who had put Archie in her place in the office, but here with very little clothes between them and experiencing new wants and desires, her innocence shone through, and it was intoxicating. Archie put her hands on Ash's hips and placed small, tender kisses around her mouth, trying to be as gentle as she could. She heard Ash's breath quicken.

"Remember you told me that you fantasized about an older woman because you wanted to feel safe, to have experienced hands touch you?"

Archie rested her palm against Ash's stomach and she felt it tense against her touch.

"Yes," Ash said breathily.

Archie trailed her fingers slowly over her stomach and brought her lips close to Ash's. Ash moved in expecting a kiss, but Archie moved her head back a few inches and smiled.

"We're going to go slow and take our time. I want you to really need me to touch you."

"I do."

Archie shook her head. "Not enough. I want you to need it so badly you'll give anything for it."

Ash's chest heaved.

Archie wanted Ash to be frustrated—she wanted to take it slowly, so that when the moment came Ash would let go completely. Archie pulled off her own T-shirt and crop top, then stood close and kept her eyes on Ash's while she untied her bikini top.

It dropped away, and Archie finally saw Ash's medium sized breasts. Her nipples were rock hard, and Archie licked her lips. If she didn't show some sort of control, she would be sucking and rolling them in her mouth this second.

Instead she ran her palm from Ash's stomach to sit between her breasts and held it there, waiting for Ash's reaction. She got it when Ash grabbed her wrist and tried to lift it onto her breast.

When Archie didn't let her, Ash grasped and squeezed her own breast in defiance. That both amused her and turned her on. Archie moved her hands and held them firmly at Ash's waist while she kissed her neck and shoulders.

"Archie, touch me."

"You know what I'm thinking when we're at work and I gaze over you? I'm thinking how much I want..." Archie put her lips close to Ash's ear and whispered, "How much I want to take you to the conference room and fuck you on the table."

"Oh my God, yes."

She kissed her way to Ash's chest and grasped one breast while she sucked on the other. Ash groaned, and her hips started to move with her need. Archie took pity on her and dropped to her knees. She grasped her hips and ran the flat of her tongue up Ash's stomach and used the tip to circle her navel.

Ash pressed her fingers into Archie's loose hair and tried to push her head where she wanted it.

Archie moaned. Ash's skin tasted salty from their swim in the sea. It was so hard trying to keep control of her own need. If she wasn't trying to make this all about Ash, Archie would bend Ash over against the door and thrust against her buttocks until she came.

But this was about Ash. She pulled at the sides of Ash's bikini bottoms and eased them down and off.

"Yes, yes," Ash said, "kiss me there."

Archie looked up at Ash with a grin. "Where? Show me."

Ash let her finger dip into her wetness, but before she could get any relief, Archie took hold of her hand and sucked the finger into her mouth. She felt Ash's knees buckle for a split second, but she regained control.

"You taste so good." Archie hummed.

"Oh God. Please, Archie."

"*Now* you need me?" Archie asked.

She saw how flustered and desperate Ash was becoming. Now was the time.

"Yes, yes, I'll do anything, just please let me come."

Archie thought back to the night they had shared some heated texts, and how wound up she had been. Now she had Ash, she was hers, she was going to be hers, and she wouldn't let go.

She kissed around her sex and then opened Ash up so she could lick the length of her intimate area.

"Archie!" Ash's hands gripped Archie's hair. After all the

teasing and build-up, the merest touch sent waves of pleasure through her. She couldn't believe this was finally happening. After all her fantasies about being with Archie, she had her mouth on her.

Archie teased her tongue around Ash's opening and then swirled around her clit. Ash felt her legs go weak, and she threw her hands back against the door, desperately looking for the support of a handhold that she knew wasn't there.

"It's too much."

Archie pulled back from her sex and placed her hand on Ash's thigh. "You're trembling." She got up and lifted Ash into her arms. "It'll never be too much when I'm here. I'll always take care of you."

Ash would have melted on the spot if she hadn't been in Archie's arms. Archie laid her on the bed and took off her shorts. She then lay down and slipped her hips between Ash's legs.

When Ash felt Archie press her sex against hers, she grasped for Archie, pulling her into a kiss. It was such a turn-on to taste herself on Archie's lips. Archie teased Ash with her tongue and surprised her by pushing two fingers inside her.

Ash gasped and Archie grinned. "This is what you wanted, isn't it? Me to fuck you?"

God. Those words from Archie would make her be willing to beg on her knees for Archie to touch her.

"Yes, yes," Ash moaned.

Archie kept her fingers still, but Ash's hips started to thrust. "You really do want this."

On one of Ash's thrusts, Archie pushed her fingers in deeply, catching Ash by surprise. Archie thrust in a steady, deep rhythm while she gave her mouth tender kisses.

"I feel like I'm going to shake apart, Arch."

"You won't. I'm here—just go with it," Archie said.

She felt her body tighten, tingling all over, as Archie quickened her pace. "Yes, yes. More," Ash groaned desperately.

Her body was trembling uncontrollably now, after a day of build-up and foreplay.

"Good girl, let go and come." Archie moved her head down and sucked one of Ash's nipples into her mouth.

That's all Ash needed. Her body went taut, and she stiffened while waves of unadulterated pleasure crashed over her body.

"Oh God, oh God," Ash cried.

Archie stilled and eased her fingers out when Ash's body relaxed. She kissed Ash tenderly and said, "Are you okay?"

Ash was gasping for breath. "Yeah, I think I've strained the back of my neck, though. I've never come so hard."

Archie stroked her hair. "You're so beautiful. God, I want you."

Ash's hips twitched, and Archie said, "You've got more to give me, haven't you?"

"Yeah, but I want you to come."

Archie slipped between Ash's legs and pushed her sex into Ash's and began to thrust. After a few thrusts, a second wave of pleasure set off in her sex. Archie was starting to breathe heavily.

"You came again?"

"Yes." Ash wrapped her legs around Archie's and pulled her close. "Come on me, baby."

Archie's thrusts became faster, and the only sound in the room were moans and the slapping of flesh.

Ash watched as Archie closed her eyes. "I'm going to come, Jesus." Archie stiffened, and she collapsed onto Ash.

Ash kissed her. "Was it okay?"

"Okay?" Archie said with incredulity. "You make me want to love you until I'm exhausted. I've dreamed about touching you for so long." Archie kissed her, then said, "I need more. Turn over."

Ash didn't know exactly what was going on, but she did as Archie asked.

"I want to fuck you from behind." Archie pushed her wet sex on Ash's buttock and put her hand on the back of her neck. Archie thrust herself onto Ash, and she helped by pushing her buttocks back into Archie. "Fuck, I've dreamed about doing this."

Ash's clit started to pound again. It was a new discovery that her buttocks were an erogenous zone for her. It was such a turn-on, being used for Archie's pleasure like this.

Archie soon began to lose control and thrust hard into her.

"Fuck, fuck," Archie cried. She then fell on top of Ash, trying to get her breath back.

"Archie that was amazing. I loved you touching me there."

Archie kissed her shoulder. "You were made for me."

Yes, I love you. Ash was too scared to say it out loud.

CHAPTER SIXTEEN

M aybe we should get some things at the shop. I'll buy us dessert for Sunday dinner," Archie said.

After a long night discovering everything physically about each other, Archie agreed to come for Sunday lunch with Ash and James. They were walking from Rosebrook back to Ash's cottage, and Archie was becoming more nervous by the minute.

"Thanks, okay. I always make apple crumble on Sundays. It doesn't take me long."

"What about wine?" Archie said quickly.

"Only if you want it for yourself," Ash said. "Dad only likes beer and whisky. Are you trying to delay us getting back home to my cottage?"

Archie thought she might as well come clean. "Yes. I respect your dad. Look, he's going to know we…you know."

Ash chuckled. "Arch, I told him yesterday I was going to stay the night with you. He's not an idiot. I'm sure he assumed our relationship might become physical. It's only a big deal if you make it so. We're all adults."

"I'm sorry. I've never experienced a morning-after with the parents before," Archie said.

Ash went quiet.

Idiot. Ash was probably thinking about all the other mornings-after Archie'd had. "I'm sorry. I shouldn't have said that."

Ash shrugged, as if trying to seem very calm about it. "It doesn't matter. You're older than me, and you're going to have a past. It doesn't bother me."

Archie took her hand. "It does. I know, okay? But like I said, I've never met the parents before, so you are different from every other woman I've known."

Ash's smile returned. "I suppose. I can't wait to cook for you. Sunday lunch is always special to Dad and me. Mum always made a big fuss about Sundays being family days. Dad and I have kept up the tradition."

"I can't wait to share it with you." Archie squeezed her hand.

They arrived at the cottage, and Ash opened the door with her keys. Archie's nerves hadn't gone away. How was James going to look at her?

Ash led her into the living room, and James was sitting by the fire reading the Sunday newspapers.

"Morning, Dad."

"Good morning, James."

James nodded. "Did you have a nice time at the cove?"

"It was amazing, Dad. Such a special place," Ash replied.

"It was to me and your mum. Archie, did you like it?"

Archie nodded quickly. "It's such a beautiful spot. I'm glad I could share it with Ashling."

Ash said, "You two chat, and I'll get the lunch on."

No, Archie pleaded with Ash mentally. *Don't leave me to make small talk with your dad after I've just spent the night with you.*

But Ash was off, and she was suddenly alone with James. He looked at her with steady eyes.

"Sit down, Archie."

Archie complied. Was she going to get a bollocking for staying with Ash all night? Ash might be a grown woman, but she was still his daughter.

"You look tense, Archie."

"I'm fine. Really."

"You're not," James said. He folded up his newspaper and sat forward in his seat. "I know why you're tense. I'm a man of the world, and I was in your shoes at one time in my life. Ash's grandad banished me from their house for three weeks, until my wife convinced them that I was serious about her. I was an interloper, you see, not a local, just like you."

This was as uncomfortable a conversation as she'd ever had. Why was she getting involved? A few months ago she would have run, but really, Ash was too important to run from.

"What happened?" Archie asked.

"I proved I wouldn't leave on the next boat out of Rosebrook. Plus"—James ran his hand over his beard and smiled—"little Ash came along as a surprise, and Kate's parents were happy for us to get married. But in your case, I doubt that any little surprises will pop up."

Archie laughed nervously. "No, I doubt it."

"In that case, all I'll ask is if you're serious, stay around—and if you're not serious, don't string her along. You know the ways of the world. Ash thinks love reads like a romance novel, but it doesn't always."

"I won't. I'm more than aware how careful I need to be, but I care deeply for her."

"Good. Or I'll have to take you on the boat to meet the fishes." James burst out laughing.

Ash came in the room just as her dad laughed and said, "You're getting on well."

"Yes, great," Archie said. That was the most awkward conversation she'd ever had.

James stood up. "I better get moving. I've a few things to prepare for tomorrow's boat trips at the shop, and I must cut the grass. It's badly overgrown."

Without thinking, Archie stood up and said, "I could cut the grass for you, James. Ash will be cooking lunch, so I could do it."

"That would be a good help. Thank you, Archie."

Fifteen minutes later, Archie was in the back garden, ready to start cutting the grass. It was only when she started the lawnmower and moved up and down the garden that she remembered this had always been her worst fear. Stuck in a rural village, in suffocating domesticity, cutting the grass on a Sunday.

But then she looked up at the kitchen window and saw a smiling, happy Ash looking out at her. Ash waved, and she found herself waving back like a lovesick fool, but what James had said resonated in her mind. She shouldn't string Ash along if this wasn't something that she could do.

Archie wanted to be able to have a life here, and to love Ash with all her heart, but what if her emotional inadequacies let her down? She imagined Ash looking at her with disappointment and tears rolling down her cheeks, and she felt sick.

After dinner Ash and Archie brought their cups of coffee out to the back garden. They sat on the garden bench and took in the calm evening air. Archie had been quiet since dinner earlier, like she was lost in her own thoughts.

"Is everything okay? Was the veggie nut roast okay? I've never had to cook one before."

Ash had gotten a few essential vegan options with her weekly shopping on the off-chance Archie would be eating with them.

"It was perfect. You're a good cook."

"I learned because I had to. Dad couldn't boil an egg. Mum did everything for him. But she loved to—it was her way of showing how much she loved him."

Only when she spoke those words out loud did she realize that was what she was doing. Would Archie realize that? How would she react?

"It's beautiful out here," Archie said.

Ash looked out over the scene before her. Their cottage sat high atop the cliffs surrounding the beach. This gave them an enviable view of the sea, and in the evening gloom it somehow was even more beautiful than usual.

"It is. I couldn't have asked for such a lovely home."

"Back to the grindstone tomorrow, I suppose?"

Ash remembered something she had meant to talk to Archie about. "Archie, you know my village history project?"

"Yes."

"I was thinking, could we put together an app, something the tourists could download and listen to as they walked around? Is that something that's possible?"

Archie shook her head and laughed softly.

"Was it such a bad idea?"

Archie turned to look at her and cupped her cheek. "I'm not laughing because it's a bad idea. I'm laughing because I underestimated you so much. You are such a capable, intelligent woman, and I was a fool to think anything else."

"Thank you, but maybe I gave you too much of a hard time about asking me for tea," Ash joked.

Archie shook her head. "I deserved it. We can use the app designers that Fox Toys worked with for *The Woodlanders*."

The Woodlanders game was one of Fox Toys' biggest sellers, with its ecological message and fun gameplay loved by old and young all over the world.

"That would be great. I found out that the Tucker twins remember hearing stories of Elijah and his family. I thought I could interview them for our project."

"Excellent idea. You get all your information together, and I'll contact the app design team."

Archie leaned in for a kiss but jumped back like a frightened teenager when she heard Ash's father clearing his throat beside them.

"Sorry for interrupting. I just wanted to thank Archie for her help with cutting the grass today, before I turn in."

"No trouble, James. Thanks for having me to dinner."

"You're welcome anytime," he said. "Well, goodnight all."

"Night, Dad," Ash said.

"Goodnight, James."

When he'd left them alone, Archie said, "I felt like a teenager being caught in the act."

"You're so silly. Dad understands."

"I know. But I'd better be on my way too."

Ash sighed and leaned her head against Archie's shoulder. "I wish you could stay."

"Your dad's been really good about us—we don't want to push him. Anyway, you exhausted me last night," Archie said.

"I suppose." Ash chuckled

Archie was silent for a minute.

"What are you thinking?"

"Spending the day with you and your dad, as a family, has brought up some difficult memories."

"What do you mean?"

"Being in my home village, with my mum and dad, then my mum and stepfather. Your dad is a traditional man, and yet he accepts you being gay because he loves you. He's even accepted me going out with you." Archie turned to face Ash. "Why couldn't my mum accept me because she loved me?"

Ash's heart broke when she saw Archie's eyes well up. Archie quickly looked away and cleared her throat, trying to cover up her emotions.

As mature a woman as Archie was, the hurt from her childhood still had the capacity to make her feel like that hurt little girl again.

Ash squeezed Archie's hand. "How long is it since you spoke to her?"

Archie looked up to the sky and thought hard. "Probably when I was your age, thirteen or fourteen years ago."

"You know, a lot can change in fourteen years. Why don't you give her a call? Give her a chance to have changed."

"No, I can't do that. I'm not giving her the chance to hurt me again."

"At least you would know, Arch. Think about it. Your dad's engaged and moving on, so maybe she will too. You were the one who said you now saw things from your mum's point of view. They were both wrong in lots of ways."

"I'll think about it." Archie stood. "I better be going."

"Okay."

Ash walked her through the cottage to the front door and kissed her. "This weekend has been really special, really romantic, Arch."

Archie smiled and said, "Romance is a magic we can cast ourselves."

Ash was astounded. "That's a quote from *The Laird and the Lady*. How do you know that?"

Archie just smiled and winked. "I've been reading."

"My romance books?" Ash said excitedly.

Archie nodded. "There's some good advice in them. Goodnight. I'll text you later."

Ash was gobsmacked. She read her books?

Archie made her way home to Rosebrook but slowed as she passed one of the empty cottages not far from the O'Rourkes'. It was a detached cottage, bigger than the ones that had been refurbished for the new residents.

Fox said it had once belonged to the Fitzroys' land steward, and Fox had meant it to be for Archie, until she insisted she wouldn't move down here. She walked up the garden path on a whim and looked in the windows.

She remembered it had a new bathroom and kitchen installed but still hadn't been decorated. When Archie made it clear she didn't want the place, Fox had moved their resources to other cottages. All she could see was the sitting room. It wasn't open plan like the smaller cottages.

Archie tried to imagine sitting on a couch in that room, her arm around Ash, who would be cuddled up next to her, watching *The Gatekeeper*. The image gave her a warm, happy feeling, not panic as it would have done when she was first offered this house.

But did she have the courage to turn that dream into a reality?

She heard a voice behind her.

"Archie? How's it going?" Griffin said.

"Good. You?" Archie walked out of the garden and shut the gate.

"Fantastic. I was down on the beach, meditating next to a fire I made. It doesn't get better than this," Griff said.

"You like it here, then?" Archie asked.

"It's beautiful. Is there a newcomer coming to take up that cottage?"

"Maybe. It's not certain yet," Archie said. "How are you getting on with Patrick?"

"Fantastically. He's a great boy, and so eager to learn about brewing," Griffin said.

"I'm really glad. He's had a hard lot in life and deserves a safe home and a good job."

"Agreed. How did the big picnic go yesterday?"

"You heard about that?" Archie asked.

"Small villages, people talk."

"I suppose so. It was nice, special."

"Are you two together, then?"

"I don't know for sure. I'm in uncharted territory, and I don't know the rules. We spent the day together today. I had Sunday lunch with Ash and her dad, and then I cut his grass for him—can you believe that?" Archie said.

Griffin looked at her quizzically. "Why is that significant?"

"I've always had this fear of cutting grass on a Sunday."

"Why?"

"It's the image of domesticity, wife and two-point-four kids. In the village I grew up in, after church the men went out, like robots, and cut the grass."

Griffin shivered. "I get what you mean, like suburbia. How did it feel today?"

"It felt okay. Ash is making me reassess so much about myself and my goals. You know me, Griff, I'm not the settling-down type."

"But love is changing your opinion?"

Archie needed time to contemplate all of these new thoughts and feelings. "Maybe. Listen, I better go. I've got an early morning tomorrow."

"Sure, take it easy, Archie."

Archie walked home with a million questions buzzing around

in her head and went straight up to bed. As she got changed, her phone rang. She thought it might be Ash, but instead her dad's voice said, "Hi, Arch."

"Hi, Dad, is everything okay?"

"Yes, don't worry. I haven't seen you much since you went to Rosebrook to stay. I wondered—can Stuart and I come and visit you and your village?"

"Of course, Dad. You don't need to ask," Archie said.

"Maybe you'll introduce us to this girl you like."

"Yes, that would be nice. I'd love to."

"Great," he said, "I'll call you later in the week about time."

Archie had a thought churning in her head, and she wanted her dad's opinion. "Okay, but can I ask you something?"

"Go ahead."

"Do you think I should call Mum and give her one last chance to make some sort of relationship?"

She heard her dad sigh. "I think you should never give up on her completely. She is and will always be your mother. There's been a lot of hurt between the three of us, but you should never close the door completely."

"Thanks, Dad. See you next week."

She looked at her phone contact list, and her finger hovered over the number for a few seconds. Then she threw the phone onto the bed. Archie didn't have the courage yet.

CHAPTER SEVENTEEN

Ash was so excited for her new workweek. She got to see Archie, the woman she was falling in love with, and had an exciting project. The app design company Archie mentioned had been in touch with a project template she had to work on. This was going to be her baby, and Ash couldn't wait to get stuck in.

Archie walked over to her desk and said, "I talked to my dad last night. He wants to come and visit me and see the village with his fiancé Stuart."

"That's great, Arch. It'll be exciting to meet them."

"I thought we could maybe have lunch at Rosebrook. What do you think?"

"Yes." Ash smiled and felt excitement in her core. "I'll cook us something."

"Are you sure? I was going to suggest getting something from the pub—"

"No, I'll be happy to. Honestly."

The more Ash could make Archie feel comfortable, the more she might be able to encourage her to stay here with her, long-term. It was a nagging worry in the back of Ash's mind, that when Fox and Clem returned and Archie went home, whatever they felt for each other wouldn't be enough to keep Archie here with her.

"Thank you. That would be nice. I'd like you to meet my dad. He's such a nice man."

"I can't wait," Ash replied.

"I'm just going back to the house for something. I won't be long, okay?" Archie said.

"Okay. I'll hold the fort for you."

An hour later Archie still hadn't returned. Ash had texted her a few times but had no reply, and when she phoned it went to voicemail.

Ash had a bad feeling, so she left Rupert in charge and walked up to the house. Ash went into the entrance hallway and shouted, "Archie? Are you there?"

There was no reply, so she walked down to the kitchen to check if she was there. Again, there was no sign. Something told her to check the grounds at the back of the house.

As she rounded the corner of the building, she saw Archie sitting by the bench at the pond. As Ash got closer she saw her iPhone lying on the bench, and her head in her hands.

Ah. Archie had phoned her mum.

"What did she say?"

Archie took a deep breath. "She has her life now and doesn't want to go back. My life isn't compatible with hers. My stepfather is a bishop now."

"Is that all she said?"

"She wished me luck with my life—" Archie's voice broke.

"I know it doesn't make the pain any less, but your dad loves you, and you have me and a village full of friends if you want us."

Archie stood, cupped Ash's cheeks, and pressed her forehead to Ash's. "You are the one who makes me feel better. I want you, Ash." Archie kissed her deeply and then said with a needing tone to her voice, "I want you, right now." She pulled at Ash's hand. "Please?"

Ash nodded and allowed herself to be pulled back to the house.

❖

Archie needed this so badly. After being hurt by her mother on the phone, Archie needed to feel in control.

Ash was on all fours, undulating her hips, while she fucked her from behind with her fingers and held Ash's hair tightly. She was learning so much about what Ash wanted and needed from her.

She learned that Ash loved Archie to have the control she didn't let her have in the office. They were a perfect fit. Archie was naturally dominant in the bedroom, and Ash had so much energy, and the stamina to take whatever Archie gave her.

Ash pushed back onto her fingers and swirled her hips. "I'm going to come."

Archie used her own hips to help thrust her fingers, and she knew Ash loved to feel her behind. She wished she had a strap-on to use. Archie was sure Ash would love it. She would ask Ash if she was comfortable using one.

Ash's hip started to tremble. "It's too deep."

Archie rubbed Ash's hip with her free hand and said, "It's not. You can take it."

She felt Ash's walls flutter against her fingers, so she swirled around and rubbed high up inside her.

Ash cried out, and Archie felt her fingers being squeezed rhythmically inside. After a few seconds, Ash collapsed to the bed, and Archie lay at her side. Ash quickly turned in to her arms.

Archie held her close until she calmed. Archie's body was thrumming with tension. As much as she needed control, she needed to come and release all her tension. Ash read her mind and pushed her back onto the bed and straddled her.

Archie grasped Ash's breasts and squeezed. Ash leaned down to kiss her lips, and then Archie said, "I need you to make me come. Suck me."

"Anything you want, baby."

Ash crawled down and opened Archie up. They hadn't been lovers long, but Ash knew Archie didn't like penetration, so she lavished attention on her hard clit and all around it. She felt Archie hold on to her head, keeping her in place.

She didn't get long to taste and lick Archie before she said, "Suck me, Ash. I need it."

Ash took her lover's clit into her mouth and sucked, making Archie groan.

"That's it. Fuck," Archie said.

Archie's hips got faster and her moans louder until she cried out and released the tension and worry in her intense orgasm. Ash went back up to kiss Archie and saw emotion in her eyes.

Ash held her and said, "It's okay. You don't need her in your life. She can't hurt you any more. I—" Ash was afraid to say *I love you*, in case Archie ran. "I care about you so much, and so does your dad, and all your friends here."

Archie rubbed her eyes self-consciously. "I know. I just hated all the bad childhood memories that came back after talking to her."

"You choose your family, Arch. Just relax."

Ash held Archie until she fell asleep. *I'll keep your heart safe.*

Archie stroked her fingers through Ash's hair as her head lay on Archie's chest. She felt calm now that she had Ash in her arms. She was like a balm to her soul, and Archie needn't have worried about their age difference, as Ash had the maturity to talk her through her mother's painful rebuff.

She felt Ash stroke her fingernails over her stomach.

"What are you thinking?" Archie asked.

"What are Rupert and the girls going to think? You went out of the office and disappeared, and then I did the same."

Archie chuckled. "Rupert is going to know exactly where we are and what we're doing."

"No, he won't. He won't think I'd jump into bed with you that easily."

"He thinks you're a little angel, does he?" Archie said.

Ash lifted her head, leaned on her elbow, and grinned. "Yes, isn't it obvious I'm an angel?"

"Appearances can be deceptive. Fortunately, I know better."

Ash smacked Archie's shoulder playfully. "Cheeky, no, what I think we should do is you go back to the office first, because you left first, and then I'll come about half an hour later."

"That makes it seem like we're having some sort of sordid affair. We both are free—we are allowed to have sex, you know."

Ash looked down and traced circles on Archie's chest. She didn't like to be described as free. She wanted to be tied down to Archie. She wanted to know this was permanent.

"What's wrong? You've gone quiet," Archie said.

"Nothing," Ash said flatly.

"Well, that's not true for a start. I'm old enough to know that when a woman says *nothing*, it means everything is wrong."

Ash sighed. "It's about what you said there, we're free. What are we? I want to be something to you, not just someone you sleep with. I think that's the kind of relationship you've been used to, but that's not good enough for me, Arch."

"Of course you're something to me." Archie cupped her cheek. "I'm falling in love with you."

"Really?" Ash squeaked.

"As for being free, of course I'd love to have exclusivity on your kisses, but that's up to you. I would have thought that my grand romantic picnic on Saturday should have told you how serious I am."

"Ooh, grand romantic gesture? I suppose it was." Ash placed the biggest kiss on Archie's lips. "I want exclusive rights on that."

"You've got it. Oh, and Ash, will you be my girlfriend?"

Ash pursed her lips. "I'll think about it."

Archie gave her a thwack on her bare bottom. "Not funny. I don't think I've asked someone to be my girlfriend before, so you're special."

Ash smiled and stood up out of bed. "In that case, yes, I will. Now, we better get back to work."

While Ash gathered up her clothes, Archie sat up and rested on her elbow. "Speaking of work, I had a few thoughts on The Big Idea Fox wanted to plan for."

Ash slipped on her skirt. "Oh? Tell me more."

"I think we need something that will be recurring, not a one-off publicity stunt. Something that will bring a wide, varied group together to see what we've built and what we're trying to achieve."

"Agreed, so what did you have in mind?"

Archie sat up at the side of the bed. One of the things Ash noticed about Archie, and was starting to love, was the fact that Archie hid nothing of herself. She was completely confident in her own body, and that was so sexy.

"The way I see it is this…"

Ash also loved it when Archie was super excited about something. She had such passion for her job and environment.

Archie continued, "There is one subject that people are enthusiastic about, and that links to the environment—food. I propose a yearly Rosebrook food festival, where local and national food suppliers who meet strict environmental standards come together to publicize their products. While the general public are here, they will see and understand what our eco village is trying to achieve, what it is promoting. Plus, they will be educated about our mission to make an open diverse community."

"That's brilliant," Ash said as she walked over to Archie.

She stepped between her legs and put her arms around Archie's neck. "And would it be a vegan, plant-based themed festival?"

"My initial thoughts are no, but we need to see what Fox thinks. Fox usually always wants to be inclusive and simply show the possibilities of a vegan, plant-based lifestyle. For example, the farmers who come to our festival to sell their wares could learn from the Rosebrook farmers that there are ways to take part in traditional farming and help the environment."

"You, Archie, are a genius! Let's put plans together before Fox and Clem get home."

Archie smiled. "I am a bit of a genius, aren't I?"

Ash giggled when Archie placed kisses on her bare midriff. "Don't kiss me like that again." She then felt Archie pull her skirt zip down. "Archie? What are you doing? We can't. Rupert will be annoyed."

"I'm not frightened of Rupert. Come here."

Ash laughed as Archie pulled her back onto the bed.

❖

Later on that afternoon, Archie approached Rupert. "Can I have a private word?"

"Yes, of course," Rupert said.

Luckily Ash was out of the office visiting the Tucker twins and interviewing them for her social history project. Archie pulled up a chair to Rupert's desk.

"You know the steward's cottage that Fox started revamping but then stopped, as it wasn't needed?"

"Yes. It had a new kitchen and bathrooms, if memory serves me," Rupert said.

"That's right. Fox wants the work restarted on it—have it decorated and brought up to scratch. She has a friend who wishes to move to the village."

Archie was only telling a little lie. The friend was her, and she had phoned Fox to ask her. It was such a big decision to move to Rosebrook, but she knew that's what she needed to do.

She wasn't falling in love with Ash, as she'd told her—she loved her completely. After the call with her mother, it brought home how much she needed Ash emotionally, not just physically.

She couldn't ask Ash to leave Rosebrook, so moving here was just what she had to do. But she wanted it to be a surprise. Archie was working over a few ideas in her mind of how to make this special.

"That's no problem," Rupert said, "leave it with me."

"Thanks," Archie said.

She got up and walked back to her desk. As long as her plan was secret, she did have the choice to *not* go through with it, but in her heart Archie knew she had to do this.

CHAPTER EIGHTEEN

This is beautiful, Arch," Adam said.

"Thanks, Dad."

Archie's father and his fiancé Stuart arrived on Saturday morning to visit Archie and Rosebrook. They'd arrived about an hour ago and had tea and got to know Ash a bit better before heading out to get a tour of the village. Archie had been really nervous, but Ash helped her through it and made sure everything was prepared for lunch.

It meant the world to Archie that her dad appreciated what they had built here. Archie walked with him while Ash was walking up ahead with Stuart, pointing out sites of interest as they went.

It was wonderful to see how Ashling had blossomed from someone who hadn't had her dream of further education fulfilled, with no job, apart from helping at her dad's boat shop, to a woman full of ideas, enthusiasm, and good business sense.

She was so proud to call her her girlfriend.

"Your young lady seems very nice," her dad said. "I never thought I'd see you with a serious girlfriend."

"I never thought I'd see you get married again," Archie joked.

"Touché," Adam replied.

"No, seriously, you know I've always run away from anything serious, but Ash was just different from the beginning. I was worried about her being thirteen years younger than me, but she is so mature.

She's had to be, I suppose. Her mum died of cancer when she was just leaving high school."

"That's tragic. Poor girl," he said.

"Yes, it's just her and her dad. He's a fisherman here and runs a boat shop, but he's needed a lot of support. Ash is his rock."

"And what does Daddy O'Rourke think of you?"

"He likes me."

"And I like him already."

Archie laughed. "I think he's happy she's living a life at last. But that's a lot of pressure."

"What do you mean?"

"In here"—Archie pointed to her heart—"I know I want to do nothing but love her, but in my head, there's this worry that I will get scared, run, and break her heart. I'd never forgive myself."

"Arch, you're doing really well here in Rosebrook. It looks to me like you have good friends, and friends who are family. You've come a long way since you got that drink thrown in your face."

Archie laughed. "It's Ash that's made the difference. She's taught me all about love and romance, and I'm not scared of loving her, but I've got some big decisions to make."

"Like what?"

"Ash isn't going to leave Rosebrook, and even if she wanted to do it for me, I wouldn't want her to. Her dad needs her support, so if I want a long-term relationship, I'd have to live here in Rosebrook."

He said, "I know you were always fearful of living in a village again, but your Rosebrook is night and day to the one you were brought up in."

"I know, Dad. I've been letting go of those fears by concentrating on Ash's love. I mean, I cut Ash's grass last Sunday—can you believe that?"

Her dad laughed, knowing all about her strange fear. "You are indeed changed, Arch. But seriously, both of our lives have moved on. Let's finally leave the past behind."

Archie nodded. "There's a cottage here that Fox meant for me. I've started the process of having it decorated and made ready for me to move in. Do you think it's a good idea?"

He stopped and squeezed Archie's shoulder. "I think it's a great idea. It would make me so happy to see you settled, Arch. I've always felt such guilt for allowing you to be brought up in that toxic environment."

Archie looked down. "I phoned Mum."

"Did you?" he said with surprise.

"Yes. Ash thought maybe I should give her a chance to have moved on, for my sake, more than hers. So I could let go of the pain of the past."

"And how did she react when you called?"

"Well, I told her you were getting remarried, and I had met someone I deeply cared about."

"And?" Adam asked.

"She wished me well but said she didn't want to revisit the past. Her second husband is a bishop now."

Adam held up his hand. "Say no more. I love you, and your lovely young lady loves you. You have more than enough love to go round."

Ashling shouted, "Hurry up, you two."

They started walking again. "Do you really think she loves me?"

"Hasn't she said? Because it's fairly obvious by the way she looks at you."

"I think she's frighted she'll scare me off."

"Then you take your courage in both hands and tell her."

Archie gazed at Ash up ahead and smiled as she saw her laugh at something Stuart had said.

I'm going to tell you that I love you.

❖

"It's beautiful, isn't it?" Ash said.

Ash and Archie had led her dad and Stuart to Bee World, to show them the large plot of land made purposefully to be a home to the bees. They were all leaning against the fence looking into the hives in the middle of the garden.

Adam didn't appear to be as impressed and backed away from the fence as some bees came close. "I'm not sure I would call it beautiful."

"Oh, be brave, darling," Stuart said to him.

Adam batted at one bee that came quite close.

"You'll get stung if you do that, Dad. Just don't stress them out."

"Stress *them* out? I'm bloody stressed."

They all chuckled. Ash loved Adam and Stuart. They were warm and kind, and Ash couldn't imagine how Adam had been suffocated in a marriage to a woman. It brought home how scared Adam must have felt to be prepared to do that. Archie said that her grandparents on her dad's side were extremely conservative and pressured Adam into marriage.

In the middle of the gardens, at the hives, Eliska stood in her full beekeeping suit with her instructor, who helped her learn every aspect of beekeeping.

"That's one of the first residents to move into our refurbed village. Eliska and her young daughter were caught up in the war in Ustana before moving here. Eliska's partner is also our village doctor."

"She's a very brave woman," Archie added.

"And you reward her bravery by forcing her to keep bees?" Adam said.

Ash laughed with everyone. "No, she volunteered. We like residents to get involved in the projects we have. Bees are an important part of our village, aren't they, Archie?"

"They are. Fox is very passionate about bees. They're essential for our food chain."

"Hmm," Adam said.

Stuart nudged his partner. "Don't be such a scaredy-cat."

Archie slapped her dad's back. "Come on, let's go and see the beach. You'll like that a lot better."

Ash stepped beside Archie as they led the way to the beach. "Your dad and Stuart are nice. They make a lovely couple."

"They do, don't they?" Archie took Ash's hand and began walking down the steps to the beach.

"I think your dad has met a good man. You needn't worry about him."

"No, you're right."

They all walked down to the shore. Archie pointed to the shop and pier. "That's where Ash's dad works from."

Adam turned around and said, "Look at those cute little beach huts."

Stuart said, "It's a gorgeous spot. Why don't we have a paddle? It's a lovely day."

"Yes," Ash said enthusiastically.

They both took off their shoes and ran hand in hand down to the shore.

Adam chuckled and shook his head. "I think we've both found partners who are going to keep us young and interested in life."

Archie watched Ash splashing in the water and sighed in her heart. She was convinced she was put on earth to love Ash and no one else. Why did she fight it for so long? She took off her shoes and said, "If you can't beat them, join them, Dad."

"You're right. Let's enjoy life from now on, Arch."

❖

Lunch couldn't have gone better, in Archie's opinion. Ash made a beautiful meal, and the four of them all got on so well. Archie felt a genuine feeling of family that she hadn't before. Stuart was clearly right for her dad, and Ash was the right one for her. It was time to tell her she loved her.

They stood at the front door of Rosebrook and waved off Adam and Stuart.

"That went well. What a lovely couple," Ash said.

"They love each other," Archie said. "I never thought my dad could find love after what he'd been through, but maybe you should always have hope."

"You see, that's what my lovely books have always taught me."

Archie pulled Ash into her arms and kissed her. She pulled back a few inches and said, "I should've had hope, because I love you, Ashling O'Rourke."

"I—" Ash looked surprised that she'd finally said it and was struggling for words.

She said it again. "I love you."

"Really?"

Archie nodded. "I've never said those words to anyone in my life, Ash. You are the only one who has ever stolen my heart."

Ash kissed her and moaned. "I love you, Archie."

"Can you stay tonight?" Archie asked.

"Yes, just let me go home, check on Dad, and pick up a few things."

"Hurry back," Archie said.

She watched Ash walk at a fast pace down the driveway, and Archie didn't think she'd ever felt so happy, so excited about the future. She was so lucky that a woman like Ash would show an interest, far less love her.

Archie's phone beeped with an email.

Huh. It was from the company that was planning Takada, the Japanese eco city she had read about. They were trying to headhunt her to work with them for a two year contract, then perhaps longer.

Initially she felt a surge of excitement rush through her. Something like this was her dream.

Wow.

But then she looked up, and cold water hit her as she watched Ash walk out of sight. Ash. She had just told her she loved her, and there was no way she was walking away from her, no matter how tempting it was.

She could have asked Ash to come with her, but she would never ask her to leave her dad. A few months ago, Archie would have been off like a shot, but now her priorities were so very different.

CHAPTER NINETEEN

Y ou've been quiet. Are you okay?" Ash could feel Archie was a little distracted as they lay in bed that afternoon.

"I'm absolutely fine. Listen, you know Fox asked me to get the cottage ready for her friend?"

"Yeah."

"She wants it furnished and ready for move-in condition. Would you choose some of the decorative features? Maybe some artwork, vases, rugs, ornaments, anything like that."

Ash sat up quickly. "Oh, I'd like that. I've really had no chance to put my stamp on our cottage. Dad has never wanted to change anything Mum did to the house."

Archie gazed at her lovingly and stroked the hair away from her face. "Well, have some fun. I know its new occupant will love it."

"Who is this friend of Fox's?" Just then Ash heard the crunch of gravel under tires. "Who's that?"

Archie sat up. "I don't know. We're not expecting anyone."

Ash got up and put her dressing gown on. She walked over to the window and saw Fox unpacking their camper van.

"Oh no. Get up, get up."

"What's the panic?"

"Fox and Clem have just pulled up."

"You're joking," Archie said.

"Would I be frantically picking up my clothes if I was?"

Archie grabbed her phone and saw there was a missed call from Fox, but her phone was on silent. "Shit. I've got a missed call from her. They must have decided to come home ahead of schedule."

"Just get dressed quickly. They have Lucy with them."

Archie grabbed her jeans and pulled them on. "I'm coming. I'm coming."

Archie was ready more quickly than Ash, who said to Archie in panic, "Go and stall."

"Stall?"

Ash pushed Archie. "Yes, stall. Small talk. Just give me more time."

"Okay, I'll go."

Ash felt so embarrassed. It would have been embarrassing enough if Fox and Clem caught her with Archie, but they had Lucy with them. That would be a bad first impression, to say the least.

❖

Fox took the bags out of the car and carried them to the door. Clem opened the car door for Lucy and she got out. Despite not being close with her dad, losing her only surviving parent at fifteen had a big effect on her.

She had been glued to Clem, and it was nice to see Clem in that caring role with her. A big gap had been left in Clem's life after her mother died. Her mum had dementia, and Clem had been looking after her for years. She was sure Clem was missing caring for someone in that way because she was a natural nurturer.

Lucy was attached to Clem emotionally, so Fox had made it her mission to distract her and try to make her smile. It had been Fox's idea to come back to Rosebrook earlier than planned. She thought it important to get Lucy out of her empty family home.

There were lots of positive projects for Lucy to get involved with here, and keeping her occupied was what Fox wanted to do.

"Welcome to your new home, Lucy," Fox said.

Clem held Lucy's hand and led her up to the front steps. Fox felt Lucy's hand slip into hers, so Lucy was holding on to them both.

Clem looked at Fox and smiled. "I've missed dear old Rosebrook. We'll need to take you to visit Thistleburn too, Lucy, since you're going to be countess there one day too."

The front door to Rosebrook burst open, and Fox was surprised to see a flustered Archie come rushing out while buttoning the top button of her shirt.

"So sorry I wasn't here to meet you. My phone was on silent, and I didn't get your call."

"Don't worry about it," Fox said. She had rarely seen Archie flustered in such a way before.

"You remember, Archie, Lucy?" Clem said. "You met at my mother's funeral."

Lucy nodded and said shyly, "Hi."

"Hi, nice to see you, Lucy."

Just then Ash came bundling out the door, looking equally as flustered, and her cheeks a reddish hue. She stood awkwardly beside Archie and said, "Hi, and hi, Lucy. I'm sorry about your dad."

Lucy nodded. "Hi. Thanks."

Fox studied the nervous-looking pair. What was going on here? Then she saw it. One of the buttons on Ash's blouse was missed, probably due to dressing hastily.

They hadn't. Had they? Now Archie's request to stay at Rosebrook made sense. Well, that was one way to sort out their working relationship, as she and Clem had hoped.

"How's things been?"

"Good," Archie said. "We've made lots of progress on the tasks you left us with."

"So I see." Fox tried to cover her amusement.

❖

Ash couldn't believe her bad luck. Archie had just told her that she was in love with her, and then Fox and Clem arrived home. Now

Archie had decided it would be best for her to go home to London. Fox and Clem had said Archie was welcome to stay as long as she wanted, but Archie insisted they needed their own space with Lucy now living with them.

That might be true, but what annoyed Ash was Archie's utterly blasé attitude. Ash was heartbroken they would be parted every night, but Archie didn't appear to worry in the slightest.

Was she glad of the chance for the space? Did she long for her city life again? That was what worried Ash, that Archie would be seduced by her city life, and what they had together would diminish.

Ash was sitting on her bed, looking out her bedroom window. Archie said she would stop by before she left. After another five minutes passed, Archie's car pulled in outside her house.

She hurried downstairs and out the front door. She found Archie hunched over her bonnet, rubbing it with her finger.

"What's wrong?" Ash said.

Archie stood up. "I think I've got a scratch."

"You think you've got a scratch?" Ash said with incredulity.

Archie narrowed her eyes. "Yes, is there something wrong?"

"We're being parted right after we say we love each other, and you're worried about a scratch?"

"What? I'm not being conscripted into the navy or something. I'm just going back to sleeping at my own flat. Not leaving the country."

"We won't be spending nights together," Ash said sharply. She couldn't say that she feared Archie would lose interest in her and the village when she was back in her old life.

"We wouldn't be spending them here, even if I had stayed at Rosebrook, not with Lucy there—it wouldn't be right. And you wouldn't want to leave your dad alone every night."

"Stay here with me and Dad."

"No," Archie said firmly. "I've made a good friendship with your dad, and I'm not going to risk that by putting him in a position where he feels uncomfortable. I'll see you tomorrow for the harvest."

The village was all coming together to help Casper and Christian with the vegetable harvest.

"You just don't care, do you?"

"Of course I care. I don't get where this anger is coming from," Archie said.

"No, I forgot. You're blind when it comes to emotions."

Ash walked back into the cottage and slammed the door. She stood behind the door and waited until she heard the car pull away. Why couldn't Archie see how this would change things? Maybe Archie just didn't care as much as she did.

CHAPTER TWENTY

Take another biscuit, Lucy. You're a growing girl," Agatha said.
Lucy smiled shyly and picked up another biscuit.

After they were settled back at home, Clementine's first port of call was to check on the two elders of the village.

"You didn't need to come and see us today—you've hardly been back at home," Ada said.

"No, it's fine. I wanted to. It's the harvest tomorrow, so I won't be able to pop in then. Has everyone been looking after you?"

Both women chuckled, and Ada said, "Yes, you would think we were about to kick the bucket. Ash, Archie, Kay, Mr. Fergus, and Mrs. Murdoch were hardly away from our door."

"Speaking of Ash and Archie, is there some village gossip about those two?"

"Oh yes." Agatha grinned. "Apparently besotted with each other. Spent the day at the cove all by themselves."

"How romantic," Ada said.

Clementine sighed happily. "I hoped romance would be in the air."

Agatha nodded. "Young Ashling deserves some happiness at last."

Worried that one of the ladies would reference the death of Ash's mother and upset Lucy, Clementine said, "Thistleburn was beautiful. You ladies would love it."

"Yes," Ada said, "tell us all about your holiday."

"Fox was a bit much for the residents of Thistleburn at the start—well, you know how she is—but they soon warmed up. Especially when we told them that we were going to refurbish the place."

"Young Fox could win over anyone," Ada said.

"True. The people in Thistleburn are so warm and welcoming, just like here. But they'll probably prefer Fox in small doses," Clementine joked.

"Lucy, you're going to love living here," Ada said. "In Fox and the duchess you couldn't find better people to love you and take care of you."

Lucy smiled and took Clementine's hand. "I love them both. Fox is so funny."

"Just wait," Ada said, "she'll have you with her, picking up litter at the beach and in hedgerows in no time."

"It'll be great to live near the beach," Lucy said.

Clementine smiled. She just wanted Lucy to be happy here. She'd been without parental care and love even before her dad died, so she and Fox wanted to make up for that.

"We're going to have a walk on the beach once we leave here," Clementine said. "I spent so much time on the beach as a child. You'll love it, Lucy."

❖

Archie lay in bed that night, reading one of Ash's books, *The Marquis Needs a Wife*, and missing Ash terribly. She had been spoiled, being able to spend so much time with Ash. She had texted Ash a few times since she got home but no reply.

Why was Ash so angry? They wouldn't be apart long. Once her cottage had been kitted out for her, Archie would get this flat up for sale and move to Rosebrook. Of course Ash didn't know any of this, but she so wanted it to be a surprise.

Maybe she should tell her? Archie lifted her phone to call Ash but hesitated. She wanted that moment to be special, to convey her love, just like the dastardly duke had done.

She texted instead. *I'm reading the marquis book, not quite as good as the duke book. Are you watching The Gatekeeper?*

Yes, was the one-word reply.

That was it. She couldn't stand it. Tomorrow, before they started to help with the harvest, she would show her the cottage and tell Ash her plans. Special would have to come later.

❖

The next morning, Archie got to the office as early as she could, so she could talk to Ash before they all went to take in the harvest. When she walked in the door, Fox was standing talking to Griffin and Patrick.

"Morning, everyone."

"Morning, Archie," they replied.

"Griff and Patrick were just getting me up to speed on the beer factory," Fox said. "Apparently they are planning a line of traditional ales with Isadora's brewer's original recipes."

"Yes, it's very exciting," Archie said.

"Exciting?" Griff said. "With me and my wingman Paddy here, the brewery is going to be spectacular. We better go, Paddy. We said we'd help Jonah with the food and drinks for the harvest later."

As Griffin walked off, Patrick hung back to speak to Fox. "Fox—I just wanted to thank you for giving me a new life here. It's more than I ever could have dreamed of."

Fox grinned from ear to ear. "I think it's hug time."

Archie rolled her eyes as Fox accosted Patrick with a hug. Fox didn't always respect boundaries.

Once Patrick left, Fox asked, "How are things with you?"

"Fine. You're early."

"I've got a lot to catch up on," Fox said.

Archie walked over to Fox's desk. "How was Lucy's first night? Is she coping okay?"

"Yeah, she's really bonded with us, especially Clem. She's like a real mother to her," Fox replied.

"I suppose you didn't expect to have children this early in your marriage."

Fox smiled. "Family is all I ever wanted. We're really lucky to have Lucy. Clem took her to visit with the Tucker twins yesterday, and they've gone down for a morning walk on the beach."

"It's a great place for children to grow up."

"Yeah, and we want to give her a full life here. Lucy might be fifteen, but she's not what you and I were like at fifteen, she's been very sheltered, so she needs to experience new things. Lucy's full of ideas, actually. You know that spare piece of land I've been looking for inspiration for?"

Archie nodded.

"Lucy suggested an animal rescue centre. She loves animals. We could maybe have an animal trust and use *The Woodlanders* in the publicity."

"Sounds great."

"So, did you miss your girlfriend last night?" Fox grinned.

"You know about us?"

"We appeared to catch you out yesterday, and anyway, my wife says you are the talk of the village."

"That's one part of village life that'll be hard to get used to. Everyone knows everything before you do," Archie said. "Yes, we're together. I love her."

Fox hugged Archie excitedly. "Well done. I never thought you'd let yourself find love."

"It took a special girl. Anyway, we might be together, but she's mightily pissed off at me at the moment."

"Why?"

"Because I went back to London. I think she's frightened I'll lose interest or something. I only told her I loved her yesterday, and then I left," Archie said.

"But what about your cottage? She knows you're moving here, surely?"

"No, I wanted it to be a surprise, but looks like I need to tell her now."

Fox nodded and then said seriously. "The Japanese company Takada called me while I was away. Asked for my permission to contact you, all very polite. I said I'd never stand in your way, because I know how much building an eco city from scratch would mean to you."

Archie sighed. "Yes, it would have done, but now I've met Ash, and my dreams are changing. Ash is part of my dream, and I'm not going to make her choose to be with me or lose her dad. She's been through too much in life. They both have."

"I'm pleased for you."

"Takada's come back to me with another offer, but I need to talk to Ash about it."

"So tell her," Fox said. "Don't leave her in doubt that you have a future together."

Archie sighed. "I have all these pieces of the puzzle that I've put together, and I wanted to wait and tell her in this romantic way."

Fox laughed. "Archie Archer, romantic? Will wonders never cease?"

Archie rolled her eyes. "Don't. I'm trying to be like the dastardly duke."

"The…excuse me?"

Archie's cheeks started to feel hot. "It's Ash's favourite romance book. It meant a lot to her and her mum."

Fox patted her on the shoulder. "You really have changed your priorities. So you'll make a home here?"

"If Ash will have me."

"Of course she will."

Archie cleared her throat. "Tell me the truth, Fox. Will people say I'm too old for her?"

"What? No, of course not. Age is just a number, and all relative."

"Not in all circumstances," Archie corrected her.

"True, but how much older are you?"

"Thirteen years."

"That's nothing. Clem thought I was too young for her until I persuaded her."

"I resisted my feelings for Ash for a while because of that, but I just can't help but love her."

"Then just love her. That's what it's all about."

Fox went back to her desk just as Ash walked through the office door. Archie immediately walked over to her and kissed her cheek.

"Good morning, beautiful."

Ash was stiff and pulled away from her slightly. "Morning."

"Morning, Ash," Fox shouted.

When Ash replied with a smile for Fox, Archie knew she was still pissed off. "Ash, I don't know why you're so annoyed with me. Nothing's changed. I love you."

"You didn't have to leave."

"I did. It wouldn't have been right to stay, but that doesn't mean I've left us. I've never felt so serious about anything in my life."

"I just worry that you'll think this was all a bad idea when you're around your old friends and favourite places back home."

Archie looked her right in the eye and said, "You have to trust me. I don't know much about relationships, but I know trust is meant to be extremely important. Am I right?"

Ash nodded and then leaned in for a hug. Maybe she *could* hold off telling Ash her plans, so she could do the whole romance thing the way she wanted.

Just as she finished that thought, Lucy burst into the office, short of breath. "Fox, Fox, there's a seal and her pup stranded on the beach. Clem sent me to get you. It has plastic wrapped around its snout."

Fox bounced up. "Archie, this is your area."

Archie nodded. She had volunteered quite a few times throughout her career with animal and eco charities. In that capacity she had taken part in teams helping with beached whales and animals trapped in nets and human rubbish dumped in the sea.

"Ash, run down to your dad and ask him to meet us on the beach with some cutting tools."

"Okay." Ash hurried away out of the office.

"Fox, let's get down there."

CHAPTER TWENTY-ONE

When Archie and Fox made it down to the beach, they found Clementine kneeling beside the mother seal trying to keep her calm.

"Clem?" Archie said. "Stand back with Lucy, and Fox and I will get in close. Seals can give you a nasty bite."

She did, and Archie and Fox moved up. The mother seal had a thick round ring of plastic around its snout, digging into its muzzle.

"Poor thing," Fox said.

In the background the baby was crying for its mum. Anger filled Archie. "This is disgusting. It makes me so angry that we do this to our animals."

"I know. Sickening," Fox said. "We need to use this on social media to raise awareness." Fox turned back to Clementine and Lucy and said, "Clem, video this. We need to educate the public about the horror of plastic in our oceans."

Ash and her dad came running towards them.

"Ash," Archie said, "stand back with Clementine. This is going to be difficult."

"I brought heavy duty gloves and cable cutters. Will they work?" James asked.

"I think so." Archie took a pair of the gloves and pulled them on.

"So, what's the plan," Fox asked.

The seal was at the very edge of the shore, so the waves were still breaking over it.

"I think if I straddle its back and you two try to hold its muzzle still, I can clip the plastic off. When it's off, we'll need to let go slowly, one by one. She's going to be so distressed and scared, and she might bite."

Fox and James put on their gloves, and Archie stood over the seal's back.

"Are we ready? I'll hold her snout, and then you two come down to her level and take over from me."

Archie kneeled in the surf and grasped the seal's snout. "It's all right, sweetheart. We'll help you. Stay calm."

Once Fox and James were in position, Archie let go of the snout and picked up some bolt cutters. She would have to be so careful and not hurt the seal.

Archie eased under the plastic with the cutters, and the seal started to struggle.

"Poor thing, she must be in a lot of pain," Fox said.

"We're here to help, my sweet," James said, trying to soothe her.

Archie took a breath. She had to cut with confidence and just get it done. The slower she was, the more the danger to the seal, from distress and exhaustion.

It was fiddly, but she made it through until she cracked the last of the plastic.

"There you go, sweetheart."

Archie pulled the plastic away and threw it to the side. There was a sore looking indent where the plastic sat but no open wound, and hopefully that would heal when she got back into the sea.

She repositioned her hands around the snout and looked at James and Fox seriously. "When I give you both the word, pull your hands away, and stand back there with everyone. Then I'll pick my moment and go off to the side, and hopefully get away unscathed."

They both nodded.

"Three…two…one."

Fox and James pulled their hands away. It was just her now, keeping their new friend in place.

"Be careful, Archie," Ash called out.

This was going to be tricky. The waves crashed in at her back, and her shoes and jeans were soaking. *Come on. You can do this.*

Archie gave herself a silent countdown—*three…two…one*—and dived to the side. She felt pain in her hand but got up and ran a few feet from the seal.

"Are you okay, Archie?" Fox shouted.

"Yes, hang on and see if she moves. If she's not showing an eagerness to get back in the sea, we'll need to get some help for her. She might need a vet."

But after gathering herself for a minute, the seal started to turn to the sea and called for its pup. They both inched their way back into the surf and swam away.

Fox whooped and shouted, "You did it, Archie."

Everyone else clapped, and Ash ran over to her, throwing her arms around her. "You're my hero, Arch. I love you."

"I love you too. You see? There's so much to do here. You think I wouldn't want to be here?"

Ash took her hand and when she winced, Ash quickly scanned her glove and pointed to a jagged tear. "You got bitten?"

Archie pulled off the glove, revealing a deep gash in her palm.

"We need to get you to Dr. Campbell," Ash said.

"She didn't mean it. She was scared," Archie said.

"I know, but still. It looks deep. Let's go."

A few weeks later Ash was at the abandoned school making some final notes for the history app, which would guide visitors around their village. The repairs hadn't started inside the schoolhouse, but the land around it had been cleared by the landscapers Fox used.

The script for the app was on her iPad, and she checked off the facts as they were written. Ash's phone beeped with a text. It was from Archie.

It read simply, *Look in Elijah's desk.*

"What is this about?"

She made her way into the school. Happily, the roof was patched up now to protect the space. Ash walked to Elijah's desk and lifted the top. In it lay a brown paper bag. She pulled out a book—a pristine copy of *The Dastardly Duke*.

"I don't recognize this cover."

Ash opened it to the first page and stared. "Oh my God. A first edition?" This was something she'd never dreamed of owning. "Why did she do this?"

A small envelope poked out from the next page. It said on the front, *To my dearest Miss O'Rourke.*

Ash opened the envelope quickly. The note read, *My dear Miss O'Rourke. Please join me at the steward's cottage at your earliest convenience.*

Something sounded familiar about that line. Excited about this new development, Ash left the school and made her way to the steward's cottage. That was where Fox's friend was meant to be moving in. She'd helped Archie choose some of the furnishings and knick-knacks.

She walked through the gate and saw a note taped to the door. *Look behind you.*

Ash turned around but saw nothing immediately. Then a second later, she heard the sound of hooves on cobbles. From around the corner a buggy led by two horses trundled slowly into view.

Ash gasped and held her hand over her mouth when she saw the driver of the buggy. It was Archie dressed in full male Regency costume, topped off with a top hat.

"Oh God, what are you doing?" Ash giggled.

She only noticed then that Patrick was at the front with the horses, dressed in traditional livery.

"Patrick, what has she got you into?"

Patrick smiled at her and winked.

Archie brought the horses to a stop and jumped down from the buggy. She retrieved a cane from the buggy and walked through the gate.

"You're the dastardly duke?"

"I am, madam." Archie bowed elaborately. "At your service."

Ash couldn't believe this. Her heart was fluttering already. "What are you doing, Archie?"

Archie leaned on her cane. "I wanted to show you my new house."

"What?" Ash was shocked. "You've been refurbing this for yourself?"

"Yes, I wanted it to be a surprise."

"That's why you didn't seem worried about having to move back to London," Ash said.

Archie smiled. "Exactly, I wanted to make everything perfect before making a commitment to you, because there's not going to be another woman in my life."

"There isn't?" Ash could hardly breathe. Was this really happening?

"Now to business, Miss O'Rourke." Archie's countenance became a lot more serious. She took Ash's hand. "Since I first met you, I have been bad-tempered, moody, and impatient, but my heart was made cold and distant by grief…"

It was the dastardly duke's speech near the end of the book. Her heart was fluttering so much, Ash thought she might faint.

Archie continued, "You were the only one who could thaw the deep ice around my heart, and I am decided that I cannot live without you."

Archie dropped to one knee, and Ash said, "Oh God."

"I live the life of but a simple country squire. I want nothing more than to love you, and you in your turn, for the rest of our lives. Would you do me the honour of moving in with me, and marrying me?"

"Oh my God, yes, yes, I will."

Archie looked up into Ash's tear-filled eyes and couldn't stay in character any longer. She got up and kissed Ash deeply. "I love you."

"I love you, Arch. You made this so special."

Archie took her hand. "It's not over yet. Would you like a ride in my carriage?"

"I'd love it."

Archie helped her up in the seat, and Patrick said, "Congratulations."

"Thanks, and thank you for helping Archie make this special."

"No bother."

Archie took the reins and said, "Off we go, Patrick."

"I never knew you could drive a cart."

"I can't—I mean, I've been practising. Mr. Murdoch let me borrow his cart and horses. I asked Patrick to help lead the horses."

"Where are we riding to?" Ash asked.

Archie furrowed her eyebrows. "Don't tell me you've forgotten the last part of your favourite book?"

Ash remembered. "The ride through the village?"

"Exactly."

After accepting the dastardly duke's proposal, he drove them back through the village, and all the villagers came out to wave, cheer, and clap. They wanted to show their appreciation to Diana for changing their once grumpy, bad-tempered landlord with her love.

The first person they spotted was her dad, standing by the beach entrance. "Congratulations, my girl."

"Thank you, Daddy. I love you."

They then rode through the centre of the village, where everyone else gathered by the pub. They clapped and cheered, and Archie slowed the buggy so everyone could come and talk to them.

Ash turned to Archie and said, "And you thought romance novels were trashy."

Archie smiled. "My mistake. Thank you for setting me straight and loving me."

"I'll always love you, Arch. But tell me, can you see yourself cutting the grass on a Sunday for the rest of our lives?"

Archie laughed, then kissed her lips softly and whispered, "I can't wait."

CHAPTER TWENTY-TWO

James lifted the last holdall from his truck and laid it by the gate of Archie and Ash's new cottage.

"This is the last of it," James said to Ash.

Archie came out the front door and lifted some of the bags, while James took the rest.

Ash smiled watching the two people who she loved most in the world working together so well. She was lucky her dad liked Archie so much. Granted, he didn't understand the vegan thing, but they'd bonded over their determination to keep the ocean pollution free, and their love of her.

As they walked inside with the bags, Ash looked up at the sky on this warm sunny day and spoke to her mum. "I hope you're happy for me, Mum, and you like Archie. But I know if Dad does, you would have too."

She looked at her watch. Still plenty of time. Not only was this her moving in with Archie day, but it was also the day the new tourist app was launched. It was Ash's baby and told the story of the village through a few residents through the years, but their hero was Elijah Winters, the man whom Ash had first discovered.

In the afternoon, the village and dignitaries from the local council were meeting at Elijah and his partner's rebuilt farmhouse to unveil a rainbow plaque in honour of the two brave men. It was all very exciting.

Ash walked into the house to join Archie and her dad, who were surrounded by the many bags they had to unpack.

"The cottage is looking lovely, Ash," her dad said.

"Thanks, I think it's going to be a lovely home." Ash slipped her arm around Archie, who kissed her on the cheek.

He gave Archie a mock glare and pointed at Ash's hand. "Remember, I expect to see a wedding ring on that finger soon. Commitment comes with living together."

"Dad, we're engaged—that's commitment." Ash looked down at the engagement ring she had chosen on a day out to London recently.

"James," Archie said, "I'd get married tomorrow, but your daughter is planning a special day for our wedding."

Ash chuckled, remembering the day Archie found her Pinterest wedding board on her iPad. She was worried Archie would feel the noose tightening, but instead she just laughed and joked about making her wear a big white dress.

Archie really was committed, and Ash couldn't love her more. "Yeah, Alanna's helping me plan. I'm the hold-up, Dad."

Archie squeezed her and said, "Just tell me where and when, and I'll be there with bells on."

"Good," her dad said. There was a silence and he stood awkwardly. "I suppose I better let you get unpacked."

Archie nudged her and communicated with her facial expressions to help her dad. Ash walked over and looped her arm through his. As they walked to the door Ash said, "I'll see you this afternoon at the plaque unveiling, and we'll be having Sunday lunch together, remember."

"Yes, I know. Don't worry about me, darling girl. It'll take some getting used to, but I honestly can't tell you how happy I am that you've found love. Archie is a good woman. I couldn't have parted with you to anyone else."

Ash hugged him. "Thanks, Daddy."

"Your mum would be so proud of you, and I know you're going to have a great life. I love you."

"I love you, Dad."

❖

The villagers and some dignitaries from the local council were gathered around Elijah's former home. Archie held Ash's hand as their council representative gave a speech about the work done in the village, its diversity, and the village's diversity in the past.

James stood beside them, and up at the front, Fox, Clementine, and Lucy listened together. Archie smiled. Fox had taken to becoming a parent like a duck to water, and Fox's mum and dad, Cassia and Donny, now visited Rosebrook every other week because they had an adopted grandchild.

Lucy herself was slowly coming out of her shell and enjoyed living in the village. Archie looked over to the left and saw Griff, Patrick, and Alanna standing together. But what Archie noticed most of all was Blake beside them, with her arm around Eliska, and little Ola snuggled into Blake's other side. Their relationship was progressing. Maybe Ash's romance novels helped Eliska too? They'd certainly helped Archie come to terms with her feelings.

Archie nudged Ash and indicated to the group of newcomers. Ash smiled and whispered, "Yeah, our little village of love is working its magic."

"Really?"

"Uh-huh. Blake and Eliska have been getting so close. Eliska is as besotted with Blake as Blake is with her, but they're taking it slowly, given Eliska's history."

"Isn't love wonderful?" Archie said with a grin.

"Is that grumpy Archie talking?"

They chuckled and then turned their attention back to the ceremony.

The councillor said, "It gives me great pleasure to unveil this rainbow plaque to commemorate two men who loved and lived together, in a time when they risked their lives and liberty. But that comes as no surprise, as Elijah Winters served his country with honour and bravery, dying trying to save a fellow soldier. It is so important to keep our history alive, and we have a local woman, Ashling O'Rourke, to thank for uncovering this important part of queer history."

Archie couldn't have been prouder and smiled when Ash's cheeks went a delightful colour of pink.

"Ladies and gentlemen, I give you Mr. Elijah Winters and Mr. Gavin Burton." The councillor pulled the cord, and the small curtain parted to reveal the special rainbow plaque.

"I'm proud of you, darling," Archie said.

After the ceremony everyone retreated to the pub to enjoy some food and drink Jonah had laid on for their guests.

Archie stood at the bar with Fox and Patrick. Across the room Ash was sitting in one of the booths with the duchess, Alanna, Kay, and Lucy.

Griffin said hello to the group in the booth, then walked towards the bar and said to Archie, "I wouldn't go over there anytime soon, mate. They're looking at wedding dresses."

Fox smacked her on the shoulder and joked, "There's no getting out of it now, Archie."

In days gone past you wouldn't have seen Archie for dust at such a suggestion, but now she only smiled and said, "I wouldn't dream of it."

As Archie looked over, Ash lifted her head and smiled at her. She was reminded of the last passage of Ash's favourite book:

> *The dastardly duke thought his heart was impenetrable, but that was until the obstinate Diana Carlton came along, and his heart had been pierced by Cupid's arrow. All that had seemed important, like the glamourous London parties, the many women he persued and seduced, gambling at the cards table, and travelling all over the world, were now so unimportant. All that mattered was making a home for Diana at Glassford Castle and spending forever loving her. The dastardly duke was now the deeply loving duke and all because of the power of love.*

Archie never imagined the feeling that true love could give you, or the feeling of love a community of people could give you. Now she had both.

Home was not a word she'd fully understood before. She had sworn many years ago to only ever make her home in a city, but her dad had been right. Home really was where the heart was, and her heart was very much here in Rosebrook with the love of her life, and always would be.

EPILOGUE

Friday was Ash's favourite day of the week, especially now that she was living with Archie. They had so much fun together, doing domestic things and spending time with her dad.

Ash was sitting on her deckchair on the beach, the small waves rolling across her feet. They had only returned a few days ago from their month-long working holiday to Japan, and as exciting as it was seeing a new country, nothing felt like sitting on Rosebrook beach.

Archie was catching up with work at the office, so Ash took the opportunity to visit her happy place. In the distance she could see her dad's boat puttering back to shore, and she had a new book in her lap to read. It didn't get much better than this.

She picked up her book and was just about to set off on her new adventure with *The Parson and the Admiral's Daughter* when she heard a voice at her side.

"The parson? That can't be too exciting." Archie sat in the sand at her side.

"You'd be surprised. I think we'll add this to your reading list."

"Hmm," Archie said doubtfully, "I don't think I'll look forward to that one. Anyway, I won't have time for reading this weekend."

Ash laughed at Archie's childlike excitement. While they had been away, the new season of *The Gatekeeper* had landed on Netflix, and Ash had promised they'd start on it this weekend.

She had to admit it was a really good show, and it hadn't taken her long to catch up.

"Remember, you promised we could binge-watch the season."

"How could I forget your bookkeeper show. It's all you've talked about the past month," Ash said.

Archie smiled. "Don't try to kid me. You love it too."

And she did. It was lovely to share something like that. They'd had some really cosy nights on the couch watching it.

"We can, as long as you can find the time to cut my dad's grass."

Archie put her hand on her heart. "Grass cutting is my specialty."

Ash noticed her dad was tying off his boat on the pier. "We better go and say goodnight to Dad."

Archie stood and brushed the sand from her jeans, then offered her hand to Ash.

"How gallant," Ash said.

"Gallant is my middle name. Come on. I'll put the deckchair back."

Once Archie put back the chair, she walked hand in hand with Ash along the sand.

"Only a month to go," Ash said to Archie.

"What happens in a month?"

Ash play-hit her fiancée. "If you don't remember when our wedding is, I might not marry you."

"I'm kidding, I'm kidding. Fox and I have our final fittings for our suits this week."

"You getting cold feet yet?" Ash asked.

"Never. Are you?"

"Just nervous. I hope it's as nice a wedding as your dad's. That was special."

"It will be perfect. Oh, Fox has offered her camper van for the honeymoon."

Ash almost growled at Archie. "Don't you even jest about that."

Archie laughed. "Don't worry—we're going somewhere hot, with lots of sand, but that's a secret."

Ash stopped and put her arms around Archie. "I really can't wait to be married to you."

"Me too." Archie kissed her softly. "Come on, your dad is waiting for us."

Ash looked up and saw her dad waving from the pier. She had everything she ever wanted here in Rosebrook, and she couldn't wait to live her life with those that loved her.

Archie walked forward a few steps and held out her hand. "Are you ready?"

Ash smiled. "I'm ready for anything with you."

About the Author

Jenny Frame is from the small town of Motherwell in Scotland, where she lives with her partner, Lou, and their well-loved and very spoiled dog.

She has a diverse range of qualifications, including a BA in public management and a diploma in acting and performance. Nowadays, she likes to put her creative energies into writing rather than treading the boards.

When not writing or reading, Jenny loves cheering on her local football team, cooking, and spending time with her family.

Jenny can be contacted at www.jennyframe.com.

Books Available From Bold Strokes Books

Flight SQA016 by Amanda Radley. Fastidious airline passenger Olivia Lewis is used to things being a certain way. When her routine is changed by a new, attractive member of the staff, sparks fly. (978-1-63679-045-9)

Home Is Where The Heart Is by Jenny Frame. Can Archie make the countryside her home and give Ash the fairytale romance she desires? Or will the countryside and small village life all be too much for her? (978-1-63555-922-4)

Moving Forward by PJ Trebelhorn. The last person Shelby Ryan expects to be attracted to Iris Calhoun, the sister of the man who killed her wife four years and three thousand miles ago. (978-1-63555-953-8)

Poison Pen by Jean Copeland. Debut author Kendra Blake is finally living her best life until a nasty book review and exposed secrets threaten her promising new romance with aspiring journalist Alison Chatterley. (978-1-63555-849-4)

Seasons for Change by KC Richardson. Love, laughter, and trust develop for Shawn and Morgan throughout the changing seasons of Lake Tahoe. (978-1-63555-882-1)

Summer Lovin' by Julie Cannon. Three different women, three exotic locations, one unforgettable summer. What do you think will happen? (978-1-63555-920-0)

Unbridled by D. Jackson Leigh. A visit to a local stable turns into more than riding lessons between a novel writer and an equestrian with a taste for power play. (978-1-63555-847-0)

VIP by Jackie D. In a town where relationships are forged and shattered by perception, sometimes even love can't change who you really are. (978-1-63555-908-8)

Yearning by Gun Brooke. The sleepy town of Dennamore has an irresistible pull on those who've moved away. The mystery Darian Benson and Samantha Pike uncover will change them forever, but the love they find along the way just might be the key to saving themselves. (978-1-63555-757-2)

A Turn of Fate by Ronica Black. Will Nev and Kinsley finally face their painful past and relent to their powerful, forbidden attraction? Or will facing their past be too much to fight through? (978-1-63555-930-9)

Desires After Dark by MJ Williamz. When her human lover falls deathly ill, Alex, a vampire, must decide which is worse, letting her go or condemning her to everlasting life. (978-1-63555-940-8)

Her Consigliere by Carsen Taite. FBI agent Royal Scott swore an oath to uphold the law, and criminal defense attorney Siobhan Collins pledged her loyalty to the only family she's ever known, but will their love be stronger than the bonds they've vowed to others, or will their competing allegiances tear them apart? (978-1-63555-924-8)

In Our Words: Queer Stories from Black, Indigenous, and People of Color Writers. Stories Selected by Anne Shade and Edited by Victoria Villaseñor. Comprising both the renowned and emerging voices of Black, Indigenous, and People of Color authors, this thoughtfully curated collection of short stories explores the intersection of racial and queer identity. (978-1-63555-936-1)

Measure of Devotion by CF Frizzell. Disguised as her late twin brother, Catherine Samson enters the Civil War to defend the Constitution as a Union soldier, never expecting her life to be altered by a Gettysburg farmer's daughter. (978-1-63555-951-4)

Not Guilty by Brit Ryder. Claire Weaver and Emery Pearson's day jobs clash, even as their desire for each other burns, and a discreet sex-only arrangement is the only option. (978-1-63555-896-8)

Opposites Attract: Butch/Femme Romances by Meghan O'Brien, Aurora Rey & Angie Williams. Sometimes opposites really do attract. Fall in love with these butch/femme romance novellas. (978-1-63555-784-8)

Under Her Influence by Amanda Radley. On their path to #truelove, will Beth and Jemma discover that reality is even better than illusion? (978-1-63555-963-7)

Swift Vengeance by Jean Copeland, Jackie D & Erin Zak. A journalist becomes the subject of her own investigation when sudden strange, violent visions summon her to a summer retreat and into the arms of a killer's possible next victim. (978-1-63555-880-7)

Wasteland by Kristin Keppler & Allisa Bahney. Danielle Clark is fighting against the National Armed Forces and finds peace as a scavenger, until the NAF general's daughter, Katelyn Turner, shows up on her doorstep and brings the fight right back to her. (978-1-63555-935-4)

When In Doubt by VK Powell. Police officer Jeri Wylder thinks she committed a crime in the line of duty but can't remember, until details emerge pointing to a cover-up by those close to her. (978-1-63555-955-2)

A Woman to Treasure by Ali Vali. An ancient scroll isn't the only treasure Levi Montbard finds as she starts her hunt for the truth—all she has to do is prove to Yasmine Hassani that there's more to her than an adventurous soul. (978-1-63555-890-6)

Before. After. Always. by Morgan Lee Miller. Still reeling from her tragic past, Eliza Walsh has sworn off taking risks, until Blake Navarro turns her world right-side up, making her question if falling in love again is worth it. (978-1-63555-845-6)

Bet the Farm by Fiona Riley. Lauren Calloway's luxury real estate sale of the century comes to a screeching halt when dairy farm heiress, and one-night stand, Thea Boudreaux calls her bluff. (978-1-63555-731-2)

Cowgirl by Nance Sparks. The last thing Aren expects is to fall for Carol. Sharing her home is one thing, but sharing her heart means sharing the demons in her past and risking everything to keep Carol safe. (978-1-63555-877-7)

Give In to Me by Elle Spencer. Gabriela Talbot never expected to sleep with her favorite author—certainly not after the scathing review she'd given Whitney Ainsworth's latest book. (978-1-63555-910-1)

Hidden Dreams by Shelley Thrasher. A lethal virus and its resulting vision send Texan Barbara Allan and her lovely guide, Dara, on a journey up Cambodia's Mekong River in search of Barbara's mother's mystifying past. (978-1-63555-856-2)